I0716633

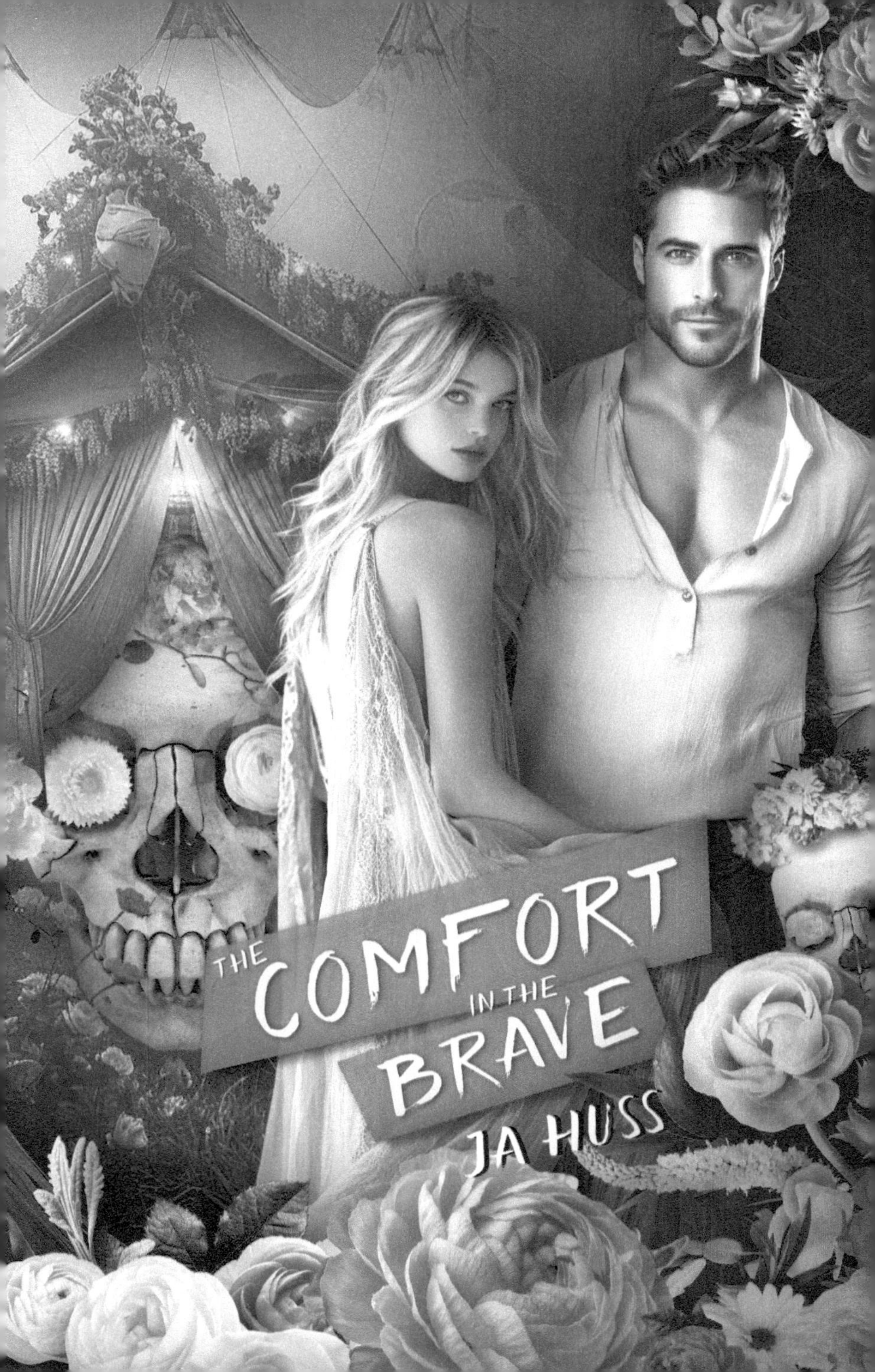

THE COMFORT IN THE BRAVE
JA HUSS

THE COMFORT
IN THE
BRAVE
JA HUSS

Edited by RJ Locksley
Cover Design by JA Huss
No part of this cover was made with AI

Clover Bradley was having the worst day of her life and then she got kidnapped. In her own home. Well, her empty and currently being renovated childhood home on the edge of Disciple, West Virginia and not her former cozy cottage on the grounds of the Dixie Yonder Hotel where she was working and thriving until that very morning. But it still counts and definitely makes her very bad day much worse.

But that's not even the crazy part. The crazy part is that she's falling for her kidnapper. A handsome man, if a little morally challenged, who is probably very dangerous and has threatened to kill her half a dozen times over the span of just one day, but what can one do? The attraction is there.

Riggs is just trying his best to stay out of prison. Which seems at odds with his current actions, but need-to-know nuances make all these nonsensical pieces fit. And even though Clover isn't a model captive—she's a complainer of the princess variety— he finds himself getting attached. If he hadn't been forced to kidnap her to save his own hide, he could see a future where the two of them end up together.

So he figures… why not save her life by endangering her some more?

And she figures… well, it's better than being left to rot in her own basement.

And that's, of course, when things get interesting.

The Comfort in the Brave is an ironic twist of fate inbred to a really bad decision. It's a captive romance turned ride-or-die in a crazy escape from Blackberry Hill—but this time Collin Creed isn't coming to save anyone, he's looking for revenge.

CLOVER

CHAPTER 1 - CLOVER

I *enter the Dixie Yonder* bright and early Monday morning, ready for what's next after an exhilarating weekend of perfectly-planned wedding events. Nearly the moment I enter the hotel my boss, Clarissa, is calling out my name from across the expansive lobby as she strides towards me. "Great job, Clover! That wedding yesterday—fan. Tastic! Went off without a hitch." She's reached me now and Clarissa is a toucher, so her hand claps down on my shoulder and gives it a squeeze and her big brown eyes sparkle with excitement. "Wedding season is just about over and I know how much you love summers because they're so busy, but don't worry, girl, we've got parties booked every weekend through December."

"Wonderful!" I tell her, flashing back a smile as big as her own. Because I can find the joy in any season, really. Even ones that don't typically come with weddings. "You're right," I tell her, "wedding season is my favorite, but party season is like a Christmas star, shining in the sky!"

"And with you planning the parties, they'll sparkle in the darkness like fireflies in the night." Then she leans in to me, lowering her voice. "Mr. Sutter has asked to see you in private as soon as you have time. And if you ask me"—she pauses here to flash a huge, all-teeth smile—"I think you're getting a promotion." She practically sings out that last word.

"What?" I say, feigning surprise. "Really?" I've been working at the Dixie Yonder Hotel for nearly seven years now. I didn't start in weddings—I was Clarissa's Girl Friday for three and a half of those years making a pretty meager salary. But she and I clicked immediately and she's been pushing me up the ladder of high-society event planning ever since. So, I've kinda been expecting this.

"Well"—Clarissa removes her hand from my shoulder—"I don't know for sure, but why else would Sutter call you in? And yesterday's wedding—oh, my God." She puts a hand over her heart. "It's being featured in *Vanity Fair*, you know that, right?"

"I do." And boy, was I nervous about that. My name will be mentioned for sure. And while it's an honor, it's also a lot of pressure. These elite people we cater to can be a bit obnoxious at times, but I aim to please and when my Dixie Yonder clients come to me with a request, I get the job done.

I hold up my hand and cross my fingers. "Here's to my promotion. But... what about you? I mean, your job is the only one I'm qualified to do."

"Oh, sweetie, I got my promotion this morning."

"What!" I jump up and down a little. "Holy crap! You finally got promoted to general manager?"

"Yep!" She shrugs up her shoulders real big. "Finally. But not here."

"*Whaaaaaat?*" This word comes out as a whine. "Not here? You can't leave me!"

"I've been promoted to general manager of the Wicked Scrod in Boston."

"Boston?" My smile falls. "*Boston?*" I'm so shocked, I say it again. Like maybe I just heard her wrong. "You can't go to Boston."

"Ooooooh, you're so sweet, Clover. I know we've been a great team, and I seriously owe you everything. Without your support I would never have gotten this far. But you're gonna be just fine, I know it. You're gonna nail this."

"But... it's not boss you I'm going to miss. It's friend you, Clarissa." I pout. Because even though we don't really hang together outside of work, she's my best friend these days. I tell her everything. And when things go wrong, she's the one who makes life better. Without Clarissa, I wouldn't have scored the cottage I live in on the Yonder grounds. It was hers before it was mine. And when she moved out to rent a little house in the nearby village, she told Sutter I should get it.

Which is the whole reason why I can afford to keep renovating my childhood home back in Disciple. One day—hopefully before I grow old—I will turn that old mansion into my own niche hotel and plan events on my own estate grounds. It's my dream. Clarissa has been helping me make my dream come true and now she's leaving.

I cannot hide my disappointment.

"Aww, I feel the same way, Clover," Clarissa says. "And I'm gonna miss you like crazy. But we're meant for bigger things, friend. And this is the next step on our journeys. We need to spread our wings."

"Yeah… I know. But we need to make sure we meet up. Once a month, just like I do with my childhood bestie, Lowyn, back home in West Virginia."

"It's a date." And she smiles at me, cementing these words into a promise. "Now go. Have your meeting with Sutter. I'm on my way to the airport." She points to a pink wheelie suitcase that I hadn't noticed.

"You're leaving *now*?"

"It's just a one-week trip to get a feel for the place. Don't worry, I'll be back and we'll have a proper goodbye then." She twiddles her fingers at me. "See ya soon!" Then she takes off at a determined walk towards the revolving front doors of the hotel, her heels clicking on the polished marble floors, and a moment later, she's gone.

I let out a long breath. I love working under Clarissa. She's very upbeat, her smile is wide and contagious, and even when people mess up, she only has encouraging things to say.

I want to be sad about this turn of events for a few more hours, at least. But I owe it to my boss to rally and meet the moment with dignity. And anyway, it's not a setback, not at all. This is a good change and now that I'll be the boss it will be my turn to pay it forward and mentor an up-and-coming event planner, just like Clarissa did for me.

So I straighten my back, turn on my heel, and head straight to Sutter's office.

TEN MINUTES *later* I'm sitting in an oversized leather wingback in front of Sutter's massive mahogany desk with my mouth open.

"Did you just say… I'm fired?" I blink at him. Like seven times in a row, because this can't be happening. "How—"

"Look, Miss Bradley, you've done a great job here. I'm not unhappy with your work at all."

"Then why?"

He shrugs with his hands and sits back in his chair, making the leather creak. "Downsizing. The economy is terrible. The Dixie Yonder has been losing money for over a year now. Something has to be done."

"But we have events scheduled for the entire year, Mr. Sutter! If Clarissa is leaving for Boston, then who will do the events if not me?"

"Brian can handle it, I'm sure."

"*Brian?* But he's my assistant."

"Exactly. He's mostly qualified and makes half as much as you do. And… well, that's really all that matters. The bottom line is king, as they say."

"But he's only been here six months. He can't possibly produce the quality of event that Clarissa and I did."

"You're right." Sutter sighs. "He won't. He'll muck it all up, I'm sure. But this isn't my decision, Miss Bradley. It came straight from corporate. They told me to fire you. I'm sorry. I really am." But then his sympathy fades and his business face returns. "Now. About your cottage."

"Oh, my God. You're not kicking me out of the cottage!"

"I'm sorry about this too, but I was ordered to book

it up and… well, the first guests are arriving tomorrow."

"Tomorrow! But how will I pack—"

"Oh, don't worry about packing." He waves a careless hand through the air. "It's been done. All your things have been loaded into a rented Haul-It trailer, courtesy of the hotel. You have a hitch on that that brand-new SUV you drive, right? I'm sure I saw a hitch and it's a monster of a car, so the load shouldn't be a problem."

For a moment I can't speak. Hell, I can't even think. What is happening here? "You… packed up my cottage?"

"No need to thank me, it's the least I could do. I'll email you all the details for returning the trailer—it's booked for two days." He shuffles some papers on his desk and then smiles as he finds what he's looking for. "Here it is. Your final paycheck." And then he slides it across the desk. "Good luck, Miss Bradley."

I DON'T CRY as I drive myself and all my worldly possessions across the state of Virginia and into the hills of my home state. I am numb, actually. Still in shock at how my life could be turned upside down in a matter of minutes.

Of course I tried to call Clarissa, but it went to voicemail and I didn't leave a message because… well, it's her parade and raining on it feels gross. At least for a few days.

I didn't call my parents, either. I didn't call anyone. I didn't even call Lowyn, even though I'm headed to Disciple right now.

I might be having trouble processing.

So I just… drive. And the next thing I know I'm pulling into my childhood home, just off the Loop Highway, in Trinity County, West Virginia. I cut the engine and sit in my driveway, gazing out at the rolling green hills and distant woods of the estate. Allowing myself a few minutes to come to terms my new reality.

What just happened? I was doing so well. I was on a trajectory and now I'm not falling, I'm… fall*en*. It is done. And I had no say in the matter whatsoever.

It doesn't make any sense. What did I do to deserve this?

At least I have someplace to go. That's a lucky break. But I still can't get over how a corporation that I've given my life to for seven years could just throw me away like this. I mean, what if I didn't have a childhood estate to run home to? What would I have done? Rented a motel, I guess. You can't just find an apartment on the turn of a dime in these times. It's a process. Not a fun one, either.

"Count your blessings, Clover," I tell myself. "Just be grateful that you still have this place."

My childhood home sounds good on paper. An historic country estate in the hills of West Virginia sounds very fancy-fancy, as Lowyn would put it. And it *is* quite spectacular—a four-story, twenty-two-room Victorian Queen Anne-style mansion that originally started out as a one-room log cabin in the early nineteenth century, but was gradually added on to and converted into what it is today over a period of a hundred years.

The old cabin is still here. As it was originally built as an earth-sheltered home with three sides already underground and just one side open, it was a sensible decision to build the new house right on top of it. Today, that old cabin is only accessible by a trapdoor in the library. When I was a kid, it was my playroom. I loved it. It was like having a secret fort inside your house. Lowyn and I spent whole summers down there in the underground coolness because the AC units barely worked back then and don't work at all now.

I sigh just thinking about those days. I had a great childhood filled with ponies, and horses, and rafting on the river. We had big summer garden parties, and lavish winter Christmas parties, and every year on Easter Monday—which is a school holiday in these parts—my parents organized a giant Easter egg hunt because, of course, Easter Sunday is Revival opening day and all us kids were required to be there working.

Egg hunts were pretty much the only way Disciple, West Virginia, celebrated that holiday. But it was fun. I love this estate so much, I bought it from my parents when they decided to sell it and move out of state. They let me buy it for a tenth of what they could've gotten for it because, well, no one in town was gonna pay that amount of money for a house—not even Jim Bob Baptist—and you're not allowed to sell a home in Trinity County to an outsider, so they were never gonna get top dollar for it.

Add in the fact that the moment I went off to college, they went down to Florida and never came back, and well, this place turned into a bit of a mess. It hadn't been kept up.

I hadn't needed to tap into my Revival trust for college because my parents paid for all of that, so that's what I gave them in exchange for the deed. One and done. An entire country estate for thirty-thousand dollars.

It was a great opportunity and certainly an amazing deal, but the place is a freaking mess, a top-to-bottom money-pit mess, and it's cost me a small fortune to even get this far in the renovations. Which is not far enough to even start thinking about paint colors, let alone event planning.

I guess I will have to join the Revival again. The season is well past half-over now that September is here and that means it's only one weekend a month until Christmas, but whatever I earn, it will be better than nothing.

Next year, I'll go full time and the January first after that, I will probably have enough to finish the electrical and start on the drywall.

Wow. I'm trying to rally here, I really am, but when spelled out in no uncertain terms, my future is depressing.

There are no workers and no work being done at the estate this month because I used this month's reno budget for a down payment on this huge SUV—which feels like a really stupid thing to do because the payment is fifteen hundred dollars a month and who the hell needs something that seats seven? But I was smitten with it in the showroom, not to mention flush with money at the time, so here I sit.

I look around at the interior of my Navigator, taking in all the luxury perks. The heated leather seats, the heated leather steering wheel, the massive display and reversing camera. It's got three rows of seats and can pull a horse trailer. That's why I got it. I was gonna buy myself a horse and start showing again next year and the extra-roomy interior was going to come in handy when hauling all my gear.

But I guess that dream is bust now.

I'm probably gonna have to turn this thing in and go beg Ethan Sardis, Disciple's town mechanic, to sell me some used compact thing he got on special from a dealer auction. It'll be a stick-shift and I'll be lucky if I have electric windows and rear defrost by the time all this dust settles.

How? How can a life get so derailed in the span of one morning?

I don't get it.

So I sit there for a few more moments, just blinking in surprise.

However, things must be sorted. I need a place to live and I'm not even sure this place is habitable. I've made incremental progress, but the only room that hasn't been ripped down to the studs is my childhood bedroom in the attic. And while there are worse things in life than sleeping under a lacy, white canopy on a twin bed in your princess bedroom of yesteryear when you're pushing thirty, it definitely wasn't on my bingo card.

I might have to move in with Lowyn. Nothing like crashing your bestie's new good thing.

Whoo. I need to pull myself together. So I shake my head. "All right, Clover. Rally, girl. You're fine. You're home. No one in Disciple is gonna let you sleep in your luxury SUV. It's all gonna be fine."

Once the pep talk is over, I get out and start

rummaging through my purse, looking for my keys, as I make my way up the back porch and to the door.

I have a panic moment when I can't find the little keyring and start picturing how I'll have to break one of my new, very expensive, custom-made windows in order to get inside when I feel the cold metal between my fingertips.

Wow. I am not in a good place. My imagination is as wild as that horse I had as a teenager.

I twist the key, open the door, and step inside.

It's… hmm. Not a total wreck. In fact, there's drywall already up down here. It doesn't have tape or mud yet, but there are walls! That's something.

Maybe this isn't gonna be as bad as I thought? Maybe it'll be…

This optimistic train of thought comes to a screeching halt in my head as I notice a sleeping bag on the floor in the far corner of the front room, near the fireplace. "What—"

But that's as far as I get, because… is that the sound of a shower?

I stand still for a moment, convinced my wild stallion of an imagination is getting the better of me, but then the sound of water stops and the familiar creak of a door—a creak I grew up listening to—filters down from the second floor.

What the hell is happening?

Is someone living in my house?

Should I run? Should I scream? Should I call Abel Bettington down at the police station?

These thoughts take up several precious seconds in real time and I still haven't come to a conclusion when a naked man comes bounding down the stairs, his junk bouncing every time his foot hits a step.

My mouth drops open. I am in shock. Also unable to tear my eyes away from this man's nether parts. "What the—"

That's as far as I get. Because this massive, muscular (and unfortunately very handsome) man comes rushing at me, and the next thing I know, he's got his hand pressed against my mouth, his naked wet body is pressed up against my back, and I'm being dragged down the hallway.

A moment later, he stuffs a rag in my mouth, ties my hands behind my back with a leather belt that is cinched so tight, it cuts into my skin, and I'm thrust face-first into the closet under the stairs.

The door bangs closed just as I hit my head on the floor, and everything goes black.

CHAPTER 2 - RIGGS

W*hen I come out* of the shower, I'm talking myself into the idea that this job is going well.

Being sent into Disciple, West Virginia, to set up surveillance on the town and going up against the new security force Jim Bob Baptist hired to protect his Revival isn't going to be a disaster. It's going fine. I've spent the last three weeks putting up dozens of discreet cameras and no one has even looked at me twice. Of course, that was August when the Revival was every weekend and it's September now, so the tourists only come one weekend a month, which means it's much harder to blend in. But the job is basically done. All I have to do now is make sure everything's working and troubleshoot any bugs.

I deserve this shower. I earned the right to squat in this empty house. No one else is using it, and I've been paying attention to it all month. It looks like it's in the middle of being renovated, but there have been no workers here since I started watching. Not a single one.

So yesterday, I moved in. If no one else is gonna enjoy this place, I might as well help myself.

And anyway, I'll be out of here in three days and no one back home will ever know that I stayed here a few nights instead of the woods. I mean, why should I camp out in the fucking forest, roughing it in the mud, when this perfectly good mansion has nothing better to do than give me shelter?

This house was the ideal solution for what could've been a very unsatisfying ending to a very stupid job. And I can use the perfection right now. Because the last six years of my life have been dark, depressing hell.

I can't go back to those tunnels. I won't go back. I'll do anything my father tells me to do in order to never go back.

Despite spending the last six years in the deepest, darkest hole of a prison imaginable, I'm not a fuck-up. I come from a good family. A really good family with Colony roots that span two hundred years. I was educated, and privileged, and given all the best opportunities growing up.

Which is what got me in trouble in the end.

Every kid who is born into an upper-class family in the Colonies gets told the truth when we collectively turn eighteen on June first. But up until then, we all think the world we grew up in is all there is.

It's not true. As nice as they can be, there's more to this world than underground cities.

There's sunshine, and grass, and trees, and oceans. Not to mention women.

And men. Like Collin Creed. Who was not the reason I went AWOL, but he definitely played his part.

But of course—if you run, they hunt you.

So they caught me and I've spent the last six years in prison for it.

Not prison like they have up here with cells, and guards, and shitty food. A Colony prison is nothing like that. There are no cells. There are no guards. You get sent to the tunnels and spend your days and nights drilling and thinking about nothing but dirt, and rocks, and darkness. You're so deep underground you don't even get to *see* an access shaft until you're ninety days out from release.

I about lost my mind. It's not so bad if you've never felt sunlight on your back before, but everyone who gets sent to the tunnels was a runner who got caught. All of us knew what we were missing down there. There weren't even overhead lights, just headlamps. Everything was a shadow. I lost track of time. The stress of being underground again gave me nightmares and at one point, I was thinking about giving up.

I think they wait for that moment and then they

pull us out and explain that we all have jobs to do, and we're all important, and they are sure we've learned our lessons. They tell us what disappointments we are to our fathers. Wouldn't we like another chance to prove ourselves to be honorable, and loyal, and dedicated to the Colony? Wouldn't we like to go back up top to work? Only this time, we will be good, obedient Colonists and complete our assignments and return home.

Just the thought of being back up top again was enough to make me promise them anything.

Anything.

I can't go back to those tunnels. I *won't* go back to those tunnels.

And now I won't have to because this job is basically done—early, I might add—and even though I'm squatting in an old mansion, I'm gonna get away with it. No one down below will ever find out that I didn't camp in the woods and bathe in the river like a good little Colony worker.

All of this is what I'm thinking as I realize I forgot to bring my towel into the bathroom with me. But this isn't enough to quell my overflowing, and smug, satisfaction over how I will spend my last few days up here in relative comfort instead of being tortured with the misery of primitive accommodations, and how I will be congratulated when I get back and given more up-top jobs to take advantage of.

I did it.

I made it.

I'm back.

These words are flowing through my head when I come bounding down the stairs and see the woman.

Her mouth is open, her eyes are wide, and she is about to scream.

Luckily, all my advanced training kicks in. I jump down the remaining stairs, cross the space between us, slip behind her, and have my hand slapped against her mouth before that scream comes out.

Not that anyone would be able to hear her—this house is nearly half a mile from town and the estate is so big, there are no close neighbors. It's not the scream I'm worried about. It's the time ticking off that makes this whole situation worse, because the longer I wait to respond, the longer she has to get a good look at me.

So all my actions are instincts. I drag her down the hallway to the kitchen where my clothes are, stuff an old rag in her mouth, wrap my clean t-shirt around her head to blindfold her, pull her arms behind her back, ratchet a belt around her wrists, open the nearest closet, and throw her in, slamming the door behind her. There is a loud *thunk* as she hits the hardwood floor.

The whole thing takes about ten seconds.

Then I stand there—back pressed against the door,

still naked and breathing heavy—as my mind finally catches up with my actions.

And that's when I realize how fucked I am.

She saw my face.

I go back upstairs, my mind spinning with my limited choices as to what to do next, when I reach for my jeans and pull them on. I grab yesterday's t-shirt off the bathroom floor, pull that on, and then peer out the window, trying to determine if she's alone.

There's a huge black SUV in the driveway with a trailer hitched to it, but there doesn't seem to be anyone waiting for her outside.

I take a breath, hold it, then slowly let it out, trying to calm my racing heart.

She's the owner of the house, obviously. Moving back in, maybe?

I don't know why that would be the case. This place is fine for squatters, but this woman doesn't look like she's into roughing it. She's wearing fancy clothes, high heels, and lots of makeup. Which, in my experience, translates to… ambition.

And ambitious women, in my personal opinion, are dangerous.

None of that really matters. What matters is how many people know she's here. How many people will I have to silence to cover up my mistake?

Down on the first floor the woman starts kicking the closet door, trying to scream past her gag, but I don't pay any attention to that. I'm busy thinking about my now very short list of choices.

There is no way I can let her go. It's not gonna happen. She saw my face. And while she doesn't have a clue as to who I actually am, this is a Disciple house and that means she's a Disciple resident.

She doesn't *need* to know anything. All she needs to do is report me to Jim Bob Baptist, who will then take this information straight to Collin Creed, and from there… I'm fucked.

Absolutely fucked.

I am three days out from completing this job and earning my way back into the good graces of my father and there is no possible way I will allow this woman to get me sent back to those tunnels.

I will not spend the rest of my life drilling in the dark. It's not gonna happen.

I go back downstairs and pace the hallway, ignoring her kicking feet and muffled screams. Then I start opening doors, looking for the basement because I'm gonna throw her down there and tie her to a beam or something while I finish the job I'm here to do and leave.

What happens to her after that is not my problem.

I know there is a basement because I saw the boarded-up windows from the outside. But despite searching the entire first floor, I cannot find the access point.

This is when I remember I need to get rid of her car.

How many Disciple townspeople have passed the house and noticed it already? How soon before one of them recognizes it and comes to see why she's here? Clearly, moving back in at this point in the renovation wasn't the plan.

I walk to the closet, open the door, push her down, grab her kicking feet, flip her over, and sit on top of her. It's not a comfortable position because her hands are tied behind her back, so I know the pressure I'm putting on her shoulders is nearly unbearable. But I need her to shut up and listen, so I lean in to her neck and whisper, "Stop kicking, stop screaming, and if you do that, I'll ease up. But I'm not gonna put up with your bullshit. Either you listen to me and cooperate, or I'll kill you." She was wriggling up to this point, but the threat makes her go still. "Do you understand me?"

She nods her head as best she can and relaxes.

"Good. Where are your car keys?"

She mumbles some words through the gag, but I can't understand her, so I pull it out. "I think I dropped them near the doorway."

I look over my shoulder, and spy them under a chair. "Good." I stuff the gag back into her mouth, get off of her, leave, slamming the door closed as I curse under my breath.

I need to move that car, so I go outside, move the

car and trailer around the far side of the barn, and then head back to the house. I'm just coming around the barn, about fifty feet from the back porch, when the door comes crashing open and the woman comes stumbling through it.

She's still gagged and bound, but the t-shirt blindfold has slipped down her face and is no longer covering her eyes. It's really not that hard to open doors with hands bound behind your back, so her ambition has kicked in and she fancies herself as one of those save-yourself girls. Because she sees me and starts making a run for it.

It's about twenty feet to the driveway and from there, another thirty to the highway. But she's got to navigate those porch steps in five-inch heels and I'm going full speed across flat grass, so I catch up with her just before she gets to the driveway and tackle her, taking her down into a weedy flower bed.

She screams past her gag and I think she hits her head pretty good on the side of the house, because then she starts crying.

I sit on her for a few moments, catching my breath, then spy the boarded-up basement window again. It's not big enough to fit through—it's actually rather long and skinny. And the framing around it is out of place with the rest of the house because it looks like a log cabin. Like maybe it was the original structure on this land and they built the mansion around it.

I lean into the crying woman's neck. "Where's the basement? How do I get in there?"

She doesn't answer, just starts cursing me through the gag.

"Lady, I've already explained that you've got two choices here. Do what I tell you and make things easy, or I kill you. Which do you want it to be? Because I don't care either way. You're not gonna fuck up what I'm doing. You're just not."

Just like before, she gives in and her body relaxes. So I let out a breath. But it's not relief. Because she saw my face. Again. That's twice now.

I stand up, pulling her up with me, and refasten the blindfold. She's sobbing and on the verge of hyperventilating when I turn her around and shake her by the shoulders. "I'm gonna ask you one more time. Where is the basement and how do I get you in there? And if you don't tell me, I'm just gonna kill you and stuff your dead body into that trailer you were hauling. Then I'm gonna drive it to the lake out there in the woods and back it into the water. It might take months for people to find your disgusting, bloated body."

Even from behind the makeshift blindfold I can see her wince. My threats are pretty gruesome, but I'm not sure how tenacious she is and I don't really have time to figure out how much threatening she needs in order to comply with my demands.

This level seems to work, because she starts mumbling.

I pull the rag out of her mouth and stuff it in my pocket. "What?"

She takes a deep breath, still sobbing. "There's a trapdoor in the library."

I grab her wrists and shove her back towards the porch. She lost one of her shoes in the dramatic escape, so she limps her way up the stairs and into the house.

"Which room is the library?"

"Down the first hallway and to the left."

With a firm grip on her bound hands I push her forward, keeping a good hold on her as she stumbles. A minute later I find the library and sure enough, once I look closely, I can see the outline of a trapdoor in the hardwood floors. I pull it open and stare down into the darkness. "Are there lights?"

"There's a switch on the side of the wall."

I position her in front of the trapdoor and give her a nudge. "Get in."

She huffs. "I can't go down those stairs blindfolded and with my hands tied behind my back. You're crazy."

"Well, give it your best shot because if you don't, I'll just push you."

Her whole body stiffens. "You're evil."

"And you're annoying. Go down. Right now."

She gets down on her knees, swings her feet out in

front of her, kicks off her one remaining shoe, then scoots forward on her butt until her feet are dangling over the side of the opening.

"See? With the right motivation, you can do anything."

She mumbles something under her breath in response—"fuck you," I think. But she does as she told, cautiously feeling out each step with her feet as she lowers herself down one step at a time. It takes forever because she's whimpering and cursing, but once she gets down far enough, I go in after her, feeling along either side of the wall with both hands, until I find the light switch and flip it on.

When she gets to the bottom she stumbles forward across the small room, trips over a bunched-up rug, and falls.

This obliterates the last of her resolve because she just starts sobbing uncontrollably, her face pressed into the rug. When I don't make a move to help upright her, she yells, "Who are you? Why are you in my house? What do you want? There's nothing here."

My words come out with a sneer. "I'm not here to rob you. I told you, I'm in the middle of something. It's unfortunate that you walked in on it, and I'm sure the next couple of days are gonna suck real bad for you, but there's nothing I can do about it. You're not gonna get in the way of me completing this job. You're just not."

"What happens in a couple of days?"

I don't answer her. Not because I don't know what happens in a couple of days, but because she's being cooperative and, generally speaking, cooperative prisoners stop being agreeable once they understand this won't help them live in the end.

I walk over to her and the sound of my footsteps must be enough to scare her back into silence, because she stops crying and goes completely still.

I kneel down and attempt to stuff the rag back into her mouth. She protests by shaking her head, then she starts begging. "No! Not the gag. You've got me tied up and blindfolded. I don't need a gag! No one can hear me if I scream!"

My first instinct is to ignore her and just stuff the gag back in, but I realize I need more information from her. "Was anyone meeting you here?"

"No."

"Then why are you here? The house isn't really livable. What's in the trailer?"

"I was fired from my job this morning. I worked at a hotel and lived in a cottage on the grounds, so they kicked me out of it. I didn't have anywhere else to go."

"What about your friends? How soon before they miss you?" She opens her mouth to say something, but I put up a hand. "Don't lie to me, either. Because if you say 'immediately' thinking I will let you go, you don't understand my situation. I need three days to finish what I came to do and nothing you say will prevent me from reaching this goal."

She lets out a breath like maybe she was gonna lie, then takes a few moments and gives me the truth. "No one. No one is gonna miss me because my boss, who doesn't even know I've been fired yet, is in Boston on business. She won't be back for a week and even if she does try and call me, she won't get suspicious until Thursday."

"Well, that's three days away. Sounds a little convenient to me."

"Whatever. It's the truth."

"What about your friends? The people in Disciple?"

"I haven't lived in Disciple for over a decade. I haven't even been back to visit in a few years. I don't even come home to check on the progress of the house. My friend, Lowyn, does that. And usually, when we want to hang out, she comes out to see me in Virginia at the hotel. I didn't have a chance to call her and cry about my bad luck yet, so no one knows I'm here."

Lowyn. As in McBride. As in Collin Creed's girlfriend.

If I have to kill this woman things will get messy, so obviously, it's better that I don't. But she doesn't need to know that. Still, this doesn't mean I'm gonna let her get all comfortable and shit either. I reach out, pry her mouth open as she starts to scream, and shove the gag inside.

"Keep quiet until I come back and then, *maybe*, I'll take the gag out. But if I hear one more noise, the deal's off and you'll sit down here in this little dungeon until some unsuspecting construction worker finds your dead and decaying body six months from now."

She recoils at my threat, but she doesn't make a noise.

I walk away, go back up the stairs, flipping the light off as I pass, and then close the trapdoor.

Three days and I'm out of here.

This woman will not be the reason I get sent back to the tunnels.

She won't.

CHAPTER 3 - CLOVER

*B*eing *blindfolded* and sitting in the dark below ground means it's impossible to tell how much time has passed since the man left me down here. Every once in a while, I'll hear a creak upstairs, but that's it. It's been a long time, though. I know this because my lips are so dry they're cracking and I'm so thirsty, even if the gag wasn't in my mouth, I doubt I could even swallow because the rag, which smells and tastes like turpentine, is sucking up all saliva inside my mouth so there isn't a drop of moisture.

I need a plan. I need to figure a way out of this because my interactions with him probably total up to two minutes and in those two minutes he threatened to kill me three times.

I'm just gonna kill you and stuff your dead body into that trailer you were hauling.

You'll sit down here in this little dungeon until some unsuspecting construction worker finds your dead and decaying body six months from now.

Both of those were bad, but it was the middle one that really jolted me into compliance. *I'll just push you.* Meaning down the stairs.

I would die. I would break my neck if he pushed me down those stairs. And even though the other two were more vulgar, they were abstract. More of a warning than an immediate threat.

The stairs were right in front of me and the action he would take was seconds away.

Focus, Clover, I tell myself. Because the other two threats might have only been a warning, but there's something in this man's voice that tells me he's totally serious. He's here for a reason and if I get in his way, he's not going to hesitate.

You're not gonna fuck up what I'm doing. He said that too. *You're just not.*

I'm not getting out of here alive. Even if I do comply with everything he tells me to do. Maybe I don't live in Disciple anymore, but I've heard my share of what's been going on up here since Collin Creed came back to town.

First Lowyn was in danger, then Rosie. And it's all because of some place up in the hills that I didn't even know existed, but is suddenly involved in some very serious shit.

Lowyn didn't tell me much about what happened to her up in some remote village in the mountains, but she said more than enough for me to figure out that it's got something to do with Collin and what he's been doing these past twelve years.

That was bad enough, but I don't live here anymore and I'm not involved in the daily life of Disciple, so it was easy to forget about it. Until Rosie's son was kidnapped and that too had something to do with Collin.

Now this strange man is squatting in my half-renovated home and he tells me he's here to do a job. There's no way this has nothing to do with Collin Creed's return.

I don't even know what he was up to all those years he was gone and Lowyn wouldn't go into details about that either, but it's gotta be bad.

Which means I need to be smart or I'll end up the next girl in trouble.

Hell, Clover, who are you kidding? You are the next girl in trouble! You're gagged, and bound, and in a secret basement. If you don't get out of here before this man finishes whatever it is he's doing, you probably won't get out of here at all.

This is when the danger of my situation turns into something very real and my heartrate kicks up, thumping in my chest. My hands begin to shake behind my back. Then my whole body is trembling, like I'm freezing cold, but actually, I'm so hot that sweat is dripping all down my body. My head starts pounding.

Take deep breaths, Clover. Take deep breaths. You're going to give yourself a heart attack if you don't try and calm down and be rational.

I've heard of people dying of fright, but never thought it was true. But the way I feel right now, I can easily see myself going into cardiac arrest over this because I can't stop shaking.

I breathe like I'm in a yoga class. Long breaths in, controlled breaths out. And after a little while of this, the shaking starts to subside. I still feel like I'm cold, but at least my muscles are no longer on the verge of spasming.

Once my body calms down, I work on my mind. Because that's the danger. The mind is where fear lives. Fear leads to panic and panic leads to mistakes.

I can't afford to make a mistake. Not when my kidnapper is throwing gruesome threats around like confetti.

I breathe for a little longer as I try to envision the room around me. It's been a long time since I've been down here, but it hasn't changed. And it's not part of the reno. I would never renovate this room. It's a piece of history.

There are four windows. Two of them are underground now though, covered up with flower-bed dirt. The other two are boarded up. So even if I could get my hands free, I doubt I'd be able to get out one of those windows without a hammer to pry the nails off first.

So the only way out is up the stairs. And there's no point in getting up the stairs if I can't open the trapdoor. And right now I can't because I have no hands and there's a latch you have to release before pushing on it.

That leaves… him. I need him to open the door. Then I need him to come down here so I can… what? What could I do? Kick him in the face, stun him, then make a run for it?

Even if I could kick him that hard, I don't think I'd make it. I had a pretty good head start that last time and he caught up with me frighteningly fast.

It's not going to work. He's stronger than me, he's bigger than me, and he's got all the control.

The only weapon I have is psychology.

I took a psych class in college as an elective. But honestly, as a woman, I don't need a psych class to get the best of a man. If… that man is interested in me.

I might not be as pretty as Lowyn or as cute as Rosie, but I'm definitely an eight. At the very least, a seven point five. And that's just regular old me when I'm not trying to save my life with flirting.

This guy is my age. Maybe a little bit older, but not much. He's young. Which means, like all men, he's horny and his dick controls his life.

If I want to control him, then all I have to do is control his dick.

He might be a ruthless piece of shit, but all men are the same. A pretty woman with a hot body can make them do just about anything.

I spend a little while trying to make a plan for how I'll flirt with him without him knowing. Winning this game, and saving my life, depends on deception. I need him to believe that I'm really interested in him and from what I've seen so far, he's a rather suspicious guy. It can't be obvious. In fact, I need him to feel like it's *his* idea to like me. He needs to fall for me first before I flirt.

Then, and only then, will he care about my wellbeing.

So I spend a good amount of time trying to come up with ways to play on his sympathy while simultaneously looking hot and turning him on.

There's one problem with this line of thinking. I am an eight on my best days. A seven point five on my down days. But this isn't a down day, this is like… the worst day of my frickin' life. There's nothing sexy about being sweaty, and smelly, and bloody. And I know I'm bloody because I hit my head when he threw me into the closet upstairs, then again outside in the flower bed, and a third time when I tripped on the rug down here.

I can't be sure that I've got a goose egg on my

forehead, but I suspect that's the cause of my pounding headache.

A burst of inspiration hits me. Maybe I could win him over by making him feel sorry for me?

Yes! I will use sympathy to play up my hotness.

But he hasn't come back. What if he never comes back? I need to get his attention. Which feels like an impossible feat when my mouth is gagged and my hands are tied. I won't even get a chance to put my plan in motion if I can't get his attention.

The only thing I've got going for me is that my feet are free.

I squirm around, trying to get up on my knees again, but my shoulders are so sore now, every time I move a painful twinge shoots up my arm.

I can rotate my body though, so that's what I do. Then I place my bare feet against the cabin wall and kick.

The noise this produces is a dud. It's not even a thud. I forgot that the walls are made of logs and mortar, which makes it feel a bit like kicking cement. And the sound doesn't carry. There's no way he can hear it from upstairs.

I picture the room again and decide the only thing I can kick are the stairs. And they are like ten feet away. But this is literally my only option, so I slowly begin scooting my body in that direction.

It takes forever to move inches. My shoulders hurt

so bad and my headache is now a migraine. I'm out of breath too. Because this stupid rag is blocking half my airway and soon, I'm gasping through my nose.

I have to stop and rest every minute or two, so I'm sure it's actually hours later when I'm in position at the bottom of the stairs with my bare heels propped up on the lowest step. I rest, then wake up with a jolt and realize I fell asleep.

For how long? Who knows?

I feel like I've been in this basement for weeks at this point. Surely my three days are over. Which means he's gone. He's left me here.

I shake my head, trying to snap myself out of these unproductive negative thoughts, and then raise my feet and bring them both down on the step with as much force as I can muster.

It does make a good, loud sound. So I pause, listening for footsteps above.

Nothing.

I do it again. Harder this time.

But there's no sound from above.

I pound my feet again, and again, and again but if he hears it, he ignores it. Because he doesn't come. So much time passes as my pounding continues, I fall asleep from utter exhaustion. Only to wake up and do it all again.

Months have passed at this point. I'm sure of it.

My lips and mouth are so dry now, the corners become painful cracks and I taste blood.

I cry, sobbing into the smelly rag as the tears streak down my cheeks, and I wish that one of them would drip into my mouth, but they don't. They only find the cracked corners of my lips and make them burn.

I sleep again, then wake up.

And I decide this is it. One more try and then I'll give up. I'll just stay here and die of thirst. And my body will rot, and decay, and some unsuspecting construction worker will find me months from now.

My feet come down one last time, making the loudest thud so far, and as the pain shoots up my legs the trapdoor above me opens.

I feel him before he speaks.

An angry presence.

He's not going to help me and I've got no chance in hell of tempting him with my womanly ways to earn his sympathy.

So I just cry.

CHAPTER 4 - RIGGS

I *flip on the lights* and stare down at the woman at the bottom of the stairs, trying to make sense of what I'm seeing. "What the…" There is blood *everywhere*. "What the fuck did you do?"

I descend and a moment later, I'm jumping over her bloody feet and reaching under her arms to pull her away from the stairs.

After I left her this morning, I stuck around for a little while, listening to see if she'd start making noise or just in case she managed to get free, because I was organizing all the equipment that still needed to be put up before I can start testing things and go home.

When I didn't hear anything, I left and was gone for about four hours. But as soon as I opened the front door, I heard the banging.

Looking at her now, it appears that she's been kicking her feet against the bottom step for quite a long time because her heels are a mess of broken skin and blood.

She's crying, so she hasn't bothered to answer my question.

"You stupid, stupid woman." I bend down, reach under the t-shirt blindfold that's flapping over her face, and pull the rag out of her mouth.

She starts gasping for breath in between sobs, which makes the whole scene even more dramatic than it already was.

"If you were trying to piss me off, you've done a good job."

"You left me!" she screams. Her voice is hoarse and raspy. "You piece-of-shit asshole! I've been down here for days with no water! No food! No nothing! What am I supposed to do? Just sit here and die of thirst?"

I kinda chuckle. Not that it's funny, because it's not. She's a mess. It's just... wow. Dramatic. "Well, that's an impressive bit of theatre. I suppose you learned all about acting, growing up in this fake-ass town."

"Acting!" She's still got the t-shirt over her face, so she can't see me and I can't really see her either, but it's pretty clear she's angry. "I'm not acting! I can barely breathe. I'm starving, and thirsty, and I have to pee! I'm not acting!"

"Woman." I shake my head and roll my eyes. "It's been like six hours. You're not starving or dying of thirst. What you *are* doing is overreacting."

"Over—" She scoffs, then starts again.

"Over*reacting*? I was fired from my job, kicked out of my cottage, and came home ready for a good cry and I was kidnapped in my own house! I am not overreacting, you bastard. My behavior is entirely appropriate!"

"Well, you're definitely screaming, so… tone that down a little, because it's too loud for me."

"Too *loud*?!"

"Should I gag you back up and leave?"

"If you leave me here, I swear—"

"You'll *what*?" Even though she can't see me, my eyes go squinty. I'm pretty sure all this annoyance is conveyed in my tone because she doesn't finish her threat.

Instead, she takes a deep breath like she's trying to pull herself together and gather up the last of her self-respect. After a few seconds of that she says, "May I please have a drink of water and may I *please* use the bathroom?"

When I first threw her down here, I didn't actually think about how much trouble a prisoner might be. I was only thinking about how much I want to be done with this job so I can go home and show my father and the Colony directors that my word is good now, and have that final hearing where they say my debt has been paid and I will not be sent back down to work the tunnels.

But I see that I have grossly underestimated what a

pain in the ass this woman will be. So I sigh.

"Listen," she says, clearly interpreting my sighing as frustration. "I wasn't trying to escape. I just needed you to come help me. I can barely talk, mister. I can't swallow. My mouth is so dry, my lips are cracked and bleeding."

"It's only been an afternoon, lady. You're fine. It was a panic attack."

"I'm not fine! Look for yourself. I need water. *Now*."

I flip the t-shirt up and study her mouth.

"Please," she begs.

The corners of her mouth are dry and if I look real hard, I can see a few speckles of blood, so maybe it stings a little—like a papercut—but she's really overreacting. However, it's not that hard to give her a drink and let her use the bathroom. Especially if it'll keep her quiet for the rest of the day. So I guess I'll do that.

I grab hold of her upper arm and tug. "Come on, stand up."

She lets out a long breath, like she's been holding it in. Then she manages to get to her feet with my help.

I push her in the direction of the stairs and then grab her shoulders to make her stop at the bottom. "I'll untie your hands, but if you run, or do anything to even make me *think* you're gonna run, I will throw you back down these stairs and leave you here for good. Do you understand me?"

She nods her head enthusiastically. "Yes. I understand. I won't, I promise."

"The blindfold stays. If you touch it, you're dead. If it even accidentally falls down, you're dead. If that blindfold moves in any way, you're dead. Do you understand me?"

"I won't touch it, I swear. Just please, give me something to drink and let me use the bathroom."

"Fine." I release the belt from her wrists and notice that the leather, while soft because I've had this belt for years, has cut into her wrists. If I were her, this is what I'd be complaining about, not those pinpricks of blood at the corners of her mouth. But whatever.

She groans as her shoulders bunch up and she stretches out her arms. "Thank you." It comes out mumble-y and low, like she doesn't want to feel grateful for the relief, but is obligated to nonetheless.

"Let's go. I'm busy and I don't really have time for this."

"Well, you don't have to keep me. I won't say anything, I swear."

I don't even bother responding to that with words, I just simply scoff and give her a good push right between the shoulder blades. "Go."

She reaches out with her hands, feeling for the stairs, then she starts climbing, using her hands to guide her up since she can't see. This affords me a good look at her backside. Her dress is light green and tight. It's all stained with grass and dirt, since I did tackle her in that flowerbed. But that can't hide the fact that she's got a nice ass.

"What's your name?" I ask her.

"Clover. What's yours?"

"Clover?" I laugh as we get to the top. "That is such a West Virginia name, I don't even know what to say about it."

"No, it's not. It's a very normal name. And you didn't answer my question, what's yours?"

"It *so* is. I've never met anyone named Clover. And you're not getting mine. If, by some accident you do get mine—"

"Let me guess," she interrupts, her tone dry and empty. "I'm dead."

"That's right, you're dead."

"You throw that threat around pretty easily. Like it's just another word for you. What are you? Some kind of serial killer?"

I huff. "Do you want to go to the bathroom and get a drink or not?"

"If my other choice is getting pushed down the stairs, then yes. I choose bathroom and drink."

"Good. Then keep quiet and walk." I grab her shoulders and push her down the hallway towards the bathroom.

It's her house so she doesn't need to see to know where it is. She places her right hand on the chair rail and follows it all the way to the little powder room. Then she pauses and aims her face in my direction. "Is the bathroom stocked with necessities?"

My laugh comes out unexpectedly. "If you mean toilet paper, then yes, Your Highness, it's stocked with necessities. You've got one minute."

She walks forward, feeling the panels on the door, then she starts pushing it closed.

I kick my foot forward, putting an end to that immediately. "The door stays open."

Her scorn comes out in her tone. "So you can watch?"

"Woman, I'll watch anything I want. But no, I'm not into bathroom kink. I'm just done taking chances with you. Now hurry up, or you won't go to the bathroom at all."

I'm pretty sure she's weighing the idea of not using it, but she gives in pretty quick and blows out a frustrated breath of air with her words. "Fine. Turn your back, though."

I roll my eyes, shuffle my feet, and then say, "It's turned."

She points her head in my direction for a few seconds, like she knows I'm lying. But she doesn't dare pull the t-shirt up to take a look. Just gives in again, letting out another breath, and feels her way over to the toilet.

I'm really not into bathroom kink. Like, at all. As

in, never once entered my mind, not even as a teenager. But I have to admit, there's something kinda sexy about watching her hike up her dress and pull down a pair of silky white panties.

She doesn't sit, she balances like she's peeing outside, which make me roll my eyes again, but this time I smile a little and then I really do turn my back.

"Thank you," she says.

"For what?"

"Finally turning around."

"Whatever."

When she's done, she rearranges her clothes, spends a good minute washing her hands, and then starts reaching around for a towel.

I hand her a rag, which has old paint on it and smells pretty bad. Her body shivers for a moment, but she doesn't say nothing.

I grab her shoulder and point her in the right direction. "Come on, then. To the kitchen for water and… whatever I can find to eat."

"Oh, I get food too? That's nice, thank you."

"Don't start being all polite and shit. I don't like it."

"What kind of person doesn't like when people are polite?"

"It's not the polite part I don't like, it's the fake part. I don't like fake people and everyone in this town is fake."

"Well, I'm very sorry my parents brought me up

proper and my good manners annoy you. Would you like me to call you names instead?"

"How about you just shut up?"

"Well, *someone's* mama didn't care much about manners."

"My mother was sick from the day I was born and died when I was five, so I guess she just didn't have the time for teaching me manners."

My revelation makes her go quiet. It's not even a lie, either. My mother did die when I was five, so I was raised by my father. And being a general, he very much cared about when and how I spoke. I would not call it manners, per se, more like protocols and etiquette.

But this one here isn't gonna get any military etiquette from me.

We reach the kitchen and Clover starts feeling around for the table. When she finds it, she takes a seat, stretching out her legs and letting out a breath of air that comes off as relief.

Which makes me glance down at her feet. "You really did a number on those heels of yours."

"Tell me about it. They hurt."

I walk over to my backpack on the floor and bring it back over to the table. "Don't blame me for that. I never told you to kick the stairs until you were bloody."

"It was the only way I had to get your attention.

And I can live with the consequences if you're gonna give me a drink."

"You could've drunk the tap water in the bathroom." I can't see her whole face because of the t-shirt, but I can see part of her mouth and she's scowling. "Something wrong with the tap water?"

"Well, I thought of that, but it smelled rusty. Was it rusty?"

"I didn't notice, but I wouldn't drink it." I'm reaching into my pack as I say this, and my hand bumps up against a stainless-steel container. I pull it out, unscrew the cap, and place it in front of her. "There. Take as much as you want. It's been filtered."

"I'll drink it all. You're not thirsty?"

"Just worry about yourself, princess. I'll take care of me." Then I take a seat across from her and kick out my legs.

She's taking a sip of her water when she stops, pointing her face in my direction. "Do I get to eat? I didn't eat this morning because I was so stunned about being fired. Oh, my God, how is this the same day? I can't believe they fired me. After all my hard work. And kicked me out of my cottage! Do you know what that asshole did?"

"What asshole?"

"My boss! He fucking packed up my cottage, put all my shit in a trailer, and then told me to haul it away. He didn't even pay for the trailer! I have to pay those people when I drop it off. Back in *Virginia,* by the way! Like… what the fuck, ya know? All this time I thought he was a nice guy, but I was wrong. I hate when I'm wrong about people."

I spy a pout form underneath that t-shirt and now I'm kinda thinking about how she might actually be pretty. I didn't really have a chance to get a good look at her when I was busy tackling and tying her up this morning. But she is. Even with the blindfold mostly covering her face, I can see it.

She suddenly sits up a little straighter. "And you know what else sucks?"

"What?"

"Well, Clarissa, my other boss, and pretty much my best friend—in Virginia, anyway—she doesn't even know I was fired. Right before she left for her out-of-town meeting, I was talking to her in the lobby, and she thought Mr. Sutter was gonna *promote* me!"

"He's the asshole?"

"Yeah. The one who fired me. She was all, 'You're getting promoted!' and I was all, 'What? But what about you?' And then she was all, 'Oh, this is my promotion! I'm taking over Boston!' And I was all, 'OMG! I'm so happy for you!' And then she was all—"

"Clover?"

"Huh?"

"I don't care."

She scoffs. "Well, sor-ree. My mistake. Sorry this is

the worst day of my life and instead of whining and complaining to my best Disciple friend, I'm a prisoner in my own house, stuck here with *you*." She blows out a long breath and leans back in her chair, kicking her bloody feet out in front of her.

I smile. Just a little. And only because she can't see me. "You're taking this kidnapping thing better than most."

She makes another face. This one is shock, I think. "How many times have you done this that you have an expected outcome in mind?"

"You're actually my very first prisoner."

"Huh."

"You're surprised?"

"Well, you're pretty liberal with your threats, buddy. And, by the way, they were very colorful. You threatened to kill me and stuff my dead body into the trailer, leave me to die and decay in my own basement, *and* throw me down the stairs."

"And yet you're still here."

"Well." She exhales so hard, the t-shirt fluffs up around her mouth. "I don't think you're serious."

I scoff. "You would be wrong. You have no idea how badly I need this job to go well. I don't care how cute you act, little princess. This ploy of yours? It's not gonna work. If it comes down to me or you, I choose me, Clover. So don't get too comfortable."

CHAPTER 5 - CLOVER

I can hear the threat in his voice. I actually do believe him. About all of it. The killing, the decaying body, and the stair-pushing. But again, the only thing I have is me. Myself. My cuteness. This is my weapon so I have to use it. Because I refuse to let this man turn the worst day of my life into the last day of my life.

There is a bit of desperation in his voice when he talks about this job he's doing. Even now, when he's much more relaxed than he was this morning, I can hear it. He's serious about completing it.

But there's still something there I can work with. Yes, he was mad when he opened the basement door, but he gave in to the idea of water and a bathroom break fairly easily.

Yes, he did watch me in the bathroom, but he turned around at the last moment.

That's why I didn't drink the tap water in the bathroom. Sure, the water from the tap did smell a little off, and I grew up in that house so I know that it turns a bit rusty if it hasn't been run in a while.

But it would've run clear, and been just fine, if I had given it another minute. I just replaced the well pump and pressure tank last year—to the tune of fifteen thousand dollars, thank you very much. I even got a reverse osmosis system, so the water had better be good, for fuck's sake. But if I had taken my drink right then in the bathroom, he would've put me back downstairs and I wouldn't be sitting here in the kitchen, charming his pants off with an expressive retelling of how my bad day started.

I mean, fine. I'm probably not charming him. Yet. But at least he's not yelling threats at me.

His chair scrapes across the floor and I know he's gonna stand up and this little reprieve will be over, so I hurriedly say, "Hey."

"What?"

"What about my feet?"

His pause here indicates that he's looking down at them. "What about your feet?"

"Aren't they bloody?"

"They are."

"So… don't you think I should clean them up? And do you have any lip balm? I could really use some lip balm."

He stands. Scoffs. Laughs. "You did all that to yourself and those feet of yours are already starting to scab. You'll be fine. Come on, it's time to go back down."

Then he's gripping my arm—tight—and pulling me up from my chair.

"*Wait!*" I'm desperate now and it's coming out in my tone. "What about… can I change my clothes?"

"The next thing you'll ask for is a shower."

I brighten at the idea. "Can I have a shower?"

"Only if I can take it with you."

My heart skips here. Because while I am sorta flirting with him, it's absolutely, one-hundred-percent fake and only for the sake of my own self-preservation. "Um…"

"Then no, Clover. You can't change your clothes or have a shower." He starts pushing me down the hallway.

"What about food? I didn't eat. I haven't eaten all day."

"I forgot. I only have one MRE with me right now, and it's mine. You've just been lying around all day. I've been working. You'll survive. You can go way longer than three days without food."

"Wait, what? You're not gonna feed me *at all*?"

"I told you, I only have one meal and I'm not going back to my camp until this job is over."

By this time, we're well down the hallway and I know the library is a mere few feet away. Once I'm in there, there's no more chances to change his mind. So

I stop, planting my feet and making him bump into me.

"Keep walking, Clover." He growls this into my ear.

"I'm hungry. I don't eat much, I promise." I need to make him give me something from his food ration. Anything. Even if it's a single cracker. I need him to take responsibility for my wellbeing. To see me as a person he's taking care of instead of something he can throw away. Because while he has been mostly accommodating for the last ten minutes, I'm still ninety-percent sure I'm not getting out of this kidnapping alive. "Something small. A cracker."

"No. There's just not enough for you."

"There's a diner in Revenant. You could go out and get us both food. Or—I know! I could go with you!"

"Fuck off. How stupid do you think I am?" He shoves me forward, making me stumble. "I'm not going into Revenant and I'm certainly not letting you leave this house."

"But you have to drive past there, anyway. I mean, when you leave. It's the only way out without passing through Disciple."

"I don't travel on *highways*, Clover. I'm leaving the way I came. And I came through the hills."

I think about this as I take those final few steps into the library. "You're one of them? The hill people that Lowyn told me about?"

"One of *them*?" He says the word 'them' with

derision. Like the thought offends him. "No. I'm not one of those hill people. I'm from out west. I'm just using their…" He pauses here. Like he's choosing his words carefully. "Their… infrastructure. That's all. I'm not from around here. Obviously, since I don't have one of those hick accents like all you people."

My mouth falls open with this insult. *Like all you people*? "I don't have an accent."

He laughs. "You *so* do."

"I mean, maybe it's a bit… Eastern seaboard, but—"

"Eastern seaboard?" He laughs again. "Woman, you talk like a country western singer."

"What?"

"And I'm not talking about, like, cowboy kinda accent, either. I'm talking hillbilly country western."

I blink my eyes underneath my blindfold. "I beg your pardon?"

"Never mind. Just turn around." Then I hear the snapping of the leather belt and my heart jumps.

When I don't turn, he forcibly does it for me. "No. Do not tie me back up! Please!" He grabs both my wrists and tugs them behind my back. "At least tie them in front!"

"So you can escape like you did this morning? Nice try."

"I won't, I promise."

"Well, I might believe you. If you hadn't already proved yourself untrustworthy. I don't forget or forgive shit like that. When I make a mistake, I only make it once."

Then he cinches the belt around my wrists, winding it around and around until it's painfully pinching into my skin and he can buckle it. He keeps a hold of my wrists as he nudges me forward with his body and for a moment, I really think he might push me down those stairs.

"Wait," I say, the desperation in my voice very clear. "When will you be back?"

"I dunno. But you're not going to die. At least not down there and from thirst or starvation. You can go three days without water and weeks without food."

"But—" I try and turn, but he stops me. "You'll be back tonight though, right? I mean, I just gulped down a whole bunch of water. I'll need to use the bathroom."

He doesn't answer me. Just pushes me forward again.

"Please! Don't leave me here. It's unnecessary!"

"Go down. And be quick. I'm behind schedule. And if you want me gone soon, we don't wanna screw that up now, do we?"

"But—" I lean back, pushing myself into him.

"Unless, of course, you've changed your mind about the shower? If that's the case I can carve out another fifteen minutes and allow myself a little fun time with you." He says these words with amusement.

And when I ease up on my resistance, he actually laughs. "Thought so. Get down there."

Then he gives me a push, sending me falling forward. I am fully expecting to dive face first into the trapdoor, but at the last moment, he grabs my shoulders. I feel like I'm inches from the opening, but then he says, "Bend down and put your legs into the hole, Clover. If you do that, and you're a very good girl, maybe I'll feed you later. We can split that MRE."

My stomach rumbles at the mere thought of eating. "OK." And that's it. That's all the fight I have at the moment. And the moment I say that word, the disgusting rag is shoved back into my mouth.

And this is it for me. I give in and stick my feet down into the trapdoor, then scoot down the steps on my butt.

He waits until I'm all the way down before whispering, "Nighty night," closing the door above me.

THERE'S *no way* to keep track of time, but there's also no way that this is still the same day when I wake up. It's raining outside, water is pelting against the boarded-up windows, and I'm thirsty again. It could be three in the morning, it could be the next day, I just can't tell.

He doesn't come back.

And as the hours tick off and the day goes on, and on, and on I realize—he's never coming back. That's why he said those things about dying of thirst and hunger. I can go three days without water and weeks without food.

He only needs two days now. By the time I'm dying of thirst, he'll be gone.

Just as I think that, the door above my head creaks open and the lights flip on.

Immediately I start struggling and trying to scream. Not because I think it's someone here to help me, because I am pissed.

"Hold on, hold on." He says these words like I'm some child in the middle of asking for something unreasonable.

His boots thud down the wooden stairs, and then he grabs my arms and stands me up as I struggle under his grip. The rag comes out and with it my anger. "You asshole! I thought you left for good! You're trying to kill me of thirst, aren't you? You're evil. You have no heart, or feelings, or—"

"Calm down, for fuck's sake."

"Calm down? You leave me down here for days, scared and helpless, and I'm supposed to calm down!"

He laughs.

"Oh, I'm so glad you think me dying a slow death is funny."

"It's only been three hours, Clover. Pull yourself together."

"Three hours!" I scoff. "Three *hours*? You're lying. It's been like two days! I fell asleep six times."

"You're crazy. Look." Then he eases the t-shirt blindfold up just enough for me so see and thrusts his wrist underneath it. "It's nine-thirty. You haven't even been in here a whole day." Then he laughs again.

I study the watch on his wrist, first noticing that it's very military-looking, and then reading the numbers. Twenty-one hundred hours. I do a quick military-time calculation and sure enough, it's nine-thirty at night. "But… that's not possible. I *have* been down here for days."

"Yeah, well, the darkness does that to you."

"Does what?"

He withdraws his wrist from my view and readjusts my blindfold so my eyes are covered again. "Fucks with your head like that. You don't realize how much humans depend on light to keep track of things like time until you have no light. You lose all sense of reality."

"What are you, some kind of time expert? How would you know?"

He leans in to me now, his face right up against my neck. So close his words tickle the little hairs there and send a shiver through my whole body. "Because I spent six long years in the dark, Clover. That's how I know. And that's why I cannot fuck up this job. Because if I do anything wrong up here, they'll send me back down *there*."

"Send you back down... where?" I'm so confused.

"Never mind. It's not important. Are ya hungry, or aren't ya? Because I'm starved and I'll be more than happy to eat that MRE myself."

"I am," I say quickly. "But I don't believe you about the time. It's probably nine-thirty the next day."

He huffs out a laugh. "Whatever. Come on, let's go." Then he releases the belt from my wrists, roughly turns me around, and gives me a push. "Go up."

I carefully climb the stairs, then wait at the top as he follows.

He leads me into the hallway and stops at the bathroom I used last night. "Need to go?"

"Yes." Then I shrug off his grip and feel my way in. "Can I close the door this time?"

"No. But I'll turn around. Just be quick."

His feet shuffle like he's turning, but whether he really does it or not, I can't tell. I can't do anything about it, either. So I put it out of my mind and relieve myself, then wash my hands and dry them using the rag from last night. It leaves a turpentine smell behind, but at this point, I don't care anymore.

And he's lying about the time. Maybe it is nine-thirty PM, as his watch said, but it's certainly not the same day. I've been down in that dungeon for more than twenty-four hours, that's for sure.

He pushes me in the direction of the kitchen and I picture it all in my mind's eye as I go down the hallway, feeling for the little dinette table that's been in the corner for my whole life, then take a seat. It stayed behind when I had the furniture moved out because it was a throwaway piece and the workers were using it for paint cans and stuff. The chairs stayed too. Almost everything else was packed up and put in the barn until the reno is done.

Everything except my childhood bedroom in the attic. It's exactly as it was the day I left for college. Not one thing has been removed or replaced. Keeping one's childhood bedroom intact after leaving for college is a long-standing tradition in my family.

When my mother left for college, the door to her attic bedroom on the fourth floor was closed and everything remained the same until I was born and old enough to move upstairs. I was eight. It was my birthday present that year, along with a pony. And opening that door was like falling into a time capsule. It was filled with things from the Seventies and Eighties. A record player—or hi-fi, I think they called them. She had stacks of albums. All classic rock like the Doors, and Led Zeppelin, and Ozzy.

My mother, listening to Ozzy! I didn't understand

how crazy that was back then, but now... I just have to laugh.

"What's so funny?"

I blow out a breath and wave my hand in the air, dismissing the memory. "Nothing. I was just thinking about the past. That's all. Nothing you need to worry about."

"It must've been a pretty good memory."

"It was." There's a silence after I say this and even though I can't see him, I know he's staring at me. I feel his gaze like it's heat. "What? Why are you looking at me?"

I hear him sighing, then the sound of rummaging through a bag or something. Another second later, and then he's unwrapping something.

"What flavor is it?" I ask.

"Does it matter?"

"Well, of course it matters. I won't turn it down no matter what it is, but yes, it matters."

He pauses here, like he's reading the label. "It's chicken and noodles in sauce."

"Oh, that one's good. What about the sides?"

He laughs. And it throws me a little because I think it's a real one. Like he's smiling too. "What do you know about MRE sides?"

"My best Disciple friend, Lowyn, she runs an antique store. It's kinda famous now, but back when she first started, she used to buy storage units sight unseen and she got one that was filled with boxes of MRE's. We tried them all."

"How long ago was that?"

"Mmmm. Eight years, maybe?"

"Which flavor was your favorite?"

"Turkey, gravy, and potatoes. Hands down the best. Like no competition."

He sighs here. "Yeah, that's a good one. They're hard to come by though."

"Tell me about it. Lowyn had seven cases of that one. Like someone was hoarding Thanksgiving dinner and was planning on making a fortune one day. There was a bidding war over them."

"That's funny." But he doesn't laugh, and I don't think he's smiling, either. "Anyway. It comes with…" He's taking things out of the package now. "Applesauce, crackers, peanut butter, and candy. Plus a drink. Wanna call dibs?"

I smile. "You don't mind?"

"It's just a stupid MRE."

"Fine. Don't be excited. I'll take the applesauce and the candy. If you're not picky, you can have the crackers and peanut butter."

"Did she make a lot of money?"

"What?"

"Your friend who found the MRE's. How much did the cache go for?"

"Oh. I have no idea. I never thought about that stuff again until just now."

He goes quiet after that, getting things out of the package and setting up the heating pouch. I don't have anything else to say, and when he doesn't say anything either, it gets awkward quick.

But once he tears open the main meal package, my mouth starts watering from the smell. "Oh, I'm so hungry. It's been days."

He scoffs, but says, "Open up."

"What?"

"You want food, right? Open your mouth."

"I can feed myself, thanks. I don't need your help."

"There's only one fork, Clover. And while I don't care if you eat the shitty applesauce or the crap candy, you're not getting my half of the chicken and noodles. So if you want me to share, open your mouth."

He gets to tie me up, blindfold me, watch me pee, and now I am to be spoon-fed?

It's so humiliating. I'm glad I can't see his smug face right now. That way, when he leaves and I'm still alive, I will never have to picture it in my nightmares.

"Do you want it or not?"

"I do." Then I sigh and open my mouth.

CHAPTER 6 - RIGGS

Clover's *blindfold* doesn't cover her whole face like it did yesterday so I can see her mouth just fine when she opens it. Her lips are very dry, but they've got a nice shape. I can't see her properly, of course, but I can tell that she's pretty and she is one of those women who cares a lot about her presentation. Nice dress, nice shoes, fancy hair and nails.

I put the fork in her mouth and she recoils for a moment. "It's hot."

"Do you want me to blow on it?"

"If you don't mind."

"I'm not blowing on your food, Clover. You're a grown woman."

"And yet you insist on spoon-feeding me."

"I can stop any time you want and scarf this hot meal down all on my own."

"No. Just… it burned my mouth, OK? Fuck. Just hold it in front of me and I'll blow on it myself. Is that too much to ask?"

I take my own bite, then load the fork up again for her. "Here. It's in front of you. Blow."

Her lips pucker up and then, ever so gently, she blows. The next thing I know she's reaching for my hand.

I pull away. "Don't touch."

"I can feed myself. Just hand me the fork."

I slap her hand away. "That takes all the fun out of it, Clover."

"I knew it! You're getting off on this spoon-feeding thing, aren't you?"

"Well… I would not go so far as to say 'getting off,' but it's entertaining. And if all you wanna do is complain and ruin it, I'll just—"

"Eat it yourself. You've threatened me with that a billion times already."

"Twice. I've said it *twice*. But three strikes and you're out. So one more grumble from you, and I'll just—"

"Throw me down the stairs? Kill me and put my body in the back of my car, then push it into the river? Or leave me in the basement to die and decay?"

"You're really dwelling on those threats, ya know that?"

"Well, why wouldn't I? You seem to have an endless number of death scenarios at your fingertips."

"All I want is your compliance. You know this, and yet you keep insisting on asserting control over me.

Which is a waste of time, Clover. Because you have no control here. I'm the one in control. And a smart woman would realize that and play along, so my final assumption about you is that you're stupid."

"Fuck you."

"That's it." My chair scrapes against the floor as I stand up and grab her arm, yanking her to her feet. "Dinner's over. It could've been a nice break for you, but I'm not in the mood to listen to you complain."

"Wait! I'll be good! I swear!"

"Too late. I'm done."

She struggles as I pull her down the hallway, planting her feet and leaning into the wall. I yank her so hard she falls forward. Luckily her hands aren't bound and she uses them to avoid a faceplant. Still, she lands pretty hard and cries out in pain.

"For the record," I say, "you did that to yourself."

She looks up at me, her blindfold askew. And I see one eye staring right at me. I should move. Pick her up. Cover her eyes again. But I don't. I just... stare back. She gets to her feet, and she doesn't fix her blindfold.

Instead, she spits insults. "You jerk! You manhandled me until I fell! I didn't do that on my own."

I reach over, pull her blindfold back up, and take her arm again.

Again, she plants her feet. "Wait. Just *wait*! One

spoonful of noodles isn't enough! At least let me take the applesauce with me!"

"I don't know what it's like to grow up in this world you live in, but where I come from, when someone gives you three warnings and you disregard them, there is no reward, Clover. There is only punishment."

"Punishment that involves darkness?"

"*What?*"

"You said—"

"Never mind what I said." I yank her arm again.

"Wait! Can't I at least sleep in my own bedroom? It's got one of those hundred-year-old locks on the door that can be locked from either side with a skeleton key."

"What difference does it make if you're locked up or down? There's no furniture in the bedrooms. I checked."

"You didn't check the fourth-floor attic. I bet you didn't even know we had an attic." She smirks at me. "Just like you didn't know we had a basement."

"I did know you had a basement. I could see the windows from the outside."

"But you couldn't find it. Not without my help. So you don't know about the secret room at the top of the house and I do. And it's just as good a prison as the basement cabin. It is. I swear, it is."

"No." I yank her again.

Again, she plants her feet. *"Please."*

"No. I'm sick of saying everything three times. Why can't you just accept the first answer I give?"

"Because your first answer is unacceptable."

She's frustrating me to the point of anger. But then, I know how to shut her up. So I lower my voice and lean in to her neck. "How about this… I'll let you sleep up there if I can sleep next to you. In fact, I think I need a shower. Don't you? Take a shower with me and we'll sleep in that bedroom of yours. Tit for tat, as they say. Quid pro quo. And that's my last and best offer."

Immediately, she's recoiling from me. I want to laugh, but I don't want her to hear, so I settle for a smile. "What do ya say? Deal?"

Her words come out as a growl. "No deal."

"Great, then let's go." I spy the belt I've been using to bind her hands and reach down and grab it. Then I drag her back to the trapdoor and put her right in front of it, her bloody feet perched on the edge. I lean in to her ear as I bind her wrists back up, making it as tight as possible. "Even though you don't deserve it, I'll leave the gag out. But if I hear one fucking peep out of you, Clover, I'll make good on one of those threats of mine that you're so worried about. Now get down there."

She wants to talk back. Badly, I can tell. But she holds it all in and lowers herself down to a sitting position. Then she scoots her way down the stairs. I don't even wait until she's all the way down, I just close the trapdoor and let out a breath.

Fucking woman. I know what she's doing with all that polite conversation she was trying to have with me. She's trying to make me see her as a person instead of an obstacle in the way of reaching my goals.

But it's not gonna work.

ONCE I LEAVE **the library** I go back to the kitchen and resume eating. But the chicken and noodles are cold now, and taste like shit, and I don't like sweets, so I have no inclination to eat the applesauce or candy.

So my meal—the only meal I have left—ends up being unsatisfying and not nearly enough.

Why couldn't she just shut up and sit here? Why is that too much to ask?

It's like she *wants* me to kill her. Like she's trying to get on my nerves. And that remark about the darkness? Did I mention that I was in the tunnels? I don't think so. All I said was that I didn't want to get sent back down there.

And she knew that 'there' was a dark place.

She's smarter than she lets on. Which is very bad

for her. Because if she would just play dumb, I might be able to talk myself into believing it.

She saw me again too. And I let her.

I let out a long breath and shake my head.

This is not going to end well.

But then I remember what she said about the bedroom on the fourth floor and I go up the stairs, all the way up to the third floor, and I start opening doors, looking for the secret entrance to the room with a bed.

A *bed*.

Something I haven't had the pleasure of sleeping in for a long time now. Before this job, I spent a few days in a holding cell on the main level of the city. But there was no bed. Not a proper one. Just a cement cot attached to the wall by steel brackets. It didn't have a mattress on it.

Prisoners where I come from don't get anything but hard labor, and darkness, and hunger, and cold.

There's no door on the third floor that leads to the top of the house. Not even one of those attic access ones in the ceilings. So I go down a floor and sure enough, I find a stairway in the back bedroom. Two flights later I come to another door, which does, in fact, have an old-timey lock with a skeleton key sticking out of it.

I open the door and find the light switch, flicking it on.

A laugh bursts out of me before I can stop it. And I'm smiling too, because this is the most ridiculous princess room I've ever seen. Actually, it's the only one I've ever seen but that doesn't make it any less absurd.

There are unicorns everywhere. The walls are pink, the curtains are yellow, and the bed is a canopy, of course. Something a six-year-old up-topper would sleep in. No self-respecting Colony kid would be caught dead sleeping in a bed like that. Not even a girl.

But… I have to admit, it does look pretty comfy. I walk over to it and sit down.

It's a mistake. Because this mattress is so fuckin' soft, there's no way I can't slump backwards into the pillows.

The next thing I know, I'm sound asleep.

I WAKE UP WITH A JOLT, sitting straight up. For a moment, I'm not sure where I am. But a gorgeous sunrise greets me from the other side of the dormer windows.

A smile creeps past my lips as I remember what this room is.

Her room.

All the furniture is white, all the walls are covered in pictures and posters, and there is a whole wall of shelves displaying trophies and ribbons.

Her childhood bedroom. Why? Why is this thing still here when the rest of the house is empty and in the middle of renovation?

I get up and study the hundreds of photographs that cover at least a dozen corkboards.

Clover. Every stage of her life is on display up here, from a little baby being cradled in her mother's arms, to a very alluring teenager wearing a bathing suit and standing in front of a river with another, equally attractive, friend.

Lowyn McBride, I realize.

I bet Collin Creed would try to kill me ten different ways if he knew I was gawking at the teenage version of his sexy girlfriend.

Snickering at that thought, I start back at the baby pictures and follow Clover's life as she grows up—birthdays, ponies, swimming and, of course, hundreds of pictures of her in Revival costumes. In many of them, she's on stage, singing in a children's choir. There are framed certificates and awards on the walls. Even her college degree.

But the one picture I get fixated on looks recent. Maybe a couple years old. She's standing in front of the house holding a piece of paper. I squint and lean in, wishing this picture was digital, so I could zoom.

But I decide it's the deed to the house. It's a big day for her and she is all smiles wearing a pastel spring dress.

She's very pretty. I've only gotten small glimpses of her whole face up until now, but there's no way to deny it. Clover Bradley is hot. And even though my offers have been mostly a joke, I actually would like to take a shower with her.

I pluck that picture off the wall and stuff it into one of my pockets.

Then I go back downstairs to the library and open up the trapdoor. "You still in there?"

For a moment, there's no answer and my heart skips a beat thinking that she escaped while I was sleeping soundly in her soft, comfortable bed on the fourth floor.

But then I hear a small, "I'm still here," and the panic recedes. "Is today the last day?"

"No. It's day two. I told you last night, it's only been one day."

"Well, that's just fucking great. Close the door and go away."

"You're not even gonna ask for a bathroom break?"

"Unless you're gonna free me, close the door and go away."

"Fine. Like I give a fuck if you wet yourself." And I slam the trapdoor back down with a booming bang.

I'm gonna have to kill this woman. I can feel it. She's too stubborn. Obstinate. Proud is probably the better word. She's too proud to be able to trust her not to talk. If she's alive when I leave here, the first thing she'll do is run to her best friend, Lowyn. Which means she'll actually be running straight to Collin Creed.

And then he'll come for me.

I already know they have access to the tunnels from that compound of theirs. For Edge Security, it's a huge asset. They don't lead straight to the ones below Blackberry Hill, but they might as well. One way or another, every tunnel is connected. All you need is a map.

When my father pulled me out of prison for this job, there was an air of panic in the room. So while I cannot be sure how much advantage Collin and his fellow townies gained by finding those tunnels, it must be considerable—and highly classified—for my father to pull me out early and have me do a job up here.

There's a part of me that wants to believe it's about trust. He's testing me, maybe.

Or he gave me this job because he doesn't care if I get caught. I don't know anything. Collin Creed could torture me to the point of death and I wouldn't be able to give him a single bit of intel because I've spent the last six years in the literal dark.

Sending me here to deal with Collin and his crew was an easy decision that required minimal effort.

But for me, this is my way back. This is my chance

to prove my loyalty so I'll never have to spend another day in the dark again.

I'd do anything to make this happen.

Which means... I need to take care of Clover Bradley.

It's **late afternoon** by the time I check on her again. But this time, I'm doing it for a specific reason.

"Sorry," I tell her. "I was caught up in the job. I'm gonna leave you a case of water."

"Well, I'm failing to see how that's helpful since my hands are bound behind my back."

"I was gonna untie you too, smartass." I throw her a disdainful glare. "You know, you're not very good at this prisoner thing. You'd get a lot farther if you'd just be agreeable."

"I thought you didn't want me to be polite? I thought it was fake? 'I don't like fake people and everyone in this town is fake.'" She makes her voice go whiney and childlike as she quotes my words back to me.

But I just smile and take her blindfold off. Mostly because I wanna see her face. But there's no point in keeping mine hidden anyway. She's seen me several times now.

Clover is so stunned, she stares at me with her mouth open for a few seconds before stuttering out her words. "What... why... what the hell are you doing? Why are you showing me your face?"

I shrug with one shoulder, unconcerned with her panic. "Why bother. You've seen me." Then I grab her arm, pull her up to her feet, and take off the belt around her wrists.

She spins around. "What are you doing?"

"Cutting you loose so you can drink the water."

"You're going to leave me down here, aren't you? That's your choice? Dead and decaying body found by a construction worker six months from now."

All I can do is shrug again. "If ya want, I can take the water with me."

She scoffs, her eyes wide. Then she makes a break for it. I grab her by the waist, swing her around, and try not to body-slam her, only marginally succeeding, as she hits the ground. She grunts and then starts moaning.

"That was a stupid thing to do, Clover." I growl this at her. "But lucky for you, I'm not the kind of guy who holds a grudge. So I'm still gonna leave the water." Then I turn and go back up the stairs and flick off the light.

"Wait!" she calls. "What about the bathroom?"

I look down at her, sitting there all pretty and desperate as the darkness threatens to swallow her up. I smile. "You wish."

Then I slam the trapdoor down and start drilling holes for the padlock I bought at a store in Fayetteville this afternoon.

She screams, pounding her fists on the wood, but the drill mostly drowns it out.

When I'm done, I leave and get back to work.

The sooner I finish up, the sooner I can leave this woman behind.

CHAPTER 7 - CLOVER

As soon as he's done putting a lock on the trapdoor—that's what he's doing, that has to be what he's doing—I get up, climb the stairs, and turn the light on. Now that my hands are free, I can make a real attempt at an escape. So I work the latch and push my shoulder against the door. It gives, but only about half an inch.

I'm sure whatever lock he used, it's industrial-grade.

Which means there's no hope of me busting through. I know for a fact that the trapdoor is made of solid hickory. It's like three inches thick. The windows are covered with the same wood. And they were bolted on good and tight because they've been like that for the entire six years I've been renovating because the cabin has always been a family secret. Lowyn is probably the only person outside my immediate family who knows it's here.

The workmen might come back. Perhaps one of them forgot a tool? But it's unlikely because I barely had enough to pay them for last month. All of this month's money went towards that stupid Lincoln Navigator. Which means they have moved on to more lucrative projects and any tools left behind would've been collected weeks back.

This SUV feels like one of my dumber purchases right now. If I had stayed on schedule for the reno, none of this would be happening because this man would not have dared use my house as some kind of secret home base for a clandestine job if workers were showing up on the regular.

So basically, my desire for a luxury SUV to pull a fantasy horse inside a horse trailer is gonna get me killed.

How amazing.

I go back down the stairs and stare at the water. There are twenty-four bottles. How long can I live off twenty-four bottles of water and no food?

I don't know. Two weeks?

What I do know is that however long it is, it's going to be miserable.

He's not going to kill me. He doesn't have to. He's just going to let me slowly waste away down here. It's cruel, that's what it is. It's evil. And this water is just a way to ease his mind about the whole thing. That's it, nothing more. Sure, it's ruthless. But my death won't happen by his own hand. I guess he can live with that. I guess his conscience is now clear.

I press my back against the wall and slump down, rubbing my scabbed and sore wrists as I think about this.

Because my theory might be flawed.

Maybe his conscience isn't clear? Maybe leaving me to die isn't his first choice. Maybe killing me, whatever way that happens, is weighing on his mind?

And maybe that weight is heavy.

He didn't *have* to bring me water, but he did. And it's quite a lot. From my perspective, this amount of water feels like torture because all it's going to do is prolong the inevitable.

But perhaps, from his point of view, it's mercy. Or maybe he's trying to give me time to escape.

He doesn't know the door and windows are made of three-inch-thick hickory. And if I were him, a man —a big, strong one, at that—I probably *could* kick my way through it.

Long story short, I think he's hedging.

He *wants* me to escape.

He just doesn't want to be responsible if I do.

It's not much—hell, it might not even be true—but it's all I've got.

An idea begins to form in my head. And a little while later, I think I've actually got myself a plan. But it will only work if he comes back.

And I'm just not sure he will.

MANY, *many hours* pass before I finally hear footsteps above me.

I get to my feet, tired—exhausted, actually—and bleary-eyed. But also ready. This is my last chance. Whatever reason he has for coming back doesn't matter. I need for him to let me out. And I only know one way I can get him to do that.

When the trapdoor opens, I'm standing at the bottom of the stairs. I look right into his eyes, trying to not think about how kinda handsome he is—though that was my deciding 'pro' in the mental 'pros and cons' I was listing in my head for actually talking myself into what I'm about to do.

If he were ugly, it wouldn't be impossible, but it would be harder to endure.

"Hi," I say, giving him a smile.

"One more bathroom break? I won't be here much longer, so I figured I'd ask."

"Yes. Please." I nod my head enthusiastically and smile bigger.

"Come up, then." He takes a step back as I begin to climb. When I get to the top, he pans his hand to the hallway.

When I reach the bathroom, I go inside, leaving the door open like every other time.

But he closes it and doesn't even say anything.

I relieve myself, cursing under my breath because he's lost interest. The time to make this proposal was two days ago. It's too late now.

But I can't think that way. If I do, I'll end up back in that prison cell and that's where I will die. So when I come out of the bathroom—which is just a powder room, actually—I look him straight in the eyes. "How about that shower?"

His eyebrows knit together in confusion. "What?"

"Can… can I take a shower? Before you leave? It's been days. If you're gonna leave me here to die, at least let me have one last shower."

He shakes his head, ready to say no.

But before he can blurt out his negativity, I say, "With *you*, of course. A shower with you. Wasn't that what you wanted?"

He frowns. Not an angry frown, either. But a pity frown. "It's not gonna work, Clover. I don't even know you. I don't even like you. Taking a shower with you would be like taking a shower with a whore. Something owed. Something meaningless. Something to be forgotten."

I nearly recoil at this insult, but control myself just in time. Then I smile and lift up one shoulder in a nonchalant shrug. "So? What do I care? I'll be dead in… two weeks? Maybe sooner? Why not go out with a bang, ya know?" I chuckle at my pun, but he doesn't.

It's not working. And the moment I realize this, I frown. Then, before I can stop it, my chin is quivering and I'm on the verge of tears.

"Fine," he says. "Take a shower. What do I care?" Then he pans his hand down the hallway.

There are two bathrooms on the first floor, but they are both power rooms. So we have to go upstairs. I'm halfway between the first and second floors when I smell the shampoo.

He's already taken a shower today.

When we reach the top of the stairs, he motions to the bathroom. "Go ahead." Then he backs up to the wall and slides down it.

"You don't want to join me?" I ask, hope in my voice.

"Nah. But don't let me stop you from enjoying it." Then he turns his head and looks down the hallway.

Why? Why, why, *why* didn't I enact this plan from the start? We could've been friends by now if I hadn't been so difficult. Instead, I'm left looking like a desperate fool.

I go into the bathroom and close the door.

The water is barely hot, the only towel is still damp from when he used it, and there's no shampoo, just a bar of industrial soap left over from the workmen, no doubt, that no woman in her right mind would use.

So I don't even get clean.

I simply let the water run down my body for a couple minutes, then get out, towel off, and put my filthy dress back on.

The dress I got fired in.

The dress I got kidnapped in.

The last dress I'll ever wear.

And have been wearing for three days already.

When I come out, he's not even in the hallway. I find him sitting on the bottom step of the stairs, his head in his hands, like he's tired.

When he hears me, he turns. Then stands and steps aside, indicating that I should go back down the hallway that leads to the library. That leads to my prison.

I've failed. I know this. But when he opens the trapdoor and silently motions for me to go down, I fully internalize it. "Please." I turn to him, grab him by the collar of his t-shirt, and go up on my tiptoes so I can look him straight in the eyes. "*Please*. Do not leave me here to rot and die. Do not leave me here to decay. You don't have to do this! I swear, I will not tell anyone about you. I'll never mention you again. I don't even know your name!"

He slowly, but deliberately, pries my hands off his shirt. "It's over, Clover. I'm sorry. I've done all I can."

I want to scream at him now. Because he hasn't. He

hasn't done all he can. If he had, I wouldn't be standing here begging him not to kill me.

But there's no point. I can see his resolve in those brown eyes of his. He won't be swayed.

He's made up his mind.

So I just sigh, and turn, pulling my hands from his grip.

And then I go back down into my dungeon.

He closes the door before I'm even at the bottom of the steps.

CHAPTER 8 - RIGGS

I **will not feel guilty** about this. I refuse. It's not my fault that she showed up and saw my face. It's not my fault that I had to lock her up. And I'm not saying it's her fault either. It's just… bad luck. That's it. I was here, I thought I was safe because the house pretty much looks abandoned. Clearly, if I had known she was in the process of getting fired and kicked out of her cottage, I would've left and never come back.

But that's not how it played out. It happened the way it happened. A classic case of wrong time, wrong place.

So I do not feel guilty when I walk out of the room and get back to work.

I leave the house, go to the control room I've set up in a nearby underground access tunnel, and spent the next four hours finishing what I started.

When I'm done it's very dark.

I go back to the house, make one last cursory check that I'm not leaving anything behind, wipe down all possible surfaces that might have my prints on them, and I'm just about to pull the back door closed behind me… when I stop.

"Fuck." I mutter this under my breath as I look at my feet. She hasn't eaten anything more than one bite of an MRE in nearly three days.

The least I can do is see if she wants food.

She's probably gonna say no, and whatever. That's fine. But I will have gone above and beyond anything she actually deserves and I can leave here with a completely clear conscience.

A long sigh escapes. I just really want to get home and get my life back on track.

But I go back in, and open the trapdoor, and peer down.

She's turned the lights off, so I can't see her. But I don't care about that either.

"Have you come to gloat? What could you possibly want now?" Her voice is raspy and low. Which isn't my fault, either. I left her two cases of water.

"I'm about to leave, Clover. Do you want some food?"

She lets out a long breath and I'm fully expecting her to start a fight and tell me to go fuck myself. But to my surprise she says, "Yes, please."

"Yes?"

She scoffs. "You were hoping for a no, I take it?"

"I'm not going to argue with you. I'll be back." Then

I close the door, lock it back up, and leave.

I used her car to go into Fayetteville to buy the lock, so I guess it's fine to use it one more time. I unhitched the trailer the last time I took it, so it's not even that hard to pull it out onto the highway and head south.

There is a diner in Revenant, and I look at it as I pass, but I don't stop there. I'm sure they are used to all kinds of tourists and strangers coming in to eat, but I'm not taking any chances that someone might remember me.

My entire future hinges on getting this job done right.

So I drive to Fayetteville, order two burger meals, and drive back to the house. The food is cold by the time I bring it inside and put it on the table, but whatever. I'm sure she won't care.

Then I go back to the trapdoor, unlock it, open it up, and peer back down. "Come up. You can eat up here."

It's still dark down there and none of the light from up here is penetrating that darkness, so I don't see her until she's right underneath me, looking up. "You're gonna let me out?"

"To eat, Clover."

I know she wants to argue here. I can feel her anger.

But I also know she's hungry.

She will die of thirst before she dies of hunger, but starvation is a very unpleasant thing. I've known hunger pangs. I missed a lot of meals while I was drilling tunnels in the dark.

She holds her tongue and climbs up the stairs.

I wave her forward in front of me, expecting her to make some stupid break for it. But she doesn't. She goes to the kitchen, assuming that's where the food is, I guess, and takes a seat at the shitty dinette table.

I sit in the chair to her right.

She doesn't even look at me. Her eyes are on the bags of takeout food.

"Go ahead, eat as much as you want."

Clover opens the first bag, takes out all the contents, and greedily peels back the wrapper on the burger, shoving it into her mouth. She holds it with two hands as she chews, head bowed and eyes cast down.

Times ticks off—whole minutes of it—but she never raises her head up. Just keeps taking bites and slowly chewing her food as she looks down at the table.

I let out a long breath, stretching my feet out. "It's not my fault, you know."

Clover's eyes flit up and meet mine. They're an intense shade of blue. Not bright and disarming, like some blue eyes can be, but more like the color of a dark summer sky. "Excuse me?"

"This whole thing here. It's not my fault."

Her eyebrows go up and then she scoffs. "Are you implying that it's my fault? Because… well, let's review the facts here, shall we? I came home. That's what I did. That's all I did. I came home. And you were here. Uninvited and unwelcome. So if it's not my fault and it's not your fault, then who should get the blame when I die a slow, painful death in my own fucking basement?" She stares at me for a moment, daring me to say she's wrong.

But she's not wrong and after a few seconds, she reverts back to chewing and staring down at the table.

"It's just…" I don't know what to say.

"Save it. I don't care. And I don't want to listen as you make up excuses."

"I just…"

She looks up again. "I get it. You feel terrible. But unless you're gonna do something about this sudden flash of guilt, shut up, OK? I'm not interested."

Again, we stare at each other. And then, again, she looks back down and takes her final bite of burger.

"There might be a way," I say.

"A way to what?"

"To not leave you here."

She looks up. Then narrows her eyes. *How?*

"I could… take you with me."

Her head tips back as the guffaw comes out. Then she shakes her head and directs her gaze to me. "I'm not going anywhere with you. How is that even a solution? What a stupid choice. I can stay here and die or I can become your prisoner?"

"Ya know, you're kinda stuck up. Not to mention ungrateful."

"What?" She scoffs.

"I'm offering to save your life, Clover. At great risk to myself."

"By making me your pet, or something? No, thank you." She starts eating her fries, staring off in the distance this time.

"It wouldn't be forever. I'd set you free."

"It wouldn't be *forever*?" Another scoff. "That doesn't sound promising."

"I'm not a killer."

"I think you are."

"For fuck's sake, Clover! Why are you arguing with me? Just say yes! Yes, you'll happily come with me and endure whatever slight discomfort there is in order to save yourself. It's a simple fucking 'yes!' That's it! That's all you have to say. Just *yes*."

There is nothing but silence after this little outburst of mine. So I just keep going. "If I thought you were coming home, I would not have been here. It's not my fault, Clover. I'm just... I cannot fuck this job up. I can't."

Her expression softens slightly. "Because of the darkness?"

It takes me a moment to decide to answer her. But there's no point in denying it. I slipped up. Somewhere along the way, I said too much. She's smart and picked up on it. It's a weakness and she knows this. The longer I insist there's nothing there to find, the harder she will look and the more power over me she'll have.

The only way to neutralize this is to spill the secret.

"I don't know how much you know about what's under the ground, but that's where I come from."

Her face crinkles up in such confusion, I actually smile. "Under the ground?" She looks at the floor, then back at me. "I don't understand."

"You don't know about the tunnels?"

"What tunnels?"

"I'll take that as a no. I'm surprised, though. I figured Collin Creed told everyone in Disciple. That's what he said he did, anyway. Guess he's a liar."

"I don't live here anymore. I haven't been home in a long time. The reno, as you can see"—she pans a hand to the wreck of what used to be a kitchen—"is at a standstill. This house is going to bankrupt me. There's no reason to come home when home is gone. Well, except for my bedroom."

Without realizing it, I smile, remembering her bedroom.

"What's so funny?"

"Nothing," I say.

"You went up there, didn't you? Did you sleep in

my bed last night?"

"If you were me, would you have slept in it?"

"You did. You slept in my childhood bed while I was locked in my own basement. Which, by the way, was sort of a playhouse when I was a kid. I loved that cabin. And now I will never think of it the same way again. You've ruined a major part of my childhood by keeping me prisoner down there."

"I only kept you prisoner because you tried to escape."

"Oh, no. You will not turn this around on me, you psychopath. I only tried to escape because you were holding me prisoner!"

I narrow my eyes at her. "You walked in on me. I had no choice."

"I walked in on *you*? No." She shakes her head. "That's not how it happened. I wasn't in the wrong place at the wrong time. I was in the right place." She points her finger at me. "*You* were the one in the wrong place. *You*."

"Do you wanna come with me or do you want to die in the basement?"

"Obviously, I don't want to die."

"So you want to come with me."

"I'm not saying that. I would rather you just… let me go."

"So you can go tell Collin."

"What is it with you and Collin Creed? I don't

understand. Are you two enemies or something?"

"Never mind Collin. I'm trying to keep you alive. That's the part you should be concentrating on right now, OK? Just that. And I feel I've had this discussion with you a million times and it's only been a couple of days. Why are you so fucking difficult? Why can't you help me help you?"

I'm getting angry and she suddenly realizes this, so she doesn't reply. But I can see the hatred in her eyes for me. I can see her loathing.

But there's something else in there, too.

It's… injustice. Her arguing and pushback isn't something she's doing on purpose. She feels wronged. I am actually at fault. And it's pissing her off so much that I refuse to take responsibility for this situation, she cannot stop the attitude.

It's not fair. And Clover Bradley is, apparently, a woman who believes in fairness.

I let out a long breath, pulling my anger back. "I'm sorry, OK? Is that what you want to hear? I'm sorry. It's all my fault. Now. I'm going to ask one more time, and only one more time. Do you want to stay here and die?"

She shrugs up one shoulder and crosses her arms. "Yes. I want to stay here and die."

"Come *on*. You do not."

"I do. I want to make you responsible for my death. I want the memory of this to eat you alive. I want you to regret not letting me go. And then, when you die, I want you to go to hell for it."

I laugh. "Oh, I get it. You're one of those 'last word' kinda girls? The kind who can't stand to lose an argument so you say and do things only out of spite."

"First of all"—she holds up a finger—"I'm a ray of fucking sunshine, OK? I'm not one of 'those girls.' I can't even remember the last time I had an argument, let alone the last time I plotted to win one. I'm a pleaser. I work in customer service. I plan events at a big hotel—"

"Correction. You *did* plan events at a big hotel. You don't anymore."

"My point is"—these words come out through clenched teeth—"I live to make people happy. My joy comes from their joy."

"Well, that's fucking sad."

"There's nothing sad about that."

"So what are your dreams?"

"Like I'd tell you."

"You don't have any, do you? You go through life living off a contact high."

"You don't know me. You don't know anything about me. But even if that were true, at least I'm not a psychopathic killer who will leave young women to slowly starve to death in a basement."

"I just invited you to come with me, so from this point on, Clover, what happens to you is your choice."

"It doesn't feel like a choice. That's the part you're missing. It feels like a requirement." Her eyes lock with mine, unblinking. "It feels like a trap."

I let out a long exhale, bow my head, and rub my fingertips into my temple. "I didn't plan to kidnap you. I'm not trapping you." I look back up at her. "I'm trying to save your life. I'm sorry my plan is not to your satisfaction, but it's the best I can do." My chair scrapes along the floor as I get up, then I point in the direction of the basement. "Let's go. Your choice awaits."

She leans back in her chair, arms still crossed, unafraid to meet my gaze. "I'm not going back into the basement."

"No? Well, you just spent the last five minutes insisting that you were."

"Tell me about the darkness then."

"What?"

"You didn't say either way. Earlier, when I asked about it? Tell me about the darkness and I'll go with you."

I laugh out loud. "I don't *care* if you come. I don't need to tell you anything."

"You do care. Otherwise you wouldn't be making this offer."

"If you know I care, then why are you being so difficult? Just agree and we can go to bed, and tomorrow morning we'll leave."

"Because I want something from you to even out this power struggle we're in."

I scoff. "There's no struggle here. I'm the one with the power."

"Exactly. And as long as it's so uneven, I don't feel safe. So I can't go." I'm just about to explode when her face changes. Her eyes go soft and her lips pout. "I want to go. I want to go with you. I don't want to die. I just need…"

"An excuse?"

She presses her lips together and nods. "Yes."

"So you can live with yourself later?"

"Yes. So tell me about the darkness and then we'll be even and I will save you from yourself."

I laugh. It comes out loud. But she's absolutely fucking serious. Her eyes are even a little glassy, like she's on the verge of tears. "You want to talk yourself into the idea that I'm vulnerable, is that it, Clover?"

She shrugs up that one shoulder again. "Maybe it's stupid, but it evens it out."

I sit back down, kick my legs out, and fold my arms across my chest. "Fine. I was sent on a mission when I was twenty-two and I fucked it all up. When I got back, they punished me."

Her eyes squint up in confusion. "What did you do?"

"It's not important. What's important was the darkness, remember?"

"OK. Fine." She rolls her hand in a 'keep going' motion.

"My punishment was to work in the tunnels." Immediately, her mouth opens to ask questions. But I put up a hand to be silent. "If you come with me, you'll see. But that's the important part, remember."

"All right. You were sent to work in some kind of tunnel. How is that punishment?"

"It was dark." My mood sours and my words come out bitter. "And it wasn't a small darkness, either. It was six years. And ya know, we're born underground, and we live our whole lives underground, and obviously, our sun is artificial, so how can the darkness be punishment? But they only send runners into the deep down where they drill the new tunnels. Because that kind of darkness—the kind that doesn't come with an artificial sun and all the perks and amenities that a city affords, it's unbearable. Runners, we know what the real sun is. We've felt it on our skin. We've lived in the open air. We've seen *sky*. We know there's more out there than artificial UV light. So. It's torture."

Clover doesn't breathe, or blink, or move through any of that explanation, so when it's over, she exhales. She doesn't avert her eyes. They are staring intently into mine. Like she's picturing everything I just revealed inside her head. She blinks. "And this is your last chance, isn't it?"

I nod. There's no point in hiding that. And if she needs something to humanize me, or whatever, so that she can make the decision to save herself, so be it. "I can't fuck it up. And if I let you go, it will get fucked up. Somehow, some way, it will."

"How long were you up here?"

"Only a year."

"How long ago was that?"

"Six years ago."

"You spent six years in the dark?"

"Yep. Satisfied now?"

She lets out a long sigh. "OK. I guess I am. But we're not leaving tonight?"

"We'll wait until morning. I have to blindfold you so you won't be able to find the tunnel again once you're free and it's better to do that in the daylight."

"OK, but"—she puts up both hands, palms thrusting forward at me—"can I at least sleep in my own bed?"

"No." Then I kinda laugh.

"Why not?"

"Because I can't trust you. I'm going out on a huge limb for you, Clover. You don't even understand how fucked I will be if I get caught. I'm not giving you any more chances."

"But... you could come up there with me." She smiles here and her whole face brightens. "Wouldn't you like to sleep in the bed?"

"Oh, I'm definitely sleeping in that bed again."

"So you *did* sleep in my bedroom."

"I did."

Her eyebrows knit together in annoyance. "That's not fair. And if you're gonna be up there anyway, then why can't I just come along? It's not like I'm trying to seduce you for an opportunity."

One corner of my mouth lifts up. "Like this morning?"

"Hey, I was desperate. And hungry. It felt like my last chance."

"'Last man on earth' kind of thing?" I waggle my eyebrows at her.

"Exactly. But that's over now. We've come to an agreement that doesn't involve tricking each other."

"Would it have been a trick?"

"Would what have been a trick?"

"The two of us taking a shower and sleeping in your bed afterward? That was your original plan, right?"

She let out a breath. "Yep. It would've been nothing but a trick."

"And now we're not tricking each other?"

She's annoyed. "I *just* said that."

"Fine. If you're so desperate to sleep with me, what do I care." I turn and wave my hand at the hallway that leads to the stairs. "Come on, then. Let's go."

CHAPTER 9 - CLOVER

I'm on the second floor of the house, just heading up the stairs that lead to my attic bedroom, when I have doubts about what's going to happen next. Not just the part about spending the night together in my childhood bedroom, but the entire offer to 'save me.'

Because it occurs to me that this offer of food might've been a ruse to get my guard down. And now that I've actually formed this thought in my head, it seems very likely that it's the case. Because it worked.

When I was looking at him downstairs, I saw a person, not a kidnapper. And that's quite a switch from my perception of him earlier in the day.

How many ways did he threaten to kill me?

Several. And at no point did I ever think he was joking, either.

So why the hell did I agree to sleep in the same bedroom with him? Was it really just because I wanted a bed instead of a hard, wooden floor?

Or did my perception change because he took the blindfold off and I was able to get a good look at him?

I'm leaning towards number two when I reach the top of the stairs and take a few steps into my bedroom. I turn to face him as he reaches the top step too.

We pause, studying each other for a moment. And this makes my heart skip. Not because he's handsome. I kinda knew that since I did actually see his face that first day. More because I now have time to actually notice his good looks. There were so many other emotions clamoring for top spot in my mind, his hotness factor didn't even crack the top hundred things I was focusing on the past two days.

Now… well, now everything feels different. He has offered to save me and not let me die of thirst and starvation. And stupid me just… believed him.

"What?" he asks.

"Nothing."

"You're having second thoughts about this, aren't ya?"

"No. I mean"—I pause to sigh—"a little bit."

"I'm not interested."

"In?"

"You. Like at *all*."

"Oh, you're into men?"

"What? No."

"Then why did you say it like that? I'm not ugly or anything."

"I'm just not interested."

"You have a girlfriend down in your tunnel?"

"No. I told you. I was in our version of prison for the last six years."

"Were there women down there?"

"No."

I press my lips together and suck in a breath.

He closes the bedroom door behind him, turning the lock. Then he looks at me with a smile. "You're not my type."

"OK, then." I turn my back to him and walk over to my bed. Then take a seat on the edge and look at my feet. My heels are still very sore from all that kicking I did the first day, trying to get his attention. But at least they're no longer bloody. Everything about my body seems… tight. I'm wound up and unable to relax. And the tension inside me is looking for a release, I think, because as I try and force myself to relax, I start trembling. And no matter how many moments I take to close my eyes and breathe, this trembling feels like the precursor to an explosion. An eruption of pent-up emotions or something.

To take my mind off what's happening to my body, I look up and study the man who's been holding me prisoner. He's tall, fit and a bit on the muscular side. He's wearing black pants, a black t-shirt, and black boots. All of this lends an air of 'military' to his look. His hair is light brown, which is nearly the same color as his eyes. They almost look hazel, but not in a blue-green Collin Creed way. More like a… lion or a wolf. "You're not a werewolf, are you?"

"What?" He laughs.

"Your eyes are a bit… disturbing."

"Oh. That. Yeah. Sometimes they come off gold, but they're not. Just brown. It's a trick of the light."

"That wasn't my question."

He shakes his head at me. "No, Clover. I'm not a werewolf."

"But you say you come from some underground city. Some secret underground city. You're not human for all I know."

He sits down on the overstuffed chair near my window and starts unlacing his boots. "Trust me, doesn't matter if you're up or down, it's all the same shit."

"So what's it like there?"

He kicks off a boot and looks at me. "Am I making you nervous?"

"No. Why?"

"Because you're very chatty."

"Well, I don't even know your name."

He and I stare at each other for a moment, his eyes doing a little search of mine. "Riggs. I'm Riggs."

"Do you have a last name?"

"Of course. But you don't need to know my last name." He puts up a hand when I open my mouth to object. "And before you tell me it will even things out, forget it. That only works once and you used it up. I told you about my prison time and the way I see it, you owe me something now because I don't know anything personal about you."

My gaze travels around the room, looking at all the hundreds and hundreds of photographs that are tacked up to dozens of corkboards. Then I train my gaze back on him. "Looks to me like you got a good look at my entire life, so that's not even accurate."

"Baby pictures of you and your ponies isn't quite the same."

"You took one."

"What?" He sneers this word out.

"You took one." I point to a corkboard. "It came from that one right there. It was a picture of me holding the deed to this house. Normally, I wouldn't notice if a picture was missing, but that was the last one I put up. And now it's gone." My eyes narrow down. "So you took it."

He tilts his head a little, just the beginnings of a smile creeping up one side of his face. "Are you gonna make me put it back?"

"Is it going to be your trophy?"

"What?"

"Isn't that something serial killers do? Take something personal as a trophy?"

"Wow." He laughs. "First, you're accusing me of

being a werewolf, now a serial killer. I think you might just need to get some fuckin' sleep."

As soon as he says that, I know he's right. I'm being dumb. My mind is confused and my imagination is getting the better of me. "But this underground city stuff?"

"What about it?"

"I don't understand. It's like you came right out of the pages of a story."

"It's not magic, Clover. It's not anything like that. You just think it is because it's unfamiliar to you, and you're sleep-deprived, and you've been through a lot the past couple of days. It's military, OK?"

"Our military? Or your military?"

"They're the same thing."

"This makes no sense. You're telling me that the American government has a bunch of secret underground cities?"

"That's exactly what I'm telling you."

"Why would they keep that secret?"

"Why?" He laughs. "Why wouldn't they?"

"So there are two Americas? One up here and one down below?"

"We're not the only country with underground cities. Every country in Europe has at least one as well. Australia has three. Canada's is connected to ours via train. Same with Mexico. Shit, we could take a train all the way down to the tip of Argentina and never see the sky once, if we wanted to."

Internally, I scoff at this. *We?* There is no 'we.'

But he's being reasonable, so I don't bring it up. I need more information. I mean, of course I'm going with him. It's either that or get left behind in my personal dungeon. I need to be reasonable as well. Whether or not his offer is genuine isn't really the point. The point is that I have to play along until I come up with a better solution. So I ask questions. "Where is this place? Where will I end up when this trip is over?"

His boots are now off so he stands up, pulls his shirt up over his head, and tosses it onto the chair behind him. He walks around the other side of the bed and I turn in place to watch him. He doesn't ask me for permission to sleep in the bed, nor does he hesitate. Just slides his body right under my covers and turns onto his stomach, one eye open so he can look at me. "If you lie down and stop talking, I'll tell you all about it."

I stare at him for a few moments, suddenly remembering that we're going to be sharing a twin bed and he's already taking up most of the space. He doesn't say anything as these thoughts work their way through my head, but he doesn't have to. His eyes are dancing with amusement. Will I get in next to him? Will I sleep on the floor? Will I try and kick him out?

My first choice would be number three, but he probably saw that coming and that's why he got into bed so fast. I'm not sleeping on the floor, so… I shrug, throw up my hands, and let out a long breath as I slide my body in next to his.

It's a tight fit and our shoulders are squished together as I look up at the ceiling. "OK. I'm in bed with you. Now answer my question. Where will you take me?"

He doesn't say anything. And this silence lingers long enough to be awkward, so I turn my head and look at him. That one open eye. It's not any kind of brown I've seen before. It's very light.

"Well?" I ask.

"I'm trying to decide how much to tell you."

"Because if you tell me too much, then you'll have to kill me?" He doesn't laugh. "It's a joke."

"Yeah. I know it's a joke."

"But you didn't laugh."

"Because it's not funny."

"Oooookay." I let out a frustrated breath and pull the covers all the way up to my chin, even though they've been on this bed for years and smell stale. Because the shaking that started out as a chill a few moments ago is starting to turn into an out-of-control shiver. The kind of shivering that reminds me of when I was a young, cool teenager who refused to wear a heavy coat in the winter because it clashed with my outfit. So I would find myself standing at the bus stop in the rain and wind, shivers bursting out of my body like tiny explosions because I was so cold.

It's summertime, so the room is warm. Not overly warm, but much too warm to be shivering.

When I turn my head to side-eye him, Riggs is watching me, his eyes narrowed down a little. "I can't tell you everything, obviously. There's a real chance I *would* be killed if we aren't careful and I get caught bringing you down below."

I turn and look at him, hugging myself as I try to stop the shivers. It's panic, maybe? Fear? Exhaustion? "Then why *would* you help me? Wouldn't it be easier if you just left me here? I would promise not to say anything. I *wouldn't*. My word is good, it really is. Why risk everything by taking me with you when leaving me behind is the easy answer?"

He's shaking his head the whole time while these words are coming out. "No. It's more of a risk to leave you behind." That one exposed eye flits up to meet mine. "This operation is important. What I'm doing here, it's important."

"Because you'll go back down to those tunnels if you mess it up."

"That's only part of it. The selfish part. But the mission is something I believe in."

My whole face screws up. "What *mission?*"

"That's not something you need to know about. But there are things I should tell you. About the city, at least. So you're not looking around like a fuckin' tourist the moment we come out of the tunnel."

I turn on my side, cheek pressed into the pillow, and hug myself even tighter. "OK. I'm ready then. Let's hear it. Tell me all about your secret underground city."

That one eye squints. "What's wrong with you?"

"Nothing. Why?"

"You're shivering like it's cold in here. It's got to be seventy-five or eighty degrees in this room."

"I don't know. It's… adrenaline, or something."

His upper body comes up off the bed and he stares at me with narrowed eyes. "Do you need more blankets?"

"No. I'm fine."

"Don't get sick on me. I'm warning you. If you get sick when we're underground, we'll get caught for sure. They'll send you to the clinic and everything about that visit will be a red flag because they won't be able to match your biomarkers."

"I'm *w-w-way* too tired for words like 'biomarkers.'" My teeth are chattering now.

He actually smiles and lets out a chuckle.

"And I'm not sick. I'm just…" I let out a long breath, trying to calm myself out of this trembling that seems to have taken control of my body since he offered to save me. "It's just exhaustion. Just tell me what I need to know."

We stare at each other for a moment, him propped up on his elbows now, me still hugging myself, trying to stop the shakes. "First of all, I need to understand how well you know Ike Monroe."

"Not at all. Why?"

"Because he runs the Blackberry Hill Colony and that's where we're going first."

"I've never heard of Blackberry Hill. I've heard about Ike Monroe, but only because Lowyn got herself mixed up with him when she was younger. I was away at school when that happened, though. So I didn't even know about her story until just this year when it all came back to haunt her and Collin had to go in and get her out of Ike's secret mountain town up in the hills above Disciple."

"Well, that secret mountain town is just the beginning of what Ike Monroe actually controls. But I need to be absolutely sure you've never met him."

"Never."

"All right. Then this might work. You're going to be my neighbor from back home."

"Which is… where?"

"Kingfisher Flats. A place on the edge of the Rocky Mountains and underneath Colorado and Wyoming."

"So." I squint my eyes at him. "The whole 'tunnels

under the Denver airport' conspiracy theory is real then, isn't it?"

"No. I mean, maybe. But whatever tunnels are under that airport, they've got nothing to do with where I come from."

"So you're not an alien?"

He laughs. "What?"

"I'm pretty sure there's aliens under that airport."

"Whatever." He shakes his head a little, but he's smiling now. And it's not a bad smile. "I'm not an alien. Now stop interrupting me. This is important. You're going to be my neighbor from back home and your name is Hattie."

"Hattie?" I make a face. "Why can't I just be Clover?"

"Because Hattie is my actual neighbor and you're pretending to be her."

"Ohhhh. She's real? Well, you left that part out."

"Because it's not important."

"Oh, my God." My face lights up. "You have a thing for Hattie."

"What? No. Stop interrupting me. You're Hattie Miller. You live next door to me—"

"Oh, that's cute. You fell for the girl next door."

"Do you want to die of starvation and thirst in your basement? Because it's really starting to feel like you do."

"Sorry. Continue."

"My father *loves* Hattie." His eyes narrow down as I hold in my snort. Because it's so obvious that this Hattie and he were a thing. "She's a prissy do-gooder, so it would be just like him to send her after me to make sure I don't fuck up."

"The good girl next door. I love it."

"Clover."

"Sorry. It's just… very cliché. But cute, at the same time. I'll shut up now, I swear. I'm Hattie Miller, and your father prearranged our marriage when we were… thirteen?"

"That's it." He gets up and grabs my arm, pulling me out of bed on his side. "Back to the dungeon."

"I'll stop, I swear. Let go of me." But I'm laughing as I say this because this is all so obviously true. He had a thing with Hattie. I pull back and he lets my arm go, so he's not really serious about throwing me back into the dungeon. But I am starting to piss him off, so I back down. "I promise, I won't say another word." Then I go back under the covers and wrap myself up, my body shaking worse now after the chill of being in the open air. "Continue."

Riggs glares at me for a few moments, but he looks exhausted too. So he's not really up to the task of dragging me down four flights of stairs and locking me up tonight. "That's it. That's the plan. You're Hattie and you came to check on me. Hattie works above ground, so this explains why Ike didn't see her come through on the trains. She would've met up with me up top. This little story explains everything. We'll probably only be in the Blackberry Hill Colony for a few hours as we wait for the next train to Kingfisher. Once we're on the train, we'll ride it until we get to Lazuli Waystation. That's the stop on the border of Kansas and Colorado. We'll get off, I'll take you somewhere safe, and after a set period of time, you will be released."

My trembling body calms for a moment as my brain uses that energy to think about what he just said. "Hold on."

"What?"

"You're taking me away from my home just to drop me off and leave me at another place? Why? Why can't I just stay here and promise not to leave until this set period of time is over?"

"Because you told me your boss didn't know you were fired. She's gonna come looking for you."

"Yeah, but that's gonna happen whether I go with you or not."

"But if you come with me, she won't find you."

"So how long are you gonna lock me in this safe place of yours?"

"Three months."

I sit straight up in bed. "Three *months*! What the fuck!"

"I need that time, Clover. I *need* it. And this is a true safe place, you'll see. There's plenty of food, and water, and stuff to do."

"Stuff to do like *what?*" My eyes are still boggled wide, because I didn't see this twist coming.

"Lots of things, you'll see."

"So what happens after three months?"

"The door unlocks and you leave."

"What am I supposed to tell people when I finally come back?"

He shrugs. "It won't matter by then. The job will be done."

"Wait." I narrow my eyes at him. "*What* job?"

"Story time's over now. You've got all the information you need." We stare at each other for a few minutes, just the moonlight coming through my childhood bedroom window to light us up.

I'm not a mind reader, but I'm reading his right now.

The job is Collin Creed because Collin is a problem. A kink in a chain. A snag in the fabric of... well, something military, that's obvious. And this Riggs guy here fully expects the problem to be resolved in three months.

Done as in... dead? My shivering starts again, and

this time it's nearly out of control. "Y-y-you're going to k-k-kill him, aren't you?"

Riggs turns over on his back and lets out a breath as he stares up at the ceiling. "Go to sleep. We've got a big day tomorrow."

CHAPTER 10 - RIGGS

*S**he doesn't sleep.*** The shaking that started as we came up the stairs is nearly out of control now. She's not cold—this shaking is the remnants of fear. She was resigned to being left in that dungeon of a basement and when I gave her another option, her mind started to relax but her body was still tense.

But this shaking has gone beyond shivering now. It's more like the out-of-control gasping of hyperventilation, but in the muscles instead of the lungs. In fact, it's so bad, the bed is shaking now too.

I reach for her. "Come here."

Immediately, she's recoiling away from me. "Don't touch me."

But this twin bed is way too small for her to put up any kind of real defense, so I slip one arm under her hip and the other around her waist and pull her up to my chest, hugging her tight.

"What are you *d-d-doing?* Let go of me."

"You might be going into shock, Clover. You need to relax."

"Well, trapping me in your arms isn't going to help."

"Just take deep breaths."

"Just let me go."

She struggles, but I don't ease up. "You need to calm down. This is a fear response and if you go into actual shock, you could die."

"Shut up. That's stupid."

"It's true. This shaking you're doing? It's not the shivers like you're cold. It's because your body is shutting down. Look." I grab her wrist and press my finger against it. "Your pulse is racing. You need to calm down. Take a few deep breaths."

She's stopped arguing with me, because obviously, I'm right. But the shivers continue.

"You're OK. I'm not gonna kill you."

She lets out a breath, but it's not relief.

"You're gonna live, Clover. This is no big deal. We've figured a way out and you can relax now."

Her only response is a huff. But she does breathe. Not deep, not at first. But gradually, over the next few minutes, she gets a more even rhythm going. The shivering stops being a constant thing and instead becomes more intermittent.

A few more minutes after that, and she's nearly better.

I could let go of her now and she would be OK. Alternatively, she could *tell* me to let go of her and I wouldn't have a reason not to. But neither of us does these things.

She says nothing while I hold her.

Which gives me time to think about how long it's been since I was even with a woman. Actually, how long it's been since I even had the luxury of *thinking* about being with a woman.

Six years.

When I think about this—about the prison time I served—I usually have one of two reactions. The first is anger, of course. Over the injustice of it all. I mean, so what? I left. So what? I never asked to be born in the Colonies. I never agreed to that. As a kid, I accepted it because I didn't know any better, but after going up top I knew that it was wrong to keep the world a secret.

And I'm not saying that the Colonies are terrible places. People generally seem to be happy. But that's because they don't think they have a choice. The adults know that there's another world up top, but it's not something they teach children. In school, when you're little and your brain is impressionable, you learn the history of the Colonies. About how the people up top were out of control and destroyed everything.

Which, in certain lights, could be considered true. I

mean, no place is perfect and the up-top certainly has its vices. There are plenty of terrible things going on up there.

But these history books of ours fail to mention that our little sub-society wasn't made out of necessity, but choice.

Choices that were made generations ago now.

Choices we never got to make ourselves.

So why can't I just… choose something else?

"You, Riggs," my father told me when I asked him this, "are meant to lead. You have a role to play, a destiny to fulfill, and your petty, personal desires have nothing to do with anything."

I had just been pulled out of the tunnels. I was still covered from head to toe in dried mud the color of blood, standing there, in his office, as it flaked off my feet and onto his floor.

We were hosed off every night in the tunnels, but I had been pulled out mid-day. He did that on purpose. To contrast my new life with the old one I gave up.

But I didn't choose those tunnels either and this is when I realized how pointless it was to rebel. Because they would always find me. My father would always win. He's the *general* of the Colonies. I'm his only son. His only child. And my mother has been dead for decades now, so I'm literally all he has outside of work.

He doesn't even have a woman. Not a steady one,

anyway. I'm sure he's got his pick of the whores, but he never remarried.

So I was standing there in his office, covered in flaking, red mud, so, so, *so* ready to promise him just about anything in order to get my life back. So that's what I did.

But it wasn't an empty promise.

My father would see through one of those in heartbeat.

"It's not my fault, Clover." I don't even know why I say it because she doesn't care.

She doesn't answer back, either. And she's not asleep, I can tell by the way she's breathing. The shivers are few and far between now, but she's not relaxed enough to be asleep.

"It's not your fault, either," I say. "It's just… the way it is."

The silence that comes after this statement feels very permanent. So I'm just starting to drift off to sleep when she finally answers.

"It takes resolve to leave. I know that better than most, since I was born into the cult of Disciple, West Virginia. And I don't mean it in a bad way. It's not a bad town. Certainly better than most, I think. But I wanted to make my own way in this world and then I wanted to come back. On my terms. As someone who left. Like Collin and Amon. And Lowyn, to a point.

Though she never left, not really. She still gave it all up and did her own thing."

Clover turns now. All the way over so that we're facing each other. I can't make out much of her face since the moonlight isn't really shining through the window anymore, but I can see enough of it to understand she's… sad.

"It's not your fault," she says. "I don't know what happened to you, but I guess it was bad. So fine. You're doing this because you need it. But just because it's not your fault doesn't mean it's not your decision."

"I'm not gonna kill you. You're not gonna die. It's a few months, that's it."

She shrugs up one shoulder, not agreeing with me. "Yeah. What's a few months of imprisonment in the grand scheme of things?"

She doesn't say it with malice or even sarcasm, but she means it that way.

She thinks I'm weak.

And I'm just about to protest—not explain myself, because it's none of her fucking business what I'm doing or why I'm doing it, but just deny it.

But as I open my mouth to do that, she nudges closer to me until her forehead is pressed against my chest. Then she lets out a sigh. "Don't be mean. *Please* don't be mean. I've had enough. I can't take any more. If you're not going to be nice, just say nothing."

"Let you have the last word?" I say it a little bit

jokingly, since that was our fight earlier. But she doesn't seem to find it funny. So I sigh as well. "I'm literally trying to save your life. I'm not being mean."

"You were about to be."

I press my lips together and shake my head just a little bit. "You have no idea what you're talking about, Clover. You just do not understand."

"You're wrong. I absolutely understand. It's not even that complicated. You value… *you*. I am no one. And that's fine because it's true. I can live with this. All I'm asking is that you don't make it harder than it already is."

"By stating my *opinion*?" It comes out a little bit snide, but for good reason. "I'm looking out for you, ya know. I'm doing my best. Who the hell is looking out for me, Clover? Oh, that would be no one. You're the one making this harder than it has to be, not me."

"Good night, Riggs."

"Right. Gotta have that last word. Good night, Clover."

I stay awake for hours, despite being so exhausted I can't even open my eyes. I just keep repeating her words over and over in my head. *Just because it's not your fault doesn't mean it's not your decision.*

Fine. It was my decision. *Is* my decision.

Locking her up in a Lazuli Waystation is the only way I can think of to keep her alive. And there's really nothing to complain about. She will be alone, sure. But she will safe, and warm, and fed, and hydrated. And it's only three months. It would be one thing to be left in the bunker with no idea when you'd be allowed out, but going in with a release date should make it easier.

She can count down the days. I'll even buy her a calendar so she can cross them off one by one. Three months. She'll live. And wasn't that the only point of this whole plan? To let her live?

But being here in bed with her, with my arms around her... I dunno. I feel like the bad guy. And I hate feeling like the bad guy.

Collin Creed needs to go. The decision to kill him wasn't my call, but even if it was, I would've come to the same conclusion as my father. He knows way too much. And not only that, he knows *me*.

He needs to go. They all need to go.

I don't think that's occurred to Clover just yet. That Collin's friends will go down with him.

All my thoughts get stuck here as I let that last bit echo in my thoughts.

It's enough to keep me up for hours.

Because they're not just Collin's friends.

They're *my* friends too.

WHEN THE SUN rises and Clover begins to stir, I've still got my arms around her. I'm not sure I actually slept at all. Dozed would be a better word to describe what I've been doing for the past seven hours.

Clover slept soundly, though. So she's looking—and probably feeling—a lot better this morning than she did last night.

She wriggles free of my embrace, turns over, and then lets out a long sigh.

"That's not a good sign."

She looks over her shoulder, side-eying me. "What?"

"That tired sigh. We've got a very long day ahead of us and I'll need you to be in top performance condition when we meet with Ike."

She gives me a little scoff. "I grew up in Disciple, *Riggs*. I know how to act."

"I bet you do."

She throws the covers off, and sits up in bed, swinging her feet over the side. "I need a shower. Can I take a shower?"

"Of course. I can't take you down below looking like some kind of…" I search for a word that won't be too disparaging, but she comes up with one first.

"Kidnapping victim?"

"I was gonna say 'vagrant,' but that works too."

She stands up, clearly done with me, and heads straight for the door. "I need to get some clean clothes out of the trailer."

I get up too and cut her off by placing an arm in front of the exit. "I'll go with you."

"Of course you will."

I slip my boots on without lacing them up and we go downstairs. Outside, the sun is bright and it's a very nice late-summer morning. I parked the trailer behind the barn, but it's visible from where we're standing on the back porch, so Clover starts heading in that direction, ignoring me.

"So… we're back to animosity, are we? Even though I've found a way to keep you alive?"

She doesn't turn to answer me, but I can practically hear the eyeroll she's doing.

"I *am* saving you, ya know."

"You're the only reason I *need* saving, Riggs. I haven't done a single thing wrong."

"That doesn't invalidate my point."

She stops and whirls around, locking her angry eyes directly with mine. "You win, OK? It's not your fault, it's just my bad luck, and holding me prisoner in some underground cell for three months to keep me out of the way while you murder Collin Creed is no big deal. There. How's that? Do you feel absolved now?"

"It's the best I can do."

"Fine. I get it. But can we just stop this?" She does a little wag with her finger here, pointing back and forth at the two of us.

"Stop what?"

"The banter. I'm not interested in you. *At all.*"

I make a face. "I'm not interested in you either."

"Then stop talking to me."

Before I can say anything else, she whirls back around and continues walking, briefly disappearing around the corner until I catch up.

She goes right to the trailer and opens it up, then lets out a long sigh as she drops her head in a gesture of defeat.

"What's wrong now?"

"I didn't pack this trailer, so I have no idea where my clothes are."

I step forward and peek inside the trailer. It's a complete mess. Like it was packed by random hotel staff who knew they didn't have to deal with it on the other side of things.

I start pulling boxes out of the trailer without commenting, and after a couple of seconds, she helps. It takes about twenty minutes of time we don't really have before she finds an acceptable outfit. It's hiking pants, a long-sleeve shirt, and a modern pair of hiking boots. It's all very matchy in various two-tone combinations of black and burnt-orange. Then she stuffs a backpack with similar outfits and a few other things, and then we put all her shit back into the trailer.

We go back into the house and head to the second-floor bathroom. She stops in front of the door, crosses her arms, and looks up at me. "That shower invitation was a one-time thing."

I scoff. "I'm not trying to hook up with you. I don't even want to see you naked. You're like a six, Clover. I can do better than a six."

Her mouth drops open. "Six?" She guffaws. "I am not a six."

"Six point two five. *Maybe*. But you're definitely not a seven."

"Well… you're like a four."

"Woman, I am a nine point seven five *at least*."

She practically snorts. "You fancy yourself a Collin Creed, do ya? Because that's what a nine point seven five looks like, Riggs."

"Right," I sneer. "Good old Collin. He's everything to everyone, isn't he?"

"What is it with you and Collin? Do you know him or something?"

I want to say something snappy back, then end this

conversation, but I don't know what to say, and the seconds are ticking off, and it's one of those situations where silence says everything.

"Oh, my God. You do know him!"

"Just take your shower. I'll wait out here."

"No. Tell me how you know him. Of course, I know he was military. That's why he left town back when he was a kid." Her eyes are doing that back-and-forth searching thing as she stares into mine. Which means her mind is working overtime. "Wait." She points her finger at me. "You know him because… the two of you worked together. Whatever secret shit he's been up to these past dozen years, you were there. You were part of it too."

Again, there are things I could say here to cut off this line of thinking, but none of them come out of my mouth. So again, the silence says everything.

"Holy shit. You're *friends* with him. What about Amon?"

"What about him?"

"So you know him too?"

The scoff that comes out of my mouth is much more pronounced than I intended. "That's a stupid question. If you know Collin, you know Amon. They are shadows of one another."

Clover's shoulders relax a little as she eyes me. "Well, that's not cryptic."

"Are you gonna take your shower or not? Because we're on a schedule here."

She frowns. "You're gonna kill him too? Amon, I mean. You're gonna turn Lowyn and Rosie into widows before they even get married?"

"Can you just take your shower?"

"Can you just answer one question truthfully?"

I shrug. "Fine. If it'll get you moving. Yes. I guess the answer is yes. Your friends will be widows before they ever get married. There's no happily ever after in this life and I'm not a prince. There. Are you happy now?"

Her eyelids drop, her shoulders tense up, and her mouth turns into a flat line instead of a frown. All signs of resolve. Which is better than resistance, so I'm good with it. I pan a hand to the bathroom. "You've got three minutes. Better make the most of them."

She tips her chin up, turns on her heel, goes into the bathroom, and shuts the door on my face. The lock turns on the other side, and then, a moment later, there's a sound of water.

While she's doing that, I grab a pair of pants from my pack downstairs and search around until I find a length of cord in one of the nearby bedrooms, so when she steps out, freshly washed and changed into her new matchy clothes, I'm ready. But I'm slightly taken aback at her new coordinated outfit because she looks like she's about to do a photoshoot for a hiking catalog, so I chuckle.

"What's so funny?" These words of hers come out with a little sneer.

"Nothing. You're just very… put together."

Clover looks down at herself, then back up at me. "What's wrong with what I'm wearing?"

"Wow. You're sensitive. There's nothing wrong with it. It's just very…"

"Coordinated?"

"That and…" I shrug. "Just… it's nice, that's all."

Her eyes narrow down. "You don't have to compliment me."

I raise an eyebrow. "Is that what I did?"

"I mean, you don't have to say *anything* to me. We're never going to be friends. Why would I be friends with a man who kills his friends? That makes no sense at all. So who cares what you think about my kidnapping outfit?"

"Wow." I blink at her, stunned at her insult because it hit the bullseye for sure. I shrug up a shoulder, blowing it off. "Fine, Clover. That outfit looks like shit on you." I pan a hand to the steamy bathroom. "It's my turn now."

"So? Go take a shower then."

"Well, you're coming in with me."

She shakes her head and folds her arms. "No. I'm not."

I grab both her wrists so quick, I've got the cord around them and I'm tying the knot before she can even process what's happening. "There," I say, once I'm done. "Now go back into the bathroom and sit your ass down on the floor. Because you cannot be trusted, Clover. You've got a lot of stupid ideas running around in that head of yours. So from this moment on, the two of us are together until the end."

Her chin juts out in defiance. But she turns and does as she's told.

I follow her in, close the door, lock it, and then look down at her as I kick off my boots. "Don't move. Because, if you recall, I've got no problem at all with chasing you down naked. I will tackle you before you get to the stairs and—"

"No, let me guess." She puts up a hand to cut me off, but doesn't look up to meet my gaze. "Then you'll push me down them, leave my twisted and broken body to decay, and—"

"Just stop."

Finally, she looks up. "What? That's your MO, right? Threaten women with gruesome acts to keep them compliant? God, I can't even imagine what your ex-girlfriends went through. I bet there was a lot of therapy afterward."

For some reason, I find this funny and the laugh that bursts out is inappropriately loud, especially inside a bathroom. It startles her and she shrinks back, pressing herself into the wall as she meets my gaze.

"You're crazy," I say.

"You're evil," she sneers back.

I reach over and turn on the shower. "Just be quiet and sit there until I'm done."

She turns her head when I start unbuttoning my pants and doesn't look back. I get in the shower, wash up, reach for a towel, dry myself off, and then grab my pants and put them back on before coming out.

Clover looks up at me, her eyes lingering on my chest, wet again from the water dripping off my hair. I wink at her as I slip my feet into my boots. "Told ya."

"Told me what?"

"Nine point seven five, baby. Now let's go."

*I stop **at my pack*** on the first floor, pull on a shirt, stuff yesterday's clothes back inside, and hike the pack up onto my back. Then we leave.

Outside, Clover pans a hand in the direction of the woods just as I take a scarf out of my pocket, so she ends up pointing at me instead. "What's that?"

I look down at the scarf, then smile and look back up at her. "Your blindfold."

It's very apparent that she didn't think I'd follow

through with the blindfold. Like maybe our night together invalidated my suspicions about her. She pauses for a moment, maybe weighing the pros and cons of complaining, but she's so done with me, she holds her protests in and says nothing as I tie the scarf good and tight around her eyes.

"You'll have to hold my hand, so don't take it the wrong way, OK? I don't like you, Clover. You don't look good in those clothes, and… well, as I've already mentioned, you're not even pretty."

She just laughs out her response. "I'm so out of your league, Riggs, it's not even funny."

I don't laugh because she would hear that. But I do smile as I take her hand. I guess, if I have to kidnap a woman, I could do worse than Clover Bradley. She's obstinate, spoiled, and has no common sense at all, since she's been arguing with me for days even though I've been threatening to kill her. But she's right about one thing, she's not a four. I wouldn't ever admit that she's a ten, but… yeah. In another life, I'd hit that. "Come on, my little pet. Let's go."

She's got no time to internalize that insult because I walk forward and immediately, she's stumbling. "Slow down. I'm blind here, OK? You can't just walk off and expect me to keep up!"

"We're literally in the grass behind the house, Clover. There's nothing to trip over."

She gives me a derisive snort. "Says the privileged man with eyes."

I suck in a deep breath and hold it, looking up at the sky. I'm frustrated and we're one minute in to this very long trip. When I let the breath out, I force myself to be calm. "Sorry. I'll go slow." I start forward again, but she doesn't move. "Now what?"

"Can I hold on to your arm instead of your hand?"

Is she serious? I can't tell. "Sure. You can hold on to my arm."

The breath she lets out comes off as relief, but I'm not convinced it is. I just have a feeling that she's playing me. Her hands start feeling for my arm and then she's gripping my bicep tight with both hands. It's a weird, confining feeling and immediately, I've got an urge to push her off.

But then she says, "I swear I'll walk faster this way. I will. If I stumble, you'll hold me up."

"Fine." And I start walking again.

As soon as we enter the woods she sighs. "The shade feels good."

She's not wrong, but I don't say anything back, hoping to deter her from being chatty because I'm really starting to think this whole plan is a bad idea that might get me killed.

Apparently, my silence has nothing to do with her eagerness to talk because just a few seconds later, a story about her childhood comes spilling out of her mouth. "When I was a kid these woods were more like my first home than my second. I was mad, crazy in love with horses. Still am, really. Just no time or money to keep that habit going. But as a kid, I had every day after school and all summer long to play as I wished and my parents paid for everything."

"Must've been nice." I say this absently as I direct her to the right where a mostly hidden path takes us back around to where I actually need to be in order to find my way back to the camp I made before I went to her house and made all these fun times possible.

"It *was* nice."

"So you're like… what? A little rich princess?"

She sighs before answering. "You make that sound like a bad thing."

"Isn't it?"

"If you were a horse-obsessed girl, wouldn't you want to be a little rich princess?"

"I guess."

"So it's not a bad thing."

"You do realize that you're one of the under one percent, right? Point zero-zero-one, or whatever."

"I'm really not. My family is Disciple, West Virginia, rich, not like entire USA rich. Of course, Disciple is better off than most West Virginia towns because of the Revival. But they just decided very early on that they would sacrifice for me. They gave up the boats and the trips to Europe so I could have a perfect childhood."

"Well, that's amazing."

"Is this a sore spot? Your parents didn't do the same?"

"Weren't you just warning me not to talk to you ten minutes ago? We're not friends, remember?"

"I never said we were. I'm just passing time. It's better than walking blindfolded through the woods with a kidnapper in silence."

"Is it, though?"

"Anyway, I'm not rich now. I used all my Disciple money—we get a windfall when we turn eighteen for all the work we did as children—and I spent all mine on buying the house from my parents."

"Bet you're regretting that right about now."

"No. I'm not. I'm going to open up an event center. For weddings. That's what I do at the hotel—well, what I did before they fired me. One day it's gonna be great. All fixed up and beautiful. And every stall in the barn will have a horse in it."

"That's your dream, huh? Planning weddings?"

"It's not a bad dream. What's yours?"

"To live." I say this without thinking. It just comes out. And as soon as it does, I want to take it back.

"Wow," Clover says. "That's pretty…" She falters for a word.

"Sad?"

"No. I was gonna say… third world."

I actually stop walking to look at her and scoff. "What?"

"Sorry. That was a very under-one-percent thing to say, wasn't it?"

"'Third world' of me. Wow. I'm actually speechless."

"I'm just saying, your little underground world must be pretty messed up if your dream is to *live*. You might as well be a child slave in a lithium mine, Riggs. That's how third-world your dream is."

"As compared to your stupid wedding thing? Come on. I'll take 'live' over that any day."

"You don't like pretty things and happy days? Because that's what weddings are. The ones I plan are."

"It's just, in the grand scheme of things, kinda stupid."

"Which part? The pretty decorations? The tear-jerking declaration of love? The fabulous party? Which part of a wedding is kinda stupid, Riggs?"

"All of it."

"So you don't believe in love?"

"Ya know, I liked you better when you were locked up in the dungeon."

"Because I didn't make you think about your lack of ambition?"

"No. Because I could close the door on your face and walk away."

"Well, you'll get your chance to do that again, don't

worry. I'll be locked up tight in your little bunker soon enough."

"Which, again, is the best plan ever."

"Says you."

"Yeah. Says me. Because the alternative is leaving you to die in that dungeon of yours."

"I think someone would save me."

I stop walking again. And once again I scoff. "Is that right? Holy shit, woman. You really do think you're some kind of princess, don't you?"

"No. Well"—she chuckles here—"yes. I kinda do fancy myself a princess. But what I meant was that people would be looking for me. Clarissa, my boss at the Yonder, she's probably been calling me for days. It's midweek and she's busy with her own life, so she's not worried. Yet. But if I don't answer in the next day or two, she's gonna come looking for me."

"You're sure about that?"

"Yes. And she knows about Lowyn. She's met her. So she would call Lowyn's store looking for her to ask about me. And then Lowyn would start calling me, and me being unreachable, this would set off alarm bells. She would get in her car and drive down to my house, figuring I went home after being fired and kicked out of my apartment. Then she would find the Navigator and the trailer and she would go inside and I would have heard all this, so I'd be pounding on the trapdoor—which she knows about because we've been best friends all our lives—and she would rescue me. And then, after I told her my story, she'd call Collin and… well, your dream would be over. Because he would kill you."

I laugh. "So I should… what? Let you go and keep me and my dream alive?"

"It wouldn't be the worst answer to this problem."

"Well, that's a very nice story, Clover. And you delivered it with confidence. But it's got one fatal flaw."

"No, it doesn't."

"Oh, it does. Because your dramatic, fairy-tale rescue hinges on your boss, Clarissa. And if you were so confident that she would get this whole liberation scheme rolling, you would've stayed put. You had plenty of water to last you a week, maybe even two if you rationed correctly. Food was never going to be the thing that killed you down there. So again, it's a nice story. Something that would work in a movie or a book. But this is real life and you don't believe it."

She thinks about this for a moment, then sighs. "Fine. I hedged. The odds of you letting me live as a prisoner in a bunker were slightly higher than the ones that depended on Clarissa finding time to care about me after her big promotion."

"Well, admitting that is very mature of you."

"There's no point in lying to you, let alone myself. I have no power here. And even though I gave it a shot, you're not gonna let me go. You don't seem like a man who reevaluates bad plans."

I stop walking again, turning to look at her. "It's not a bad plan. It's the only one that keeps you alive."

"So you can kill Collin Creed before he kills you?"

"Look. I get that you grew up with him or something. So maybe you were friends. Maybe you think he's a good guy, or whatever. But he's not. You have no idea who that man is. None, Clover. You have no idea the things he's done."

"And you do?"

I don't answer her. Just start walking, making her stumble.

CHAPTER 11 - CLOVER

There's about thirty minutes of silence after this Collin conversation. Enough time for me to stumble seventeen times and fall three.

Finally, Riggs says, "We're here. Stay put while I pack up my camp."

He and Collin really do know each other.

This is some kind of personal vendetta. Or maybe not. Maybe it's just an order from whoever runs things down where he comes from. But it makes a lot of sense that there's animosity between them over some… mission gone wrong, or whatever. Collin is part of some secret military thing and this Riggs guy is too.

I push my blindfold up a little bit, looking at him. "Did he betray you or something?"

"Who?"

"You know who. The only 'who' we were talking about."

"It's not important. Just forget about it." Riggs doesn't look at me when he says this, so he doesn't notice that I'm peeking past the blindfold and this gives me time to study him. He's wearing a muscle shirt today. It's olive green in color and it's so tight, I can see every one of his stomach and chest muscles rippling under the fabric as he gathers things up and stuffs them into a pack.

His head turns, catching me. "What are you doing?"

I was checking him out, I realize. But I'm not going to say that. So I just shrug.

He's mad though. Because he growls words at me. "Push the blindfold back down and don't look up again or the whole deal's off."

I give him a good eye roll, but do as I'm told.

Then I just sit there, listening. But I got a good enough look at him to picture what he's doing. I'm keeping track of where we are. If Riggs thinks a little blindfold is enough to confuse me in my own woods, he's just kinda stupid. I spent eighteen years in these woods. Well, probably more like ten because obviously my parents didn't let me go traipsing off into the woods when I was a toddler. But I was an outdoor girl for sure. And after I got the ponies, Lowyn and I would ride these woods all day, every day, in the summers. We'd have stayed out here forever and gone completely feral if we weren't expected home for dinner at seven-thirty every night.

So the moment Riggs put that blindfold on me, I started taking mental notes. I pictured the whole walk in my head. And even though I only got a two-second look at him and the surrounding area, I know exactly where we are. I didn't even need the peek to know that. I know every boulder, every old tree, and every single creek in these woods.

I'm going to escape. I don't know when or how, but I'm going to escape. I'm sure Riggs figures he's this big, strong, capable man—and he is, I'll give him that—and he's been here a few weeks, I guess, so he's got a handle on these woods too. But he doesn't know all the hiding places. He didn't play hide and seek in here for years on end when he was small like I did.

These woods are my kingdom. I'm the queen here. And this is why, when I run, I'll get away.

"I know what you're thinking."

I turn my head in the direction of his voice. "Is that so?"

"Yep. I can practically hear your thoughts, Clover. And you're not gonna get away from me in these woods just because you know them better than me."

I scoff. "Why would I be thinking about that? We've already come up with a plan to save me." I add that little 'we' in there to remind him that it was really his idea, just in case he's having second thoughts.

He walks towards me, leaves and twigs crunching under his feet. "Because you've got the princess complex."

I don't care what he says, I reach up and pull the

blindfold down so I can look him in the eyes. "Princess complex?"

He points at me. "See, you think you're above it all. You pulled that blindfold down like my commands mean nothing to you. Like you own the world. And, Clover..." He smiles a little, but it comes off condescending. "You do *not* own the world. You literally have no idea who owns the world. So this little 'I'll save myself' fantasy you're in the middle of right now? It's bullshit. And you're gonna get yourself hurt if you keep plotting."

I want to say something back. Something that challenges his threat to hurt me. Daring him to do it, maybe. Because while I don't agree that my escape plan is a fantasy—I think I've got a decent chance of success—I do agree that I'm *over-humanizing* him.

He's dangerous. I knew it the moment I saw him. But we've had enough normal conversations now that I had started to replace the fear with... I dunno. Camaraderie isn't quite the right word, but it's close. We've schemed up a plan and we did that together. It implies a level of partnership.

At least in my mind.

But definitely not in his.

He's doing this to save himself. Not because he cares about me, but because he would've felt guilty if he had left me in the old cabin basement to die.

This choice to bring me along was about him and only him.

I was very confident in my assertion that Lowyn would find me. And I really do believe that there's an eighty-percent chance it would turn out that way. She's very clever and Collin and Amon would send in their little army if Lowyn told them I was in danger. It's pretty good odds.

But there was no guarantee I would live if Riggs left me behind and it would be a very big mistake to think there's a better chance now that he's taking me with him.

One screwup and he'll throw me under the bus. He'll sacrifice me to save himself. I truly do believe this.

So I drop the blindfold back down and sigh without saying another word.

I can almost hear his smile. But he doesn't say anything else either.

AFTER HE'S PACKED UP, the hike continues. And this time, I don't bother keeping track of where we're going in my head because we cross over my family's property line.

Actually, that's not why. I know the other properties around here just as well as my own—to a certain degree. But I've given up on the escape plan. At least for now.

He's right. I can't get away in these woods because I'd have to run and while I've done my share of treadmill time and 5K charity events, there's no way he wouldn't catch me.

And then he'd… I dunno. Maybe he wouldn't kill me, but he could just tie me to a tree and gag my mouth so I couldn't scream and let the forest take care of the rest.

If I didn't die of thirst, some animal might get me. We've got coyotes and bobcats here, neither of which are particularly threatening to humans who are not tied to trees, but there are bears too.

But even if none of the mammals got me, there are insects. Fire ants, and black widows, and mosquitoes and ticks.

"You got awfully quiet."

"Well," I huff, "you went back to being a threat."

He stops walking, making me stop as well because I'm holding tight to his arm as I navigate the terrain. "Because we made a plan and you were gonna go back on it."

"I wasn't really thinking about running. I know you

can outrun me. But I was mapping the forest in my head."

He lets out a scoff now. "So you know where we are."

"Not exactly. Not for about ten minutes now. I just figured my energy was better spent on trying not to fall on my face than figuring out where I actually was. Otherwise you might tie me to a tree and leave me out here to be eaten by fire ants."

He actually chuckles. "You've got some imagination there."

"Well, I grew up here, Riggs. It's not a far-fetched scenario."

Suddenly his fingertips are on my face, lingering on my cheek for a moment. I don't know how to react. Should I swat his hand away? Pretend like it's not happening?

But he just pulls the blindfold down and when I look up, all I see are those golden-brown eyes of his. "What did you do that for?"

"The problem is… I can't trust you, Clover."

"Well, we're even then. Because I can't trust you either."

His eyes lock on mine and we stare at each other for several long seconds. Finally, he says, "I *want* to trust you."

"Well, I would like to trust you too."

"I want you to commit to this plan so when we go

up against Ike Monroe, we're on the same side. And you just refuse to give in. My solution is not horrible."

"Well, it's not great, either."

"There is no 'great' solution. They're all bad. But this one we're in the middle of, at least we both get out alive."

I shrug and throw up my hand. "Fine. You're right."

"It's not enough."

"What do you mean?"

"It's not enough for you to say it's 'fine,' Clover. You need to say it's perfect." He knows I'm about to object here, so he presses a palm at me. "No. It's not perfect, I get that. But I need that level of commitment from you. Otherwise, I might as well leave you tied to a tree to be eaten alive by fire ants because the ending will be the same. We're in a lot of danger here. You're failing to understand this." He pauses and sighs. And I know that he's sincere. Every word he just said is true. His eyes search mine for a moment before speaking again. "I *need* you to understand this."

I'm about to retort with a, 'Fine, I'll be good. I get it.' But I've already said that. And I wasn't sincere. So instead, I nod, still meeting his gaze. "I get it. I mean, I don't, Riggs. I don't understand your world or the danger you seem to be in. But I'll do my best and I'll commit to the plan."

"A hundred percent, Clover."

"A hundred percent, Riggs."

After a few second of hard staring he reaches for the scarf, slides it around my neck, then unties the knot and takes it off. "There. You can leave it off. This is me telling you I trust you now."

I feel unexpectedly... sorry, I think. For making things harder. Which is weird and will probably require years of therapy to understand at some later time in the future, but I push the consequences of what I'm about to say away for another time. "I won't run. I'll do everything you say. I promise. But this is me trusting you to get me out of this alive."

He presses his lips together and nods. "All right. Let's go. It's just a little bit farther."

At first, we don't talk. We just keep walking. But we do make better progress now that I'm not blindfolded.

However, this silence gets awkward fast. At least for me. So I prompt him to talk with a relevant question. "What is this Hattie woman like? I mean, if I am to pretend to be her, shouldn't I have an idea of who she is?"

He side-eyes me. "I'll tell you, but no more jokes about me being in love with her."

"All right. But one question first. Did you and her—"

"*No.*" He says this so emphatically, I laugh. "You're totally off track, Clover. I can't stand her. She's a bitch. And I really don't say that about many women. She's just…" He looks at me for a moment. "Nothing like you."

"In what respect?"

"Everything. She's tall, and thick, and… manly."

I laugh.

"It's true," he says. "I'm not cutting down her looks, because she's not ugly, or anything. She's just not feminine."

"You prefer your women feminine, I take it?" As soon as I say that, I feel a blush heat up my face. Because I'm *very* feminine.

But Riggs doesn't even hesitate. "Yeah. I like the princesses." Then he shoots me a sideways look and winks.

Which makes me blush hotter.

"But anyway, she's rough. And strong. And *very* capable."

"Is that why they sent her up top?"

"No. They sent her up top because she's rigid. Not to be confused with frigid."

I laugh.

"Because she's not a prude. She's just very by the book."

"She likes rules, I take it?"

"That woman has never broken a rule in her life."

"And let me take a wild guess here. You're a natural dissident?"

"Some might say that. She turned me in dozens of

times when we were kids. Every time I wanted to do something fun, she'd ruin it. I think she gets pleasure out of ruining people's fun."

"That's… mean."

Riggs stops to point at me. "Exactly. She's *mean*."

I point to myself, eyes wide as I look up at him. "So I should be mean? If I'm supposed to be her?"

"No. The last thing we need is you coming off aggressive to Ike. Just be yourself. That's good enough."

Which is a surprisingly nice thing to say, so it catches me off guard and I stop paying attention to him, or where we're going, and just think about it for a little bit.

Being me is good enough.

It actually makes me feel relieved. Like I won't mess this up and in three months it really will be over, and I'll be fine, and I'll put the whole terrible experience of being held hostage by a man who comes from an underground military facility behind me.

Riggs is walking in front of me now, so when he stops, and I'm still not fully paying attention, I end up bumping into him.

"We're here," he says.

I follow his pointing finger until my gaze lands on a cave opening in the rocky hillside.

"Come on. Let's go in."

CHAPTER 12 - RIGGS

When I point my flashlight at Clover, her face is pale and her eyes are wide as she stares at the steel door I've stopped in front of. There's an awkward pause here, then she turns her gaze up at me and starts shaking her head.

"What? Why are you shaking your head at me?"

"This can't be real." She looks around the dark tunnel, peering back the way we came. "How the hell?" She looks at me again. "Am I dreaming? Did I hit my head? Did someone drug me?"

"What are you talking about?"

"I mean… it makes no sense. Don't you see? The world doesn't work this way. There are no secret underground tunnels. It doesn't exist. This is just… I dunno. A dream. It's gotta be a dream."

"Ya know"—I blow out an exasperated breath—"I'm surprised that it took you this long to catch up."

"What?"

"It's shock, Clover. Well, this isn't." I knock on the steel door. "This is real. The fact that you have been pretty much ignoring everything I've been telling you —or, at the very least, sweeping it under some metaphorical rug up inside your brain—is just instinct."

Her eyes narrow down. "I can't tell if that was an insult or not, but I'm not crazy."

"I never said you were. I'm just trying to explain your inappropriate reaction right now."

"Inappropriate?" She huffs at me with blinking eyes, then pans her hands wide at the dark tunnel all around us. "I'm in a tunnel, under the woods behind my house, and I'm about to enter the fucking Emerald City or something. Nothing about my reaction is inappropriate."

"Exactly. We're *here*, about to go inside a secret city, and you're freaking out on me. That's the part that's inappropriate. You've had days to think about what I've been telling you and come to terms with it, but no. You had to pretend none of this was happening and wait until we're literally on the *doorstep* of top-secret shit before throwing your little princess tantrum."

She scoffs and blinks at me again, but I keep going.

"It's fine, OK?" I hold up a hand, palm out, trying to keep her calm. "It's fine if you're confused, or whatever it is you're feeling. I understand that part because once upon a time I was on the other side of a door like this one feeling just like you are about a world up top that I never knew about. But we're here,

Clover. I'm putting a lot on the line for you. I'm saving your life. And if you go in there and freak the fuck out, and get me caught, I will throw you under the bus so fast, your fucking head will spin. Do you understand me?"

She recoils back in the middle of my threat, but now she scoffs and crosses her arms. "Well, it's good to see that my first impression of you still stands. Because I was starting to think you were a decent guy or something. But obviously, that's not true. You're just a bully, Mr. Riggs."

I laugh. Loud enough for it to echo down the tunnel. "A bully?"

"Yeah. You enjoy threatening me, don't you?" She steps forward and pokes me in the chest with a manicured fingernail. "That's how you get through life, isn't it? Threatening people with gruesome acts of retaliation if they don't act the way you tell them to."

"I'm trying to save your life, Clover. I'm sorry my delivery is a bit terse for your standards of care, but I'm all you've got. So if you're done throwing your little tantrum, princess"—I wave my hand at the door —"can we please proceed? Because the sooner I get rid of you, the sooner I can get on with my life."

She clenches her jaw, narrows her eyes, and presses her lips together. Like she wants to explode right now, but doing so would just prove my point that she's a spoiled brat.

And she's not.

Even I know she's not.

All I wanted to say to her just now was that I understand how weird it is. I get it. But she was too wound up to hear that, let alone appreciate it, so I reverted back to threats. She responds well to threats, so it's just the quickest, easiest way to snap her back in line.

Because there's a significant part of this plan that is dangerous. Everything about her being here with me is dangerous. If they catch us, she's done. If she's not killed outright, *if* she's allowed to live, then she will be a prisoner down here. And not my prisoner, either. A Colony prisoner. They won't send her to the tunnels, but she'll never have a carefree day again for the rest of her life.

I just don't want to tell her that part. It'll stress her out and high stress leads to mistakes. I'd rather have her angry with me than locked up in a cold, dark cage like a lab rat in one of our military laboratories. Because that's where they'd send her. A nice up-top girl like her with all those outside genes to poke through? Yeah, the Colony scientists would *love* to have a guinea pig like Clover to test their shit on.

"Fine," she finally says. "I'm ready."

"You're not, but it's OK. Just let me do all the talking and don't look around like a goddamned tourist, all right?"

Clover makes a face. "Why would I? It's a dirty, underground city. It probably smells like a sewer."

I just chuckle. "Whatever you say, Your Highness. Just stick to the plan."

She blows out a breath, but our conversation is over.

I exhale loudly too, then turn my attention and flashlight to the security panel to the left of the door. I open it up, key in the code to open the door, and then the locks disengage with a low rumble. I crank the long handle to disengage the seal, and the door opens with a hiss of stale air.

When I look over my shoulder, Clover is all wide-eyed again, trying her best to see past the dark.

"Ready?"

She looks up at me and nods, all traces of her little freak-out gone now, fear taking its place.

"It's gonna be fine, Clover."

"I dunno, Riggs." She sighs. It's a much softer, nicer way of expressing her doubts than the huffs and scoffs. "You might be right. I'm maybe not up to this."

I smile. Not just because she's calm now, but because she doesn't really think I'm a bully. Somewhere inside that head of hers she understands that I'm sincerely trying to help her. "Just follow my lead. And don't act all impressed and shit over the city. That's the big thing."

"I don't understand why I would be impressed by a

dirty, dark, underground city." She puts up a hand. "So no worries there."

"Yep. You've got this, my queen."

She wants to be mad about my royalty jabs, and she tries. For a moment. But then she gives in and smiles. "Fine. You're right. I'll be great."

"That's the spirit. Put on the brave face. Let's go."

The moment I point my flashlight into the next room, Clover grabs at the back of my shirt, then hooks her fingers around the belt loop underneath it.

I look down at her from over my shoulder. "Are you coming on to me?"

Her face scrunches up in confusion. "What? No. I just..." She peeks around me, like maybe there's monsters in this tunnel. "I'm just a little bit afraid, OK? But if you're going to make a big deal about me holding on to you for moral support, then—"

"I'm fucking with you. I don't mind at all. Ready?"

She sucks in a big breath, then nods. "I'm ready."

I walk forward as Clover shadows so close behind me, I can't turn around to close the door until she gets out of my way. But I don't say anything else about this little act of vulnerability she's displaying. She can cling all she wants. It kinda turns me on to think she needs my protection.

"Fuck's sake," I mutter. *Focus, Riggs! This woman is gonna get you sent back to the tunnels if you're not careful.*

"What?" Clover whispers.

"Nothing. Just talking to myself. Come on, the next door is just right up here."

She doesn't ask any questions at this door, just waits for me to unlock it, then calmly steps through. We do this several more times before entering an elevator that drops us a thousand feet in just under a minute. When we stop, the doors do not open automatically. Yet another code is required. So before I punch that in, I say, "This is it. Are you ready?"

She's still holding on to me, but now, as she waits for me to key in the code to unlock the door, she presses herself right up against me, peering past my shoulder. "I guess."

I key in the code, open the door, and we walk through.

It takes a second for the bustle of the city to overtake the absolute silence we just came out of, but then... there it is. While Blackberry Hill only houses two thousand people these days, it's big enough for twenty thousand. Which, relatively speaking, makes it empty, so the city sounds have an echoing quality that makes it a different kind of loud than a city filled to capacity like Kingfisher Flats.

I reach around, prying Clover's fingers off me, and then direct her to step out from behind my back. We're in an alley and while there are people walking past up ahead, there's no one in here with us. So it's a safe place for her to take a look around and collect herself.

When I look down at her, she's squinting, her hand partially covering her eyes like a visor. "Why is it so bright?" She looks around, then up at me. "You're tricking me. This isn't underground. This is outside. There's a sun!"

"Artificial. It's just lights, Clover. We're definitely underground. You know this. We got in the elevator. We went down a hundred floors. And it goes much deeper than that."

"It was a trick. I'm dreaming—"

I turn and grab her shoulders, shaking her a little. "That's enough now. You need to be calm. When we get to our room, you can ask all the questions you want, but right now I need you to stop. OK? Here. Take my hand." I offer it to her, fully expecting a fight. But a fight is better than panic.

She looks at it for a moment, but then puts her hand in mine and lets out a breath.

I give it a squeeze. "It's only a five-minute walk to the room we're gonna stay in and there's no one in the consulate here. We haven't kept full-time ambassadors here in Blackberry Hill for nearly a decade. It's a big city, area wise, but not many people live here these days, so most of it is very quiet and empty. Honestly, Collin Creed is the most interesting thing to happen to Blackberry Hill in a long time. So you don't have to talk to anyone. There's almost no way you fuck this up. Just as long as you don't talk, don't gawk, and keep a hold of my hand." I hold up our joined hands and give her a smile.

Her face is all kinds of confused, but this seems to settle her. For now. So she nods. "OK."

"All right. Let's go." I lead her out of the alley and immediately, she's gawking and gasping. I squeeze her again, but this time far less gently. "Knock it off, Clover. Ignore everything until we get back inside."

"But it's so big!"

"Shhh." I tug her a little to make her keep up with the new, fast pace I've set, and focus on the door to the consulate just a little way down the street.

When we arrive, I key in the code, open the door, and close it behind us. The lights come on automatically, illuminating the three-story lobby. I quickly turn to Clover and shake my head, cautioning her. "Wait." Then I point up.

Her eyes follow my pointing finger, taking in the massive wooden staircase, and she nods.

We climb the stairs all the way up to the top of the building, because I figure that since I'm the only one here, I might as well take the penthouse.

When we finally reach the top, I open the door to the apartment and wave her in. Again, the lights come on automatically. But only because the curtains are drawn across the massive bank of floor-to-ceiling windows on the far end of the main living room.

"Oh… wow." Clover steps inside, looking around the room. "I wasn't expecting this."

"It's nice," I say, closing the door behind us. "But here's the best part." I walk over to the windows, grab the curtains, and throw them aside. Sunlight—well, fake, of course—comes streaming into the room, giving the whole place a nice, warm glow. "The view," I say. "I've always liked this view."

Clover joins me at the window, saying nothing.

In the early days, when the underground cities were first being drilled, the men in charge tried to make them fit in with the esthetic and geography above. So Blackberry Hill has all the characteristics of Charleston circa 1956. The buildings are various shades of buff and red brick with some of the same ornamental features of their up-top counterparts. There are cars and a trolley system—all electric. Shops line the street below us. A corner store, a tailor, and a diner are visible from up here. Most of them are probably abandoned these days, but they don't look derelict. And if you only look down and not across, you could almost believe you *were* up top. But there's no endless expanse of sky that ends in a horizon down here, obviously. Just a fake sun shining through a massive hole in the rock walls.

"Speechless?" I ask.

She points at the cityscape outside the window. "Is that a river?"

"That is a river. You have rivers above, so there must be rivers below."

An incredulous huff escapes with her words. "I… don't know what to think about this. It's a city." She looks up at me. "Like a normal city."

I shrug. "If it makes you feel any better, I felt the same way about the up-top cities when I first saw them. I had never imagined that something could exist on the surface. To go up there and see… civilizations, well, it was jarring."

Clover points at the sky. "What is that?"

"An artificial sun. I know they have really good ones up top now, but this one is old. It's UV, but it's not nearly as strong as the one where I come from."

"But it looks like a sky up there. It looks like a bright sunny day."

"It's a hologram. Again, kind of a substandard one compared to other, better cities down here. But it's a nice touch, I think."

"A hologram. I feel like I just fell into a science fiction movie. Do the people down here know they live underground?"

"Yes. Of course they know."

"But what do they think is up there on the surface?"

"What do you think is up in space?"

Her face screws up for a moment before answering. "Stars."

"But you don't *know* there are stars out in space. You were told there are stars out in space."

"Yes. But I can look up at the stars myself. I can use a telescope and see them up close. The people down here, they go their whole lives never seeing the top?"

"First of all"—I hold up a finger—"you don't know what those tiny pinpricks of light up in the sky are. You only know what you've been told. It's the same with everyone down here. They are born here, told that this is all there is of the world, and most of the time there's no reason to question it. It's the same with the stars above."

"But it's not the same. I was told the truth. You're lying to these people."

"Second of all"—I hold up my second finger—"you have no idea if you've been told the truth. You were told *something*. And everyone around you was told the very same something. Common knowledge is a hard thing to fight."

Clover side-eyes me. "If you've got something to say about space, just say it."

"I don't. I have no clue what the stars are beyond what I've been told as well. It's a very difficult thing to question the narrative. I mean, where would I even start? Assuming I was living up top. Where would I start to study the stars?"

"College?"

"A logical option. But colleges and universities are filled with people who all think the same way. Why should they question mysteries that have been solved? These things are… *facts*."

"Why do you say it like that?"

"Because come on, Clover. Facts? Think about it. There are very few facts in this world. Very few. Not even the laws of physics are facts. They are presumptions based on equations, which is based in the idea that the universe runs on math."

"But the universe does run on math."

"Says you."

Clover shrugs. "Fine. I don't know then. Where would you study stars?"

"Well, I wouldn't. Because I don't care if the stars are true or not. But there's almost no way to get past the… *consensus*." Now it's my turn to shrug. "So why bother. But anyway, my point is that the people who live down here think the surface is like space. Unreachable and unknowable except through the lens of science and textbooks. So why should they spend one moment of their lives questioning the narrative?"

"Surely you have curious, imaginative children who dream big? I mean, I can see the adults falling into line, but kids? They don't know what they don't know. They don't know it's pointless to fight the narrative and seek a new one."

"We do have our fair share of those kids. Myself included. But at the first sign of 'curiosity,' as you call it, they remove us from the general population and conscript us into the Future Founders."

"What's that? Like the Boy Scouts?"

"Yeah. Sure. It's just like the fucking Boy Scouts."

"I'm serious. I want to know what it is. Especially if you were in it."

"Why would that make a difference?"

Clover sighs. "I dunno. I just... think it's all very interesting. So, what is this Future Founders thing? An ROTC?"

"Kind of. I mean, sure. Yeah. It's ROTC. My father is a general."

Her eyes go wide. "Oh. That's significant."

"Yeah. So, when my curiosity started causing problems, I was sent into Future Founders."

"Is it like a stayaway camp?" She's grinning at me.

"Sure. It's exactly like a stayaway camp."

Now she frowns and huffs. "So that means it was horrible."

"How do you get to that conclusion?"

"Because I hear it in your voice. You hated it."

"No. I didn't hate it. It's hard to hate being in the Founders."

Clover turns to look at me, scrunching up her nose. "Why?"

"Because we're the elites. We get all the privileges.

We can even go up top on vacation—I mean, eventually. You have to earn that and it takes most of your career. But at least it's a possibility. As a twelve-year-old kid, being conscripted was… well, fuckin' amazing. I got to leave home, for one. There's an academy in the Lumina Basin, right on the lake, and that's where I lived all my teenage years. So it's not a stretch of the imagination to say it was a stayaway camp."

Clover turns, sitting on the edge on the window sill. "Lumina Basin. What's that?"

"A huge underground crystal cavern attached to a massive salt lake. It's…" I pause here, conjuring up images of Founder Academy and the surrounding area. "It's the most spectacular thing I've ever seen. And maybe I haven't seen everything up top, but Lumina Basin is like something out of a storybook. The crystals are a dozen feet in length."

"Shut up."

"I'm not joking. That's just the average length. There are a few that are sixty feet or more. They're as wide as a house. It's almost not even possible to understand that it's a crystal, because when you're right up close, it looks like a wall of milky luminous glass. They're all like that, because they are lit up with lights, of course. They don't illuminate on their own."

"Hmm. It doesn't sound real."

"There are caves like that in the up-top. There's

one in Mexico, but that one doesn't have the salt lake like Lumina does. It's the water that keeps Lumina Basin habitable. It even rains there. So… no. I didn't hate the academy. I loved it, actually. And I was a captain of my year the whole time I was there."

"What did you want to do when you were a kid that caused you to be diagnosed with 'curiosity?'"

"I found a book in my father's study called *Journey to the Center of the Earth*."

"Jules Verne."

"You've read it?"

"Skimmed. It was boring."

I actually laugh out loud. "You're crazy. That book was the best thing I had ever read. Still is, maybe."

"What a strange book to find though."

My eyebrows go up. "Right? I mean, it was a book about surface people who journey underground and find a new world."

She laughs. "That is kinda funny. It would be like me reading a book about a girl underground who comes up top to find my world. So it's interesting, I guess. But I would not obsess over that. It's just another story in a sea of stories, if you ask me."

"That's because you're allowed to read whatever you want up there. Authors are allowed to write whatever stories they want. This book was not on any of the approved reading lists and I immediately knew that because the idea that there could be a whole other world on the surface never occurred to me until that very moment and it felt... very... *forbidden.*"

Her eyes are locked with mine for many long seconds. Then she lets out a small breath, and with it comes a chuckle. "You ran."

"What?"

"When you were sent on your mission, or whatever. You never told me what you did to mess it up and get sent to prison, but this is what you did. You ran when you got up here."

There's no point in lying about this. Clover already knows so much more than she should, she'd probably be executed for that fact alone if we get caught. So it hardly matters what I did to get sent to the tunnels. I walk over to a chair, sit down, and kick my legs out. "Yep. I ran. I only made it one year, though." Then I smile and tip my chin up a little. "It was the best worst decision I ever made."

Clover studies me for a few moments, then gives me a little nod. "Curiosity is a bitch, isn't it?"

"An ancient crone of a bitch."

"What about me?"

I shrug. "What about you?"

"How do I rank in terms of the best worst decision you've ever made?"

My grin isn't immediate. It takes a couple moments to form. But once it does, it's big. "Clover, you are tippy-top bad for me. You're number one on my long list of reckless, traitorous decisions."

"Then why are you doing this?"

"Because…" I fully intend on lying here. I fully intend on insisting that I'm some kind of good guy in this deception that's going on all around us. But I can't seem to do it, even though it's a better answer than the truth. "Because there's a part of me that knows there's no coming back from this one. Bringing you here is a death sentence for me if I get caught. But I'm angry at my father. I guess I just didn't realize it until now. I'm pissed, actually. That he would send me to those tunnels. That looking for truth is a punishable offense. And there's a part of me that wants to get caught and embarrass him a second time. Two chances, two fuck-ups." I pause here to smile. "I would die happy to see the look on his face if he ever found you here."

CHAPTER 13 - CLOVER

*H*o. *Lee. Shit.*

He's setting me up!

He's using me to get back at his father. He's gonna get us caught on purpose. He never intended to let me go. Hell, for all I know, this waystation place doesn't even exist. He brought me down to this forbidden city to rub his father's face in his own bad parenting.

"Why are you looking at me that way?"

I just stare at Riggs with an open mouth.

"Clover?"

I let out a breath. "What?"

"Why are you looking at me that way?"

I press my lips together. I've underestimated him. I fell into the idea that he has a conscience. But I knew better. He spewed all those threats at me—vile, repulsive, gross threats about letting me rot and decay in my own basement—and the very first time he turns on the charm, I fall for it.

What the hell is wrong with me?

"Clover? What's wrong?"

I need to up my game, that's what I need to do. All that talk about trust and whatever. Such bullshit! "Nothing," I say. And to my surprise, my outer voice is calm despite the inner one roaring inside my head.

He's just about to object and start questioning me thoroughly when a phone rings.

We both get to our feet and start looking around. But then Riggs is crossing the room to a table and a moment later he picks it up. "Yeah." There's a pause while he listens, then he smiles. "Yeah. Well, I didn't think I'd get done this quick." Another pause. "It's all set. There's no problem there. But hey, I brought someone with me."

He looks at me and has the audacity to smile. What a jerk.

"My neighbor from Kingfisher. Her name is Hattie. She came to check on me. You know how my father is." There's laughing on the other end, I can hear it. "But we're not staying long. Leaving on the train tomorrow, in fact." Riggs is still smiling at me, then starts nodding to whoever is on the other line. "Yeah. Sure. We'll be there." Then he hangs up. "Well, that was Ike Monroe. They know we're here, obviously. And I knew we'd never get into the city without him knowing. But he wasn't expecting you, also obviously, so now we need to have dinner with him."

I'm failing to understand how the first of these things leads to the second, but it's not even worth questioning. He's taking me to dinner with Ike so Ike sees me and this whole charade gets uncovered. Then Ike will contact Riggs's father and well, obviously, I am not this Hattie person and that's it. I'm dead and Riggs gets his revenge.

"Is that OK?" Riggs asks.

"You're trying to get me killed."

"What?" He actually has the gall to laugh. "What are you talking about? I'm saving you, Clover. Not trying to get you killed."

"You're trying to get back at your father—"

"Whoa, whoa, whoa!" He puts up both hands, pressing them at me. "That's not true."

"You just admitted it!"

"Because it's… kind of like a… consolation prize should things go wrong."

"And *then*"—I glare at him—"you accept a dinner invitation to Ike Monroe's? What the hell?"

"I can't tell him no. That would be a huge red flag. We go, we eat a nice meal, we come back here, and tomorrow morning we get on the train. That's it. It's gonna work, I swear. And as fun as getting back at my father sounds, you're dead wrong about me wanting to get caught. If I get caught…" He's shaking his head at me. "Fuck that. I'm not going back to those tunnels. Never. I'd rather die than go back there."

He puts up a hand to shut me up because I'm about to interject here with a great big 'ah-ha!' "And before you go jumping to conclusions about *that* one, I don't want you to get caught either. They would kill you, Clover. One hundred percent, they would kill you. And… well… I… you've… grown on me. You're…" He pans a hand at me. "Attractive. And… a little bit fun. Not to mention gutsy, in a princess kind of way. I don't want to get you killed, I really don't."

I blink at him. Then narrow my eyes. "Are you coming on to me?"

His smile is immediate. "Maybe."

"Well, save it, mister. I'm not interested. And I don't believe you. There's no way you're as altruistic as you're making yourself out to be. Altruistic men don't threaten to stuff my dead body into a trailer, drive it to the lake, back it into the water and let it decompose for months before being found."

"How the hell do you even recall those threats?" He blinks at me. "I mean, it was heat-of-the-moment shit, Clover. I was never gonna kill you like that."

My eyebrows shoot up my forehead and my mouth falls open. "Like that? Like *that*?"

Riggs sighs and drops down into a chair. "All right. Fine. Get it out of your system. Tell me I'm a piece of shit. What should I say back? That all my threats were true?"

"I can't trust you."

He stares at me for a moment. Glares at me for a moment. "That would be unfortunate, Clover. Because if you can't trust me, then I can't trust you. And if there's no trust, then maybe I *should* kill you."

"See?" I point at him. "There it is again."

He scrubs both his hands up and down his face, mumbling things I can't make out. When he's done, and meets my gaze again, he looks worn out. His eyes, I now notice, are bloodshot. And his face is paler than I recall it being. Maybe it's the light down here. Or maybe he's just… weary. Which implies more than just being physically tired. This weariness comes out in his voice when he speaks. "If it were up to me, Clover, I'd stay with you."

I make a face. "What?"

"In the bunker where I'm gonna leave you. I'd stay with you if I could. I'd never go back. And you know what? I kinda hate you right now for making me admit that, because it took a long time to give up on the dream. I don't wanna live underground. Maybe, back before I understood what the up-top was, maybe it would've been fine to live this way. To never see the sun or stand in front of the ocean. But once you've seen it, it's impossible to live down here. I'm never gonna be happy. Ever. So I'm mad at you for reminding me of what I've lost and making me admit it."

"Well…" I pause here, not sure how to respond to that. I land on a classic third-grade rebuttal. "I didn't make you do anything."

"You did. Because you can't trust me. That's what you said. And that only leads to me not trusting you, so…" He lets out a long breath. "So then I had to admit to myself that I like you, OK?" He shrugs with his hands.

"I don't even see the connection."

"The connection is *us*." He points to himself, then me, then back at himself. "We've started to feel like a team."

Hmmm. I consider this. The mood between us *has* turned a bit collaborative.

"And if we've got a connection, then I *can't* kill you." He pauses here to press his hands at me again. "Not that I ever would. I've never killed anyone."

"That's got to be a lie. Your threats came off… *professional*."

He shrugs while pulling out a charming smile. "It was an act."

I scoff. I don't think it was. I really, really don't think it was. He had a look to him that first day. A reckless, kind of panicked look. A desperate look. He acted out of instinct when our eyes met that first time. He saw me, I saw him, and before I could even process the fact that there was a half-naked man in my house, he had me. Just like that, he had me.

My eyes narrow down because this charm he's throwing at me right now is meant to be distracting.

Disarming. "You're lying." I don't say it with heat or anger. It's just a fact.

The charm disappears. Like… instantly. Because he knows I know and that's that. That part of the charade is over. "Fine. I'm lying. Is that what you want to hear?"

"It's not supposed to be about what I want to hear, Riggs. I just want you to be honest with me. You *have* killed people. And if I didn't worm my way into your head and make you see me as something other than an inconvenience, you would've killed me too."

He shrugs this off. A one-shoulder shrug, implying indifference. "So what? That killing was done a long time ago. Will you give Collin Creed the same scrutiny when you get back? Because he's killed a lot more people than I have."

Now I'm frowning and there's a crushing feeling inside my chest that I can't describe. It's not sadness, but something like it. A silence emerges. And then it continues for nearly a whole minute.

"Say something."

"I'm disappointed in you."

He laughs. "Is that so?"

"Yeah. Because we *were* becoming a team and now it's not even in the realm of possibility. And… well, I was starting to like you too. You're fun to banter with."

"But? Now that you know I'm a killer, you've changed your mind?"

"That's not it."

"Right. See, this is why I didn't tell you."

"So you lied to protect me?" I scoff.

"No. I lied to protect *me*. You have all the power now, Clover."

"How the hell do you figure that?"

"Because we're in my world now and all you'd have to do to ruin me is admit who you are. I'm taking you to Ike Monroe's home for dinner tonight. All you'd have to do is tell him you're Lowyn's best friend."

I huff. "Why would I do that?"

"Because he obviously loves her. So he would save you. Send you back home to tell her the whole story about how he did that. Then... you know, maybe she'd..."

"Forgive him?" Oh, my God. Underground men are so dumb. It takes a lot of self-control not to laugh at him right now. "He *kidnapped* her, Riggs. Twice. And almost killed her."

"He was never gonna kill her."

"How would you know?"

"My father's a general. I was briefed. And look, I'm not saying he's a nice guy. I'm just saying that if you wanted to stop this plan where *both* of us get out alive, you could. Very easily. Telling Ike who you are tonight would change everything." He stares at me for a moment, those weird brown eyes of his lit up with emotion. "If I wanted you dead, Clover, I'd have left you behind. But I didn't. I trusted you to keep *me* safe when I brought you with me. You've got power over me now. We *need* to trust one another. I don't want to be here." He points to the floor. "I want to be up there." He points to the ceiling. "And having you here…" He lets out a long sigh. "Well, it just reminds me of what I'm giving up."

"What does that mean?"

"I ran, remember? I lived up top. And then they sent me to the tunnels for six years to punish me for wanting something more. Bringing you here is just me admitting that I still want more. What other reason would I have to risk everything for a woman I don't even know?"

"Well, see… that's my problem with you, Riggs. I don't understand why you're doing this. If not to get even with your father, then why help me?"

His sigh is long as he rakes his fingers through his hair. He holds up his hand, one finger raised. "You're pretty." He raises another finger. "I don't want to hurt you." He holds up a third finger. "There's a part of me that thinks… maybe…"

When he doesn't finish his sentence, my eyebrows go up. He *likes* me? As in 'likes' me? And he's thinking that maybe I'll like him back?

I scoff. Maybe he's telling the truth. Maybe he's not. It's impossible to tell, so of course, I have to lean towards the latter. Because misplaced trust is far more dangerous than misplaced suspicion.

"What?" he says. "What are you thinking?"

I shake my head and turn away, just kind of looking around the room to buy myself some time because I don't really know what to say to him right now. It's a nice big room. Looks like any other penthouse suite in a hotel. Not the Dixie Yonder, since the décor is all very modern here and the Yonder was very Colonial cottage, but there's a living area with a big L-shaped couch and two sleek club chairs opposite.

The dining area has a round table and enough chairs to seat eight. There's a bar on the far end, stocked with bottles of alcohol.

I head that direction.

"What are you doing, Clover?"

"Getting a drink." I step behind the bar and study the liquor, unable to recognize a single brand. There's one bottle of everything—a red wine, a white wine, a bourbon, a brandy, a vodka, a gin, a rum, and a tequila.

Normally I'm a wine girl, but for this occasion, I choose the bourbon. I take two glasses down from a shelf, then turn and face Riggs as I set them on the bar. "Neat or ice?"

His grin is lopsided. And I'm not gonna lie, he's got a certain charm to him. This grin in combination with the rogue dark hair makes him look like he belongs in the wilderness climbing the rocky red cliffs of Utah or rounding up cows in a Montana valley. And even though this city is lit up and bright, it's a lie. We're underground. There's no sun, no ocean, no cows, I bet. So it's nothing but a lie.

He's nothing but a lie.

But I guess I can see his point. He's stuck here and when your father's some highfaluting general of a secret underground army, there are expectations.

Is it any different growing up in Disciple? I mean, no one ever asked me if I wanted to sing in the children's choir every fucking weekend. No one ever asked me if I wanted to make crafty things to sell in Lowyn's family booth. No one ever asked me if I wanted to play a part in that show—fanning myself and shoutin' 'amen' during the Revival. It was just the straw I drew.

He and I are staring at each other when he says, "Neat."

I press my lips together and nod. Then pour us both a shot of bourbon and slide his glass across the bar. He crosses the room and picks it up, locking his gaze with mine. "To trust?"

My sigh is kinda loud. "Do you want the truth? Or do you just want me to agree?"

He sets his glass back down on the bar. "Well, obviously, if we're gonna trust each other, then the truth."

I frown. Because I don't want to say something cliché. I've already done that. I've already told him the surface-level thoughts in my head. So I take a moment. Surprisingly, he allows me this time. After a long, awkward minute I land here: "I just… don't know what to think about this." I wave a hand at the hotel and then the window, so he knows I'm talking about where we are and what this place is. "I feel like I've fallen into an adventure. Which implies, as you said, that we're a team. I get that. I mean, we're plotting together, we're relying on each other to get through this, we both have things at stake, and there's a real atmosphere of danger."

"OK. So… is there a question in there somewhere?"

"There is. But it's crossing a line, I think."

"How so?"

"Because if I give in to this trust thing, I'll start to like you." His grin is so quick, and so big, and so fucking charming, I feel the faintness and heat of swooning. But I'm a grown woman, not a teenager, so instead of fainting from his charm, I pull myself together and point at him. "See? That's what I mean."

He chuckles. "What are you talking about?"

"Come *on*. You know what you're doing with that smile of yours. You're playing me, Riggs."

His face goes serious now. "I'm absolutely not."

"Then why are you risking everything to help me?"

"For fuck's sake. I *like* you."

"I understand that. I mean, I understand that's what you're trying to convey. But there's nothing between us. You kidnapped me. You tied me up, gagged me, and left me to rot in the dark of my own basement. And while we have already discussed the threats, I don't believe you, Riggs. You *are* charming, and you have this whole rogue-adventurer persona going, I'll give you that much. But you've killed people. And if you insist on sticking to the whole I'm-a-good-guy-underneath-it-all story..." I don't finish. He's already told me, in a way, what happens if I don't trust him. So I don't say it, but I do mean it. And he knows this.

He downs his drink, puts it back on the bar, then walks away. But over his shoulder he says, "We're leaving for Ike's in ten minutes. Go clean up." And then he disappears down a hallway.

CHAPTER 14 - RIGGS

*W*hen *I close* the bedroom door behind me, I'm frustrated and angry. Frustrated because she's right, of course. Why should she trust me? It's Stockholm syndrome shit.

But the anger is with myself. Because I was starting to fall for her and it's nothing but a stupid, hopeless fantasy.

What I didn't tell her, when she asked why I was doing this, was that maybe the reason I wanted to lock her in the bunker for three months was so I could sort things out and then… go back and get her so the two of us could…

I scoff.

Could what? Go on the run together? It's so fucking absurd, I'm internally cringing at my own thought process.

But the truth is… that *was* what I was thinking and I didn't even realize it until we had this conversation about trust.

I really thought I could put her on hold while I

sorted shit out, then go back and get her and keep her forever.

Not alone, in a bunker, but in her world up top.

We could find a new future together. I mean, her life just imploded. She lost her job and her place to live. It's the perfect time to start over.

Yeah, Riggs, that little voice in my head says. *She really wants to start over with a guy like you.*

Probably not. She saw right through my lies. And even if she could convince herself that I was telling the truth about liking her, those threats I made in the beginning are something else altogether. I can almost picture us as old people, after being together for thirty years and getting in a fight. She would still be quoting those threats at me. We'd have kids, and grandkids, and she'd tell the story of how we met.

Well, dear grandchildren, your Pop-Pop here kidnapped me on the worst day of my life, and then we ran away to an underground city and…

And what? What *are* we going to do next?

"Next," I say out loud, "we're going to dinner at Ike Monroe's."

I go into the bathroom, splash some water on my face, and try not to look at myself in the mirror.

One night.

All I have to do is get through this one night. Then, tomorrow, get on the train, take her to the bunker, lock her in, and never think about her again.

This was the plan.

This *is* the plan.

When I go back out to the main living area, she must've splashed water on her face too because her cheeks are a little bit flushed.

She doesn't say anything, so I walk to the door and hold it open.

We exit the room without another word.

OUTSIDE, **the lights are** dimming down to the twilight hour. The nights down here never go completely dark, but all Colonies keep a moonlight schedule so the amount of darkness will differ like it does up top. Something to do with circadian rhythms.

"When I first learned about the moon cycles, it bothered me so much I couldn't sleep for almost a week." To my surprise, I say this out loud.

Clover side-eyes me. "What?"

"The moon. The real moon. I nearly went crazy from it."

"What do you mean?"

"It was..." I shake my head a little. "It was the biggest lie I learned before I was sent up top. I mean, the lies we tell down here, they're wrapped around everything. And you'd think that learning that there was a world up top would be the kicker, ya know? The biggest lie of them all. But it was the moon."

"Why not the sun?"

"I dunno." I look at her as we walk down the street. There are people about, but Blackberry Hill isn't what we'd call a big Colony. It's spread out because there are lots of levels, so it looks big. But there are only about two thousand people living here. "I dunno," I say again. Because she's right, it should be the sun.

"Maybe because you can't look at it."

I smile. "Yeah, maybe that's why. You can look at the moon all you want. They showed us pictures of it in Assimilation, but my first night up top happened on the full moon and those pictures didn't even come close. I mean, it's a big rock in the sky, ya know?"

"Yeah. I get it. I think the moon inspires awe in everyone."

There's a lull in the conversation after this. Which is fine by me. Ike's place is not that far and I'm hoping that the silence will extend all the way to our destination. But just as I'm thinking this, Clover says, "Hattie Miller, right?"

"Yep."

"Anything else I should know about her? Other than she's rigid and boring?"

"Nope."

"Come on, Riggs. There has to be something."

"You don't need to pretend to be her. Trust me, no one down here wants to be her. Just say you're her and leave it at that."

"What did she do to you?"

I stop walking and look at Clover, shaking my head a little. And I'm about to deny it and just ignore the whole thing, but Clover holds up a finger. "First," she says, "I'm really not prying, but you're hostile."

"I'm not hostile."

"You are. You get this cold, aggressive look in your eyes whenever you speak about her. We're already fighting over our own personal shit, the last thing we need is the name 'Hattie' setting you off. I'm not gonna tell Ike who I am. I'm not escaping here through him. And you're spilling all this bullshit about me trusting you, but you can't trust me with the reason you hate this woman so much?"

I scoff. "Fine. If you must know, she's the one who found me."

Clover's eyebrows knit together as she works things out. "Found you." Then they shoot up in surprise. "Up top?"

I nod. "Yep."

"OK." She's smart. She knows there's more to this. "She turned you in."

"You could say that."

"Well, I did say that. But is it true?"

"She's a bounty hunter, Clover."

"Oh."

"Yeah. We were friends as kids. We were both 'curious' kids so we both got sent to Future Founders. And there was… maybe… a year there? Where I liked her the way you were thinking earlier. Maybe when we were twelve or thirteen, but definitely before fourteen because fourteen is when we get to select our possible assignments."

"Are these assignments a Founders thing too? Or does everyone get to choose?"

"Yes, a Founders thing. No, most people do not get to choose their path in life. Not everyone grows up the way we did. Most of them"—I wave my hand at the people going about their business on the streets—"they don't live any different than people up top. They swallow all the lies, dedicate their lives to working harder and longer to just afford something a little bit nicer. They dream big for their kids, and watch sports, and think about everyday things. But everything in the Founders is different. It's like ROTC, like you said. There are uniforms and we earned ribbons, and medals, and awards by completing our destiny checklist."

Clover stares at me for a second, then blinks. "Wow. Destiny checklist. That's quite a title. But I gotta say, this whole image you're painting in my mind is starting to come off a little bit…"

"Tyrannical? Yeah, I would agree. Hattie is a bounty hunter for people who escape."

She and I just look at each other for a moment and I watch in real time as her opinion of this place adjusts. Clover blows out a breath. "Wow." Then she turns and we resume walking. "So… she hunted you. Like actually hunted you?"

"Yep."

"Did you ever date her?"

"No."

"Did she want to date you?"

"I think she did."

"Come on, Riggs. Either she's a bitchy jilted ex or she's not."

"She's not. Not really. She never had the chance to be an ex."

"So she's a bitter, scorned woman looking for vindication?"

My smile is crooked, but honest too. "I think that would be the perfect way to describe Hattie Miller."

"All right then."

"But don't be like that. Please. Just… be yourself."

"That's the second time you've said that."

I shrug. "Well, you're likable just the way you are." She doesn't say anything and when I steal a look down at her, I find her cheeks flushed. "Why are you blushing?"

"I'm not."

"Whatever."

"It's just… you're such a contradiction. One minute you're threatening to—"

"*Clover*. My God. Can we just put those threats behind us? If I had known you'd throw my words back at me for the rest of my life, I'd have chosen them more carefully."

She chuckles. "Rest of your life? That's dramatic. Unless you have plans for me that I don't know about. Because tomorrow you're gonna drop me off in a bunker and we'll never see each other again."

"No. I mean…" I sigh and stop walking. Then point at a building. "We're here."

Clover looks over at it and lets out her own long breath. "OK." Then she turns to me. "But I would like to go on record that I think this whole night is a bad idea."

"It's fine. Ike Monroe is a bit player in the big scheme of things. Blackberry Hill is considered somewhat of a backwater in my circles. It's probably a major event to host people from Kingfisher Flats. We're gonna go up, mingle, eat, and leave. And tomorrow we'll be out of here and never think about him again."

Clover wipes her hands on her pants like she's nervous. And she doesn't agree with me. But there's no way back now, so I just walk to the door of the building and hold it open. "After you."

.   .   .

Ike Monroe's **quarters** are a lot like the penthouse at the consulate. It's all very upscale and proper. Which is a bit of a contradiction to Ike himself, who comes off as folksy and simple.

It's an act, though. Well, I'm sure that's who he started out as. He did, after all, grow up in the up-top Blackberry Hill. And from what I've heard, before he took over, it was a real shithole of a place.

Of course, what happens up there has almost no relevance to what happens down here, so this city— while tiny in comparison to the ones out west—has always been rather middle-class. Maybe even upper-middle-class.

I'm sure, when Ike Monroe came of age and was brought down here for the first time, his eyes went wide with wonder. To someone like him—a folksy, simple boy from a poverty-stricken hillbilly village— I'm sure it was nothing short of opulent.

And I do admit, Blackberry Hill has a certain charm to it. Kingfisher Flats is more of an urban city. It doesn't have the old buildings like this place. Or the historical struggles that took place up top. Even though Blackberry Hill has the forlorn and destitute feel of up-top West Virginia, it's kinda quaint and has a very small-town feel.

But that's not the look Ike was going for when he styled this penthouse. Though the building has to be over a hundred years old, and looks its age from the outside, you'd never know it from up here.

It's all modern and sleek. Floor-to-ceiling windows and stainless-steel accent tables, in combination with the ultra-modern black and white color scheme, makes the whole thing feel very metropolitan.

When we arrive, Ike is busy talking to other people and it immediately becomes clear that this isn't some simple dinner. It's a cocktail party and no one is dressed as casual as Clover and me. Dozens of people mingle. Every man is wearing a suit and every woman is wearing a dress. Not tuxes and gowns, but compared to us, in our woodsy-adventurer clothes, they might as well be.

Ike spies us from across the room, smiling big as he excuses himself from the crowd of people he's been talking to and heads our direction. I turn my head to Clover so he can't read my lips and quietly say, "Here he comes. Just smile and act... demure, or something."

Clover's comeback is cheerful. "On it."

"Riggs Russell!" Ike comes at me, hand extended. I shake it as he beams. "It has been a minute, hasn't it?"

This is a dig at my six-year absence, obviously. But

I let the taunt slide and force a smile. "It has, Ike. It has." The words come out wearier than intended, but the tone isn't entirely false.

Ike lets go of my hand, immediately directing his attention to Clover. "And you must be the infamous Hattie Miller." His eyes slide back to me. "You never mentioned how beautiful your hunter was, Riggs." He chuckles. Looks back at Clover. "I wouldn't mind having you on my tail."

Clover, having been brought up with manners, puts on a flawless customer-service face and offers her hand. Not in handshake. Fuck that. Clover is both Southern and rural, so it's one of those limp finger offerings that concludes with the kissing of knuckles.

To my surprise, Ike actually does this. He takes Clover's hand in his and, without breaking eye contact, gently brushes his lips across said knuckles.

I lean back a little, slightly repulsed. But Clover suddenly transforms into someone I don't quite recognize. She bows her head, averts her eyes, and does a little curtsy.

And I've got to say, I'm a little bit annoyed that Ike Monroe is the man who coaxed this response out of her instead of me. The worst thing is, his internal ugliness has nothing to do with his outside appearance. In fact, Ike Monroe kinda looks like a Viking. Very tall—at least six-three—and while his blond hair isn't as long as it was the last time we met, it's tousled and sloppy in a lion's-mane kind of way.

I've never seen him wearing anything but black leather and denim. Like he's some kind of biker gang leader. But tonight, he's in a casual cream-colored suit. Something very Disciple, which surprises me, since that place reeks of his archnemesis, Collin Creed.

Who, quite frankly, is my archnemesis too.

So there's a sort of paradigm shift happening in my brain, and, unfortunately, this shift looks good on him. I think Clover is as surprised as I am at how easily all our preconceived notions of Ike Monroe could be shattered in less than thirty seconds.

"Nice to meet you," Clover says, recovering from her curtsy.

"You as well, Miss Miller." He's still holding on to her hand, but he takes a step back like he wants to get a better look at her. "I was expecting something more…"

When he falters for words, Clover attempts to set him at ease by filling them in. "Hardy? Robust? Muscular?"

Which makes Ike bellow out a laugh. Practically a guffaw.

"Come on," I mutter. "It wasn't that funny." But neither of them are paying any attention to me.

In fact… are they staring into each other's eyes?

I slip an arm between them, breaking the moment.

"Yes. She's quite something, isn't she, Ike? Hattie and I have known each other our whole lives."

"I've heard," Ike says, not looking at me. His eyes are still locked with Clover's. Now he points at her. "You know what I like about you, Hattie?"

"You don't even know her," I scoff. "How could you like anything?"

Clover shoots me a warning with her eyes, then trains them right back on Mr. Viking here. "Never mind him. He's still bitter about how it all turned out."

My mouth actually drops open, and I want to grab her arm and pull her away. But Ike steals my move and the next thing I know, they've turned their backs on me and are walking across the room.

I take a deep breath. *It's fine. She's nothing to you. In fact, she's your prisoner so you should just let it go and...* I head to the bar. Get a shot of tequila, down it, then get another one and down that too.

Ike Monroe. What the hell does she think she's doing? She's gonna blow it. She's gonna ruin everything.

But as the minutes tick off, I realize she's not gonna blow it. She's actually having a conversation with him. Ike takes her around, introducing her, and there's a moment of panic here that someone will recognize her—as either Clover, or as not-Hattie. So I have an urge to go save her.

But this recognition doesn't happen, so neither

does my saving.

It makes sense, I guess. That no one recognizes her. Clover said she moved out of Disciple for college, which was a decade ago, at least. A couple of years before Ike Monroe was officially in charge down here. And no one this far away from Kingfisher Flats knows what Hattie looks like. Her identity, when she's up here hunting defectors, is a secret.

This whole charade is actually working.

So why am I so pissed off about that?

I drink a little more, notice that Clover is also drinking, and by the time the party starts winding down, she's well on her way to tipsy.

It's time to go.

She and Ike are in a crowd of people—mostly men, I notice. And all of them, even the women, are gawking at Clover like she's some shiny thing they all need to get a piece of.

I touch her arm and lean in. "Ready to go?"

"Oh, Riggs!" Ike exclaims. He's clearly 'tipsy' too. "Not yet. We're just getting started here. The night is young!"

I check my watch just for show. "It's past midnight and"—I almost say 'Clover'—"Hattie and I have a long trip tomorrow on the trains. We'd better turn in, don't you think, Hattie?" I give her arm a little squeeze when I say this. Not enough to hurt, but hard enough to get her attention.

She's about to say no, but then her eyes find mine. I think she actually might've forgotten that she's not Hattie Miller and these people are her literal enemies, because once our eyes lock, they sober up and she nods. "Yes, you're right." Then she turns to her crowd of admirers. "We'll have to catch up another time."

"Looking forward to it," one man says.

"Do keep in touch," his woman adds.

Clover leans in to have a few final words with the crowd, while Ike leans in to have a few words with me.

"Hey, the two of you… you're not together, right? I mean, tell me I haven't been stepping on your toes all night, Riggs, because I'll feel like an asshole if I have."

"No," I quickly say. "We're friends, that's all. I'm just a little protective of her."

"I've noticed. You've been lurking in the shadows behind us this whole night. Antisocial, as usual. But I have to say, I'm surprised you've remained friends. I mean, I wouldn't mind if she took me down and tied me up. But most men probably would."

"She was only doing her job," I say.

"Hmmm," Ike hums. "Funny. I've heard her name enough times to have a picture of her in my head. But that mental image and this real one don't seem to have any relation whatsoever. She's an absolute delight. And… well, if you're not with her, then… I might just take my chance. You wouldn't care, would you?"

I force a smile. "Not at all, Ike. Give it your best shot."

He laughs, throwing his head back. Then he claps me on the back. "Thanks, brother. We'll see ya next time you come through." Then he steps away, raising his hand to hail another friend across the room.

He passes Clover, stops to kiss her offered hand one more time, then shoots me a wink over his shoulder as Clover approaches.

"Wow." Her face is very flushed and while her eyes are bright and happy, they are also a bit glassy. "This was fun!"

"Yeah." I offer her my arm, not even knowing where that gesture came from because never in my life have I offered a woman my arm. It just felt appropriate for some reason. And Clover doesn't even blink when she clutches it, pushing herself into me, like she's tired.

She sighs. "Did you have fun?"

"Sure."

She looks up at me as we enter the elevator. "You didn't."

"It was fine. These people aren't my crowd." Then, under my breath, I mutter, "But apparently they are yours."

If she hears my snide comment, she doesn't respond. Just sighs again, leaning her head against my shoulder. "He's not what I thought he would be."

Here it comes. "I presume you are talking about Ike?"

"Yeah. I mean, from the way Lowyn described him, he's a monster. But he doesn't come off as a monster."

"He's like one of those pretty, poison frogs, isn't he?"

"Or… just one of the copycats. For survival reasons."

"Oh, my God, you *like* him?"

She shrugs, not even denying it.

"You're just drunk," I say, making excuses.

This makes her laugh. "Probably."

Which is a terrible answer. So we go silent after that. Thoughts of Ike Monroe lingering in our heads all the way home.

WHEN WE GET UPSTAIRS to our room, Clover heads straight for the bedroom. Once inside, she turns at the bottom of the bed, smiles, then spreads her arms and flops backwards, sending a ripple through the white, down comforter. She sighs. "I really needed this night."

I close the door behind me and step into the middle of the room. "You needed a night out with a monster?"

She scoffs and, because she is kinda drunk, it comes out as a snort. "If you're the monster, then I guess you're right."

"Whatever."

"You're just jealous."

Now it's my turn to scoff. And because I am way less drunk than she is, I *don't* snort. "There isn't a chance I'm jealous of Ike Monroe."

Clover turns on her side, awkwardly attempting to prop herself up on her elbow. Her eyes are bloodshot and her long, blonde hair is all messy. She looks tired. But… also happy. Like she really did have a good time. "It's not him you're jealous of, Riggs. It's my impression of him."

"Because you fell for his cliché good looks? Because you fell for his over-the-top fake charm? Clover, the only thing I feel about those two things is pity."

Her laugh bursts out and becomes a guffaw as she flops back on the bed and looks up at the ceiling. "This is a new side to you." She side-eyes me. "You like me, Riggs. But you're one of those unemotional men who can't stand intimacy. While Ike Monroe is the exact opposite. He's dying for some intimacy. He's looking for a partner. That's why women like him. He's looking for someone, Riggs. And you're just pushing everyone away."

I shake my head, sit down on a nearby chair, and start taking off my boots.

"I can feel it."

"You can feel *what*?" I snap back.

"Your distance."

"Whatever."

I finish taking off my boots and stand up, pulling my shirt over my head. To my surprise, I find Clover watching me.

She even takes a moment to study my body before meeting my gaze. "Will you take off my shoes too?" She lifts up one leg, with some difficulty, and wiggles her trendy hiking boot at me before letting her foot fall back to the ground with a thud.

I want to say no on principle, but she closes her eyes and turns her head to the side, like she might just pass out and sleep fully clothed if I don't lend her a hand.

So fuck it. I walk over, pick up her foot, unlace her shoe, and then do the other one.

She doesn't even move. Doesn't even open her eyes.

"Clover?"

She lazily answers me with a low, "Hmmm?"

"You're… you're in the middle of the bed."

"What?" She tries to laugh, but she's already half asleep.

"You're in the middle of the bed. You need to scoot over. I'm not sleeping on the couch."

"Isn't there another bedroom?"

"No. And if you don't move, I'll do it for you."

Her giggle is sleepy and filled with disbelief.

She doesn't move.

So I walk over to the side of the bed, grab her by the arms, and pull her up and push her over. She wakes up just enough to unbutton her pants and start wiggling them over her hips.

I watch, fascinated, as she brings her legs up, slips the pants off, and then kicks her long legs around as she tries to get under the comforter without opening her eyes.

"You're ridiculous."

She finally slips her legs under the covers, and then opens one eye to look at me while she snuggles into her pillow. "You like me."

I point to myself. "*You* like *me*."

She smiles, eyes closed again, and nods. "I do like you. It's a very bad idea, but you're just kinda…" And then she falls asleep. Leaving me dying to know what I'm kinda like.

I watch her for a moment, wondering what this liking her will get me.

Probably another prison sentence.

Possibly a death sentence.

How pissed off would my father be if he knew I had smuggled a Disciple resident into Blackberry Hill? Livid would be an understatement. It would be rage. A great rage. The kind of rage one expects from men with great power. And because it was me who did it, he would take it personal.

It would not just be a betrayal, it would be treason.

I take off my pants and get in on the other side of the bed, turning my back to Clover.

Immediately, she squirms behind me and then the next thing I know, she's got her face all cuddled up to my back.

I push her off. "Don't."

She is only semi-awake, but she musters up some energy to taunt me. "What's wrong, Riggs? You don't like me anymore?"

I push her all the way over to the other side of the bed. "There's a line here, OK?" I cut the bed in half with a fingertip. "You stay on your side, I'll stay on mine."

This makes her snort. "That's so very *I Love Lucy*." Then she snickers while making a monumental effort to open her eyes one last time. "Don't be a prude. Let me snuggle you, Riggs."

There's a pause here while I replay that word 'snuggle' back in my head.

And then she bursts out laughing and turns her back to me. A moment later, she's snoring.

I reach over, turn the light out, and then lie there in bed, staring up at the ceiling, forcing myself to think about the consequences if I don't get rid of her.

Falling for this woman would be a monumentally stupid thing to do and all the ways in which it could go wrong start playing in my head on repeat well into the early hours of the morning.

CHAPTER 15 - CLOVER

A ringing phone wakes me but I'm so confused about where I am, it takes whole seconds before I actually become lucid enough to pull together some semblance of reality.

"Yeah." Riggs' voice is low and rumbly as he answers the phone. He sounds tired and… well, sorta sexy if I'm being honest. "*What?*" Now he sounds irritated and he shifts in bed.

This is when I realize he's reached over me to get the phone and I'm actually pinned up against his bare chest. Do I move? Do I push him away?

I would, but this accidental embrace feels too good to end prematurely. So I do nothing.

"Well, when will they be back up? I'm on a schedule." His irritation has shifted into anger. "Fine. Call me as soon as you know." This feels like the end of the conversation but then, abruptly, he says, "*No.*" And now he's definitely angry. "We're busy." Then he leans over my body and drops the handset back onto the cradle, flopping back onto the bed with a sigh. "Are you awake?"

"Hmm," I hum. "Well, I don't want to be awake. Does that count as an answer?"

He scoffs. "The trains are down."

"Oh." I sit up and turn over so I'm facing him. "What's wrong with them?"

"Ike didn't say. But this feels like a set-up."

"You think they know I'm not Hattie?"

Riggs shoots me a snarl. "What?"

"They know. They're trying to keep us here until someone can come sort it out or whatever."

"*No.*" He sneers this word out. "This is all Ike's doing. I know it is. He's lying. The trains are *down?*" Riggs huffs. "Since when? The trains don't go down. Not all of them at the same time. That's ridiculous. It's such a stupid excuse. He's keeping us here because of *you.*"

"Isn't that what I just said?"

"You were implying that this was about something legitimate. But it's not. He just wants a date with you. He asked me if you were busy today."

I smile, chuckling. "You're jealous."

"I'm not jealous. It's just… fuck him. We're sharing a room, can't he take a hint?"

"You told him we weren't a thing, remember? We're not supposed to be sleeping in the same bed."

"I know that. It's just fucking rude."

"You like me," I say.

"*You* like *me*."

I smile, then turn on my side and prop myself up on my elbow so I can see him better. "Why can't you just admit it? You want to spend the day with me."

"I *am* gonna spend the day with you. It's got nothing to do with want."

"Are you gonna enjoy it?"

I get another snarl for this question. "You were so drunk last night, you wanted to sleep with him."

"And yet," I tease, "here I am in bed with you."

"You were flirting with him," he continues.

"You were snuggling me when I woke up."

"I was not. I had to reach over you to get the phone."

"Riggs?"

"What?"

"Do you want me to spend the day with you?"

"We *are* going to spend the day together."

"Why can't you just admit you want me to spend the day with you instead of Ike? Because you're not the boss of me. I don't have to listen to you. I could call Ike back and tell him I'd love to spend time with him today. Do you guys have star sixty-nine here? I bet you do. I'll call him back right now."

I scoot over, reaching for the phone, but Riggs

grabs me by the waist and pulls me back, cinching his arms around me like a belt. "You're trying to wind me up."

"You're trying to deny you're jealous."

"You're acting like you're not already mine when you are."

I nearly guffaw. "Says who?"

"Finders keepers, Clover."

"You didn't find me. I found you."

"Same thing. You *don't* like Ike. You know you don't like Ike. You're just trying to make me jealous. And…" He pauses here.

"And?"

"And… make me rethink leaving you in the bunker."

I rip his hands from my waist and make a serious attempt to get away from him, so this time, I succeed and stand at the edge of the bed, glaring as I point at him. "I am *not* doing that. And fuck you for thinking I was."

Then I turn on my heel, grab my pack, and go into the bathroom, locking the door behind me and leaning against it as I fume. I really wasn't pulling some femme fatale thing. I really do like him. And he likes me too. He does. He knows he does. We have that whole team thing going between us now.

So it makes me mad that he said that.

I open the door, find Riggs standing at the end of the bed wearing only his boxers, and then point at him again. "Fuck you. I trust you now. And you're the one who doesn't trust me."

He shoots me a smarmy smile as he steps into his pants and pulls up the zipper. "You *don't* like Ike."

I plant my hands on my hips, suddenly aware that I'm only wearing a t-shirt and underwear. But I rally, since he's half-naked too. "*You* don't like *me*."

He scoffs. "What's not to like about you?"

This catches me a little bit off guard. "Well, why are you being such an asshole?"

"Why are you trying to make me jealous?"

"I'm teasing you, Riggs."

"You're flirting with me, Clover."

"Do you hate flirting?"

"No. Nobody hates flirting."

"Then why are you being a dick?"

"Because I don't like the way you acted last night. You were slobbering all over him, for fuck's sake."

"I was not."

"You were drunk, you don't even remember."

"I was *tipsy*. And I remember everything." Sort of. But I keep that part to myself.

"You were trying to wind me up and you were using Ike to do it. He's gross."

"I mean… come on, Riggs. He's not gross. On the

inside, fine. I agree. He's got a very undesirable mind and a black heart. But he's like a frosted glass bottle filled with poison and all tied up with a shiny, satin bow. You can't not admire it. No one in their right mind thinks the presentation is ugly, even if the liquid inside is nothing but frog venom."

"You're playing with fire here. He's one of those obsessive types. If he even *thinks* you like him, he'll just claim you, Clover." Riggs points to the phone. "That's why he was calling. He's trying to claim you."

"Well." I shrug up one shoulder and shoot him a smile. "I guess he's too late. Finders keepers, right?"

His smile is slow, but it's real. "I knew you liked me."

I spit out a laugh. "Why are you so incorrigible?"

"Why aren't you more needy?"

"Oh, I see. I see what's happening here." He plays dumb and keeps his serious expression in place, but he's about to crack a smile, I can tell. "You want to be the hero."

"Well, you are a princess in need of saving."

My scoff is automatic. But I shake my head and look down. Men. They are so predictable. I look back up and meet his gaze. "Thank you."

"For?"

"Saving me. I don't think I said that, so I'm saying it now. You are a prince, Riggs. A real prince."

"I can't tell if you're being serious."

I turn and shrug up one shoulder, shooting him a sweet smile. "I'll be in the shower. *If* you want to find out how serious I am." Then I retreat back into the bathroom, but this time, I don't close the door behind me.

CHAPTER 16 - RIGGS

I stand in the middle of the bedroom, just staring at the open bathroom door as the shower turns on. A minute passes and the pattern of splashing water changes, so she's not bothering to wait and see what I do.

I could have a long internal debate with myself right now about how getting involved with Clover in this way is a very bad idea, but then I'd just talk myself out of it. And I don't wanna talk myself out of it.

So I follow.

But I stop at the entrance and watch her for a moment. Most of the bathroom is marble—the floor, but also the walls and countertops—but the shower is encased in glass all the way up to the ceiling, trapping the hot steam inside. It swirls up and around the tall narrow space, partly obscuring her naked body.

She's standing under the water, not washing, but enjoying it with her face tipped up. If she notices me—or cares that I'm here one way or the other—she doesn't let on. There is no second invitation, she's made her offer and the rest is up to me.

There are plenty of reasons—very valid reasons—why I should turn around and ignore her. But I've made a habit of making bad decisions so why stop now?

A moment later I'm naked and pulling the shower door open. Clover has her back to me and her body goes still as I step inside and pull the door closed. She doesn't say anything as I study her from the back. She's got curvy hips and a nice round ass.

Neither of us says anything as I take a few steps closer and then gather up her long blonde hair in one hand, draping it over her shoulder, while the other hand pumps some soap from a dispenser into my palm.

I rub my hands together, making suds, then start massaging her shoulders.

Immediately, she relaxes. "That feels good."

I don't say anything. Just let my hands slip down her arms, getting her all soapy. Then I start washing her back, letting the bubbles froth up. She shivers a little, even though the shower is dense with steam now and there's no way she could be cold.

If she's not gonna say anything, then I'm just gonna keep going. I take my soapy hands to her hips, then bend down so I've got a front-row seat for that curvy ass of hers. My hands slide over her hips and down her thighs, pressing my fingertips into her muscles.

As I'm doing this, she slowly turns so I'm eye-level with her stomach. When I glance up, she's blushing. Or maybe it's just the steam, but either way, her flushed cheeks make her look innocent and fresh.

She's got her arms up now, crisscrossed over her breasts, and she's looking down at me with a flat line of a mouth and very serious eyes. I bet all the reasons why this is a bad idea are flooding her mind right now too.

"I trust you," I say.

Which makes her draw in a breath.

Then I stand up so I'm looking down at her now. My hands take hers by the wrists and I push them away so I can see what she's hiding. I stare a little, noting how round and firm her breasts are, and when she doesn't protest, I figure it's game on from here.

I get some more soap in my hands, then cup her breasts and slide my fingertips under and around them as she watches me caress her nipples and make them rise up into tight peaks.

"You're not gonna say anything back?" I ask.

She bites her lip, then gives a one-shoulder shrug. "What's there to say?"

"Oh, we've got millions of things to say, I'm sure."

"Why ruin it though?"

My mouth lifts up into a lopsided smile. "It

wouldn't ruin anything. But it's fine with me if you don't wanna talk. We've got nowhere else to be, so whatever we have to say to each other, it can wait."

"It's just… sex, Riggs."

I bring my hands up to her neck, pushing her hair off her shoulders. "Is it?"

She nods her head. "It's not gonna mean anything."

I cup her face in my hands now. "Won't it?"

"No. It won't."

Then I lean down and kiss her. The first thing I notice is how wet her lips are. The second thing is that she's not opening her mouth for me.

Not yet.

I slip one hand around to the back of her neck, gripping it and drawing her closer so I can kiss her harder. I open my mouth and start nipping her lip with my teeth. She responds to this with a gasp, but it gets the job done because a moment later, our tongues are touching. I walk her backwards until she bumps into the marble wall.

We're kissing each other now. My hands are going wild feeling all up and down her body, while hers tentatively slide down to my waist.

I take one of her hands and push it down further until her fingertips are probing my rapidly growing cock. For a moment she hesitates, and I figure she'll pull back and refuse to follow my lead. But the moment passes and her hand opens, then closes again around my shaft.

I grit my teeth as the pleasure of having a woman touch me again stirs up feelings inside me. Mostly feelings of being cheated. Of losing all those years of my youth working underground inside an endless, dark tunnel.

But it's like Clover can tell I'm dwelling on things that are not her, because she begins to kiss me back with more intention, making a fist around my dick as she pumps it up and down. This pushes all the things I've lost aside and forces me to concentrate on the present.

I study her face as my hand slips between her legs, watching with equal parts fascination and lust as she closes her eyes and lets her head fall backwards and to the side, clearly enjoying it.

"I lied," I say.

She shakes her head a little, but doesn't open her eyes because I haven't stopped playing with her.

"I lied about you."

Her words come out as a whine. "I thought the talking was for later?"

"It is. But I just need to set the record straight. You're not a four, Clover. You're so out of my league, it's not even funny."

Now she does open her eyes. Then she narrows them down. And for a moment, I think... *Fuck, why couldn't I just shut up already? I've ruined it.* But then I realize she's not looking at me with suspicion, it's exasperation. "Fine," she huffs.

"Fine what?"

"You're a nine point seven five, OK? Collin Creed wishes he was you."

I chuckle a little as my fingers find her little sweet spot between her legs. And just before she gasps with ecstasy, I say, "And you're a ten. Hell, who am I kidding? Ten point two five." Her expression changes and she smiles, her eyes wide open now. "Standing next to you, Clover, Hattie Miller comes off as a burly, towering lumberjack."

Clover laughs out loud at this comparison, and while she's doing that I reach around, grab her under her ass, and lift her, pressing our bodies together as I hold her against the marble wall. Immediately, her arms come up and wrap around my neck. Her cheeks are bright pink now—either from the steam or the joke—and her eyes are shining and happy.

I'm happy too. Maybe for the first time in years, actually. But as we stare at each other, reality is rushing at us from all sides and our smiles fall in the same moment.

It's a natural segue into a real discussion. But it's not the time or place for a real discussion so I reach down between her legs, grab my dick, and push it inside her.

Then I watch her face as all thoughts of talking are set aside for later and once again, her eyes close and her head tips back.

I start slow. Easing in and out of her with deliberate care. Allowing us both to savor all the new, emerging feelings as the minutes pass. But eventually, we're worked up to the point where the time for savoring is over now too, and I go faster, pressing into her with more intention and force, until finally, she reaches the top of that hill and falls over it with a moan as her fingernails dig into my shoulders.

The look on her face is enough to send me over the edge too, and the next thing I know I've got my face buried in her neck and I'm biting the muscle just below her ear. It's not a real bite—I don't draw blood or anything—but it's hard, and serious, and makes her back stiffen as I explode inside her.

We stand there for a few moments, enjoying the residual sparks of the climax, and then she lets out a long breath and drops her head onto my shoulder.

"You can bite me back if you want."

She just chuckles.

"Sorry. I really didn't mean to bite you, it's just... something I like to do."

Her arms are still around my neck, but she holds me tighter after I say this. "I hope it leaves a hickey."

"A hickey." I almost snort as I lower Clover down and her feet find the floor. She looks up at me and for the first time I think I see the real her. An easy, relaxed version of the tense, scared woman I kidnapped and locked in a basement several days ago.

There's a thick clump of wet hair plastered to her cheek and instinctively, I slide it off her face so I can see her better. "Hi."

She smiles. "Hello."

"Would you like me to wash your hair?"

"Only if I can wash you back."

"Deal."

I turn and take her with me, pushing her back under the hot water. Then I pump out some shampoo from a container and start working it into her hair. She gets some soap and starts making suds on my chest. We don't say anything as we wash each other. We just take our time—like we've got millions of years ahead of us instead of one day—and when we're done, we wrap up in towels and go back into the bedroom.

I towel myself off as Clover finger-combs her hair in a mirror over the dresser, and then I walk up behind her—dry now, but still naked—and reach around to take her towel away. Our eyes lock in the mirror for a few moments. And even when I avert my gaze so I can towel her off too, she continues to watch me.

"You're a very nice lover," she says.

"Surprised?"

"Not really."

"That's a lie."

"No. There is a very kind person inside of you."

"Deep inside, you mean?"

"Not that deep."

"I kidnapped you. I made all those threats. I've killed people."

I know she knows this. Hell, I admitted it. But saying it so casually like this is something I've never done before. I don't want to be a killer. I'd prefer to deny it, at least to myself. But at this point in my life, it's just a fact.

Clover shrugs up one shoulder. "And yet here you are. Saving my life."

It's a consolation prize. We both know this. "I really did mean what I said."

"Which part?"

"You're *really* out of my league."

Her eyes go all squinty. "Don't say that."

"Why? It's the truth."

"Because if you truly believe this, Riggs, you won't come back for me."

"Do you want me to come back for you?"

She pouts her lips a little, taking time to think. Which I appreciate, because the honest answer here is no. She doesn't want me to come back for her. Life for us, if I do manage to get away again, would be hell. Clover has to know this.

Just as she opens her mouth to respond, I put up a

hand, stopping her. Then I answer for her with the same words I was just thinking in my head. "You don't, Clover. If I came back for you, we'd be on the run. And Hattie Miller would be our hunter. We'd never have a moment's peace."

"I know," she says. "That's why I didn't answer right away. In another life, I'd date you, Riggs. But this is the only life I have and I can't see a future where that ever happens."

"Because there isn't one."

"Well." She blows out a breath. "If this day is the only one we get, let's enjoy it."

CLOVER

R*iggs just stares at me* for a moment. Like he's in the middle of some big existential crisis. Probably wondering how the hell we got here. Yesterday morning, we still hated each other. He was still blindfolding me. One day later and we're talking about a future where the two of us are together.

Not only that, we're naked and still wet from the shower. Where we had sex.

Really, really nice sex, actually.

Riggs starts shaking his head at me.

I can't read his mind so I don't really know what he's thinking. But it's something negative or why would he be shaking his head? So I'm guessing he's thinking this is never gonna work.

And I sort of agree. It's a stupid fantasy to think I might end up loving this man—this kidnapper—for the rest of my life.

So I just take his hand and turn, walking right over to the bed and getting in. Not asking if he wants to, or playing shy, or anything like that.

There's no time for that.

We get one day. So I'm gonna enjoy it.

He gets in bed, already reaching for me. The next thing I know, he's got me by the waist and he's pulling me on top of him. There is a moment of awkwardness until he's inside me, and then my hands come down on his hard abs and as I gaze down at this man between my legs, I let out a breath and start moving.

His eyes are bright and almost dancing with mischief as he grins up at me. His hands are sitting lightly on my hips. They slide up over the curve of my waist until finally, he's cupping my breasts.

A whirlwind of thoughts and feelings are twisting up inside me. If I was rational right now—still comfortably inside my own reality—I would have a thousand things to say to this man. A million questions that would need answering before I could give up my mind, or my heart, or my body.

But nothing about what is happening to me is rational, so why should my feelings be any different? "I must've hit my head pretty hard that first day," I say.

He's been staring at me this whole time, fondling my breasts and rocking us in a slow up-and-down rhythm. His smile falters, and then the next thing I know, he's flipping me over. A fluff of air tickles my cheeks as my head crashes into the soft pillow when we trade places. He nudges my knees open with his legs, settles down comfortably, resumes our carnal dance, and places his hands along the side of my face.

I'm expecting an answer here. I'm thinking he's gonna say something. Something profound about reality, maybe. Or trust, since that seems to be our theme.

But he just stares at me with those werewolf eyes of his for so many seconds, I start thinking that he'll never speak again and all my questions will remain unanswered.

This whole time, we're still moving. He's still fucking me. But it's agonizingly slow and borders on the sublime, adding merit to the idea that this must be a dream. I'm back there in my basement, starving and dying of thirst. Alone in the dark. Tied up and helpless.

It's all fake. A delusion comin' off as real because I'm on the edge of my own demise.

But then he speaks. And his voice is as gentle as his touch. "Reality provides us with facts so romantic that imagination itself could add nothing to them."

I smile, trying to play those words back in my head so I don't lose them.

"Do you know who said that, Clover?"

"You."

Which makes him laugh. And how did I not notice how sexy his laugh is? My God. It comes off as a rumble inside his chest, and if I were still a Disciple girl, I'd be writing poetry right now about the glory that comes after.

"No. I mean, yes, I did just say that. But I wasn't the first. It was Jules Verne."

I giggle over this revelation, which delights him further.

"It's all real, Clover." He plays with my hair for a moment, pushing it out of my face like he needs to see me better. "Who needs fiction when this is the world we actually live in?"

This doesn't explain anything, but I don't even care. There is something between us now. Something of a bond. Like synergy. Like loyalty. Like... *trust.* "I think I like you, Riggs."

But his reaction to my declaration is to press his lips together, which erases his smile. He wants to say something. Maybe... *I like you too.* Or maybe something more supportive, but also a fiction, like... *It's all gonna work out. We're gonna be just fine.*

Instead, he leans down and kisses me on the forehead. Which is a pity kiss, in my opinion. A gentle way of offering moral support. My heart is starting to crack and my frown is immediate as he does this because I'm convinced that we're cursed. This whole thing is pointless.

But when he lowers down, kissing each of my eyes, forcing them to close—forcing me to take a breath— the cracking stops. It doesn't mend, it just stops.

I lie there, his hips still moving. Still rocking me. Lulling me into a sense of calm easiness.

When he speaks, his words are a whisper. Just a feathery touch against my cheek. And they are neither lies, nor fantasy. "It's not gonna work out for us, Clover. We're doomed. But I'll take doomed over nothing. This one day with you as a free man is worth more than a hundred years as a slave."

Then his mouth finds my lips and no more words are spoken.

Because there is no time for words when you're doomed.

Every moment counts.

I don't want to let go. I'm not the kind of woman who plays life like a game, who lives every day like it's my last. Even though I plan weddings, I'm a worker, mainly. Not a romantic. I like coordinating things, obviously. I like checking things off lists, and problem-solving, and results.

I really, *really* like results.

So my first instinct is to protest and hash this out until I get my desired ending. The happily ever after, if you will. I mean, isn't that the whole point of a wedding?

But I don't feel much like myself right now.

In fact, I don't have the slightest idea of who I am.

So I drift into this new reality with him where we're some kind of Bonnie and Clyde couple. Racing through this day as if it's our last.

Our movements pick up and he leans on me a little

harder. A little heavier. Still holding my face. Still kissing my mouth. And we just fuck. It becomes so intense, I find myself digging my fingernails into his shoulders, then scraping them down his back.

He bites me again. In the very same place, right on that muscle below my neck. We both come when he does that, his soft words, barely a whisper, floating into my ear. "There. You've got yourself a hickey."

Which makes it all end with a smile.

He rolls off me, but immediately pulls me in next to his chest. Even though it's morning, I have a heavy sense of fatigue and being so close together, I am warm and comfortable in way I don't ever think I'll feel again.

So I'm drifting off—it is a way to prolong the dream, after all—when his words tickle the back of my neck. "I'll come back for you, Clover. And then we'll have time."

"Time for what?" I sleepily ask.

"To fall in love, of course."

I don't know why this makes me happy because nothing has changed. Our doom is still very much preordained. But this promise, empty as it might be, is exactly what I needed to hear.

So I believe him.

CHAPTER 18 - RIGGS

I wake up hours later. I can tell by the light filtering in from the sheer drapes along the wall of windows to my right. Blackberry Hill has a rather outdated circadian program, so the changing nature of the light outside isn't as subtle as what I grew up with. But it's good enough to know it's definitely some time in the afternoon and Clover and I are still in bed.

The funny thing is, I'm still tired. It's more of an exhaustion, really. And I suspect that Clover is feeling this way as well, because even though she turns over and cracks an eye open to look at me, she closes it back up just as quickly. A signal, if ever there was one, that she's not even close to being ready to get out of this bed.

"We've got all day," I tell her.

She huffs out a little breath of air and then her response comes out sleepy and slow. "It feels a little wasteful, doesn't it?"

I slip my arm underneath her shoulders, then draw

her in tight to my chest, resting my mouth on that fleshy muscle I like to bite, suddenly having an urge to do it again. But I restrain myself. "What's wasteful about spending a day in bed?"

"We only get the one, ya know. This is it for us."

"Yup. We're doomed."

"So maybe we should put a little more thought into our last day."

"What do you wanna do? Go be a tourist?"

"I dunno. I just don't wanna waste it."

She's right, I know this. I just don't wanna get out of bed. "All right. Let's play a little game. It's called... Truth or Fantasy."

She peeks over her shoulder, squinting one sleepy eye at me. "Never heard of it."

"It's just like Truth or Dare, but for people who are already naked."

Clover laughs and turns around. And my God, her smile lights me up. "Truth or Dare for naked people?"

"Yeah. So, like... there's no weird consequences. When you dare someone, it comes with a level of angst and discomfort. But my version of the game is a fantasy. Truth or Fantasy. We all know what truth is. I ask you a question and you answer. Fantasy is... I give you a command."

She laughs again. "How is that not like a dare?"

"Well, it's entirely sexual."

Clover laughs. "It's the grown-up version of Truth or Dare."

"Exactly. But there's a catch."

"Of course there is."

"You get to choose truth or fantasy for me and I get to choose truth or fantasy for you."

"OK, so if I choose truth for you, then I ask you anything I want."

"No."

"No? How is that a no? That's how it works."

"That's how Truth or Dare works. Truth or Fantasy is the opposite. If you choose fantasy for me, then I get to have my fantasy with you."

"Hmm." She thinks about this for a moment. "And if you choose fantasy for me, I get to have my fantasy with you. For instance, I could make you kiss my toes."

I smile. "You could."

Her face screws up a little as she thinks. "I could make you… brush my hair."

"You could do that too."

"OK. I'm ready. Can I go first?"

"Please do."

"You choose…" She blushes, so I already know. "Fantasy." Her blue eyes are practically dancing right now. Like she's about to win a prize.

"You do realize I can make you do anything I want?"

"I do."

"You do realize this is a sex game?"

Her chuckle is immediate. "I get it. Now go. Fantasy."

Well… shit. I was expecting to ease into this so I'm not ready with a fantasy. I mean, I could make her suck my dick, that would feel pretty good. But that's too easy. That feels like an immediate payoff and if I just wanted to get down to business, I'd flip her over and fuck her.

That's not what I want. I want this afternoon to linger. I get one day with this woman so I'm gonna make the most of it. "All right. My fantasy is… you have to push the cover off and lie naked on top of it."

Her grin is lopsided. "You're going easy on me."

"I might be. But it's not for your benefit."

"No?"

"Nah. I just want to drive you a little crazy." I nod my head at the comforter. "Off with it."

She throws it aside, gets up on her knees—subtly flaunting her tits in my face—and then smooths the comforter out and places herself on top of it. She's propping herself up with an elbow, lying on her side, accentuating the curve of her hips. "There you go. Your fantasy, good sir."

I smile with appreciation. "Nice."

"All right. My fantasy is—"

"Woman," I cut her off. "I want truth."

"What? Truth is boring. I'm ready for the fantasy."

"I know. That's why I'm asking for truth."

She tsks her tongue. "Our objectives here do not seem to match up. I'm trying to please you and you're out to deny me."

"It's a game, Clover. You could deny me too."

She huffs out some air. "My truth is…"

Her eyes lock on mine and they stay that way for nearly ten seconds. Long enough for things to get serious again. I want to caution her here to keep it light, but it's her truth, so she can say whatever she wants.

"My truth is… you're the most exciting thing that's ever happened to me."

I smile. "Well, I'm glad that this kidnapping, and your subsequent Stockholm syndrome, has turned out so well for you."

She slaps my shoulder. "It's not Stockholm syndrome."

Which makes me wince. "It most likely is."

"Well, fine then. I don't really like you. I'm suffering from a mental condition. But that doesn't explain why you like me."

"My turn."

Her eyes narrow and I know she's thinking about giving me truth, but she can't help herself. "Fantasy."

"My God, you're killing me here."

"Well, you see… this denial thing? It goes both

ways. You can deny me, but you're only denying yourself in the end if you do."

"We'll see." I think for a moment, because she's caught on. If I deny her, I deny myself. "Flip around so your head is at the bottom of the bed, and then open your legs."

Her eyebrows go up. "That's provocative."

"It's meant to be."

She gets up, flaunts her perfectly round ass at me, crawls down to the end of the bed, and does just as I asked. "How wide do you want them?"

"Dirty."

"Hey, it's your fantasy, not mine. So how wide?"

"Just wide enough to get a peek."

She goes red. I'm talking bright red. But she plays it off by teasing me, sliding her legs together a few times before just barely opening them up. "Is that a good peek?"

I lick my lips and shake my head as I exhale. "Damn. I'm gonna lose."

This makes her giggle. "OK. My turn. And if you choose—"

"Truth."

"You bastard!"

"What? I've got you all posed, Clover. I've got an endgame in mind here. I can't fuck it up by making you move."

"Hmm." She's smiling big. "That's clever. If we ever

play again, I'm gonna use that tactic. But I'm gonna pose you like we're playing Twister when I do."

"Oh, we'll just play that for real. I'll get your ass in the air, put it right in front of my face and then—"

"My truth is…" she interrupts, propping her upper body up on both elbows so she can see me. "I'm… gonna miss you."

I let out a long sigh. "Yeah. I think the feeling is gonna be mutual."

"All right, I'm in it to win it now. So you want truth. But I get to ask the question."

"That's not how it works."

"I'm rewriting the rules. My question is what is going on with you and Collin? I mean, why do you hate him so much?"

"This is your question? Isn't there something more pressing on your mind than why I hate Collin Creed?"

She closes her legs and crawls back up the bed towards me, settling right down in front of my chest so when she turns her head up to see me, her eyes are big and close. "There are a lot of things about you that I don't understand, Riggs. Most of them I'm probably not capable of understanding. But if you tell me about this, it will make sense. I know it."

"I'm not sure it will, Clover. Because it hardly makes sense to me."

"Just tell me."

"He's a traitor, that's all."

"To who, though?"

I scoff. "To *me*."

"You were friends? And he betrayed you?"

"Yeah. I mean, there's a lot more to it than that, but yeah." I haven't thought about the actual reason I hate Collin Creed since my father offered me this job as a sort of salvation. While I was standing there in his office I did conjure up several ways in which I might pay Collin back for what he did to me. But then I let it go. Rage is a powerful motivator and has carried many a man across the finish line of whatever mission he was on, but it comes at the expense of precision and I wasn't in a place where I could afford to be sloppy.

A huff comes out of my mouth and along with it, a laugh. Because there is nothing neat and tidy about the naked woman in bed with me.

"What?" Clover asks. "What are you thinking that you're not telling me?"

"It's nothing."

"But I want to know about you and Collin. How did you meet him?"

"It doesn't matter. All you need to know is that he betrayed me. And I was fuckin' loyal, too. Collin Creed was on our list. I could've—"

"Wait. Whoa, whoa, whoa. Slow down. Collin Creed was on *what* list?"

"Our list. Hattie's and mine."

"Hattie's and yours? What, were you two partners, or something?"

"Oh, fuck. I guess I left that part out."

Clover sits all the way up in bed now, pulling the comforter around herself to cover her breasts.

I point at her. "Don't."

"Don't what?"

"Don't look at me like that and don't act like you're all shocked, or whatever."

"You gave me a few hand-picked details, but you never mentioned you were hunting partners. So you were a bounty hunter for the Colonies?"

I shrug with my hands. "Is that a big deal?"

"Well, it implies a certain level of loyalty to your government, doesn't it?"

"I am the general's son, Clover. I was twenty years old when I got sent up top with Hattie. Why wouldn't I be loyal to my own father when I had been force-fed a menu of lies my entire life?"

She draws in a long breath, then slowly lets it out. "OK. I guess that makes sense." Then she settles back down into the pillow, but our little Truth or Fantasy game is over because she doesn't uncover herself. "Keep going. Collin Creed was on your list and you could've... what? What could you have done to him?"

"Well, handed him over, of course."

"This implies that you had access to him."

"I did. I worked with him the entire year I was on the run from Hattie."

"This doesn't make sense. Why did you run and how did you get involved with Collin in the first place?"

I hesitate here and Clover sees it. "Don't." She's pointing her finger at me now.

"Don't what?"

"Lie to me."

"I wasn't gonna lie."

"You were gonna find a way around the truth, Riggs. I saw it in your eyes. How did you get involved with Collin in the first place?"

I need to make a choice here. Because Clover is way too smart for her own good. She's like a little lie detector, this woman. Which means I need to tell her the truth.

At least a little bit of it.

"OK. I'll tell you. But you need to give me the benefit of the doubt."

She squints her eyes a little. "Okaaaay. I will."

"I was sent…" I can't believe I'm gonna admit to this.

She rolls her hand at me. "Keep going."

"I was sent to infiltrate Collin's outfit."

"Why though? What is so damn special about Collin Creed?"

"You tell me. You're the one who thinks he's a nine point seven five."

Clover smiles. "You're a nine point seven five too."

"Anyway. Collin is… I dunno. Fuckin' talented, I guess. He just gets the job done. The point is, Hattie and I were sent up top to infiltrate Collin's outfit."

"All right. So… you did that, I guess? I mean, you were working for him."

"Kind of. I did work with him. I was on his team that whole year I was running from Hattie."

"Well, that's not a 'kind of', Riggs, that's a 'yes'."

"But it comes with a disclaimer. Because I wasn't there as an infiltrator, I was approached and offered a defection package from the American government. Like the legit American government, not the shady one down below. You see, there's a bit of a civil war going on between the underground and the surface." Clover opens her mouth to start asking questions about this, but I'm not gonna answer those questions, so I put up a hand. "Let me finish."

She sighs. "OK. Keep going."

"I accepted this defection package and went to work for the American government. I didn't infiltrate Collin's outfit, I was *placed* there by my defection coordinator."

Her eyes are darting back and forth, looking straight into mine. "And you left Hattie Miller behind without telling her?"

I nod. "Yep."

"Wow." She blinks at me. "First. How pissed was your father?"

"Six years, Clover. Six fucking years of darkness. That's how pissed."

Her mouth goes crooked just thinking about it. "Yeah. Pissed probably doesn't even cover it. Second. How pissed was Hattie?"

"Pissed enough to set me up."

"What do you mean?"

"She's the one who told Collin I was a spy. Which I wasn't. And then he sold me out. She made a deal with him. He set me up to be captured by Hattie and… well, the rest is history."

Clover shakes her head and makes a face. "What? But why would he believe *her*? I mean, Collin comes off as a pretty rational person." I nearly guffaw, only just managing to hold it in. "He's a thinker, Riggs. If you spent a year with him, you know that. He's not impulsive."

"No. I guess not. But you don't know Hattie. She's… formidable. And she got to him. I'm not sure how, but she got to him. And then she told him I was there to infiltrate—"

Clover points at me. "Because technically, you were."

"Technically, I guess. It started that way. But I took a defection package, Clover. I wasn't there to spy. I was on the team, for fuck's sake. I didn't have to risk my life for him for the whole year. If I was there to spy I could've delivered Collin Creed to my father per my original mission in the first week. He'd be dead now if I had done that, by the way."

She presses her lips together, thinking. Does she believe me? Or is she suspicious? "How did you get away from her? Hattie, I mean. How did that happen?"

"Why do you wanna know this?"

"Because I need details, Riggs. And you're not really giving me any."

She doesn't trust me. But I wouldn't trust me either if I was her. I mean, I did just tell her I was sent to infiltrate her friend's kill team. So why I might normally take offense at her lack of trust, I earned this one. So I say, "His name was Clayton Boseman. I poisoned Hattie—"

"What?" Clover sits up, laughing.

"I'm telling you, Clover. Hattie is no one to fuck with. She's suspicious of everyone. She never let me out of her sight. We slept in the same hotel rooms, we ate every meal together. Hell, I'm lucky she let me use the fuckin' bathroom alone, that's how uptight and suspicious she is."

Clover scoffs. "Couldn't you just tell her off, or whatever? You're the general's *son*."

"She's the Sovereign's *daughter*."

"What the hell is a Sovereign?"

"The only person who has a higher rank than my father."

Clover's lips slide together into a delightful little pucker. "Ooooooo."

"Yeah," I laugh. "Kinda explains a lot, doesn't it?"

Her face tightens up into a wince. "No wonder she's so uptight. OK. I'm starting to get the picture. So you poisoned her so you could escape. What did you use?"

"To poison her? Just ipecac syrup. She was puking so hard, she didn't even know I left."

"Wow. She hates you."

I laugh. "Ya think?"

"OK. So you got away. Then what happened?"

"You want to know about how I got away?"

"I'm still painting my picture. It's not done yet. So yes."

"Fine. The defection coordinator's name was Clayton Boseman. At least, that's what he was calling himself when we met. He gave me a new name—Raleigh Winston, and sent me in for an interview."

"And Collin liked you."

"I guess he did. I mean, he and I were never 'friends' per se. Not like he was friends with Amon. But I was on the team. And for the next year, I worked for him."

"What did you guys do?"

"Even if I wanted to tell you that shit—and I don't —I'm not allowed. It's classified."

"What were the guy's names? On the team?"

My eyes narrow down. Because I've been pretty accommodating and yet, she's insisting on more details.

Sensing my building frustration, Clover shrugs. "I'm trusting you with my life, Riggs. The least you can do is trust me with yours."

Which feels fair. "It was a small team of ten, including Collin. There was me, Jimmy, Naveed, Manuel, Roddy, Rick, Amon, Ryan, and Nash. They were doing some serious jobs, Clover. I'm not talking bodyguard kind of jobs, either. Collin was hunting people down, just like I was."

Clover's face darkens with this little revelation about Collin Creed. "Hunting what kind of people?"

"Anyone the government told him to."

She's still looking at me, but her eyes go weird and distant for a moment. Like she's trying to reconcile this revelation.

"And before you go dismissing that, you should know it wasn't *us* hunting people. It was *him*. The only reason the rest of us were even there was to set him up for the kill and then, if necessary, cover for him afterward. We were his support team. We were there to save his ass. To make sure he got out no matter what. Five men died for him, Clover. Jimmy, Naveed,

Manuel, Roddy, and Rick all *died* for him. He was the only one who mattered. Charlie Beaufort saw to that."

"Who the hell is Charlie Beaufort?"

"Well, that's who my defection coordinator, Clayton Boseman, really was. He used a fake name to make my offer—just in case I said no, I guess. But I was recruited by one Charlie Beaufort. He's a very dangerous man with the power of the government behind him. Charlie was having a greedy, power-hungry love affair with Collin Creed's killing skills. As far as Charlie was concerned, Collin could do no wrong. Whatever he wanted, he got. Because he was Charlie's loyal little attack dog. That's all Collin was, just a sick fuckin' dog foaming at the mouth for his next kill."

Clover huffs. "Come on, now. That's not Collin. I understand that he is dangerous. But a rabid dog he is not."

"You don't know him like I do."

"Maybe not, but nothing you told me adds up to the hatred you have for him. Who cares if he turned you in? I mean, if he was military and you were military?" She shrugs with her hands. "Who cares? All's fair in love and war, right?"

"Wow." I blink at her. "That's a really fucked-up thing to say."

"It's an expression, that's all."

"Well, to me? It's gross. I hate Collin because I got

him out of two messy retreats after his kill shot while I was on the team. I almost ended up like the rest of them. I put my life on the line for him. I was loyal and committed, one-hundred percent, and he sold me out. That's how I got caught. It was Collin who got me sent to those tunnels for six years. Hattie was just the tool he used to do it."

CHAPTER 19 - CLOVER

*E*verything about Riggs* has changed over the last few seconds. His eyes seem darker, the muscles in his jaw are clenching, and his shoulders are tense. "'All's fair in love and war' is nothing but an excuse."

"I didn't mean it that way."

He lets out a long breath. "I know. But it's *so* gross. It means… well, that anything and everything goes when you're at war. And the whole world is at war. There's no peace, not anywhere. And that expression, at least to me, is just a way to reconcile the evil everyone's doing to one another."

I don't know what to say to that. I don't know this man. Not really. I've seen him in a few select circumstances. I understand he's dangerous. But this is something else. It's a very serious moment. Like he's explaining something deeply important to him.

All I can do is nod. "OK. I won't say that again."

"Sorry. I didn't mean to accuse you of anything. You don't know any better."

"But now I do. So I won't say that again."

He nods his head now, accepting my *mea culpa*.

"But Riggs, how do you know it was Collin who sold you out?"

"Hattie told me. She couldn't wait to tell me."

"But she must've figured out that you poisoned her so you could escape. Maybe she lied?"

"I thought of that. But my father admitted it as well. He was very proud of the fact that they got Collin Creed to give me up for a fat bonus."

I'm shaking my head as he's saying this. "I don't believe it."

"What's not to believe?"

"Maybe I don't know Collin these days, but he's loyal. I mean, the whole reason he became a killer instead of some college football star is because a man tried to kidnap his sister. You don't fuck with a man's sister. And he saved Lowyn from that monster, Ike Monroe."

"Monster, is he? I thought he was a pretty bottle of poison wrapped up in a shimmering satin bow?"

I make a face. "He's a frog. You're the prince. I was just fuckin' with ya."

Riggs laughs and those dark eyes go light again. "Anyway…"

"Anyway." I flop back onto the bed and look up at the ceiling. "Here's your last fantasy."

"Are we still playing?"

"Your fantasy is… the two of us packing up our shit and walking out of here. We go back through those tunnels, leave the mountain behind, get my car, and start over somewhere." I turn my head to look at him, meeting his critical gaze with a weighty one of my own. "Together. And we forget all about Collin Creed and Hattie Miller. We just start over."

"It would never work."

I ignore him and keep going. "We could drive south, maybe. Down into the Ozarks."

"We've got bases in the Ozarks, Clover."

"We could drive down to Texas, cross the border—"

"We've got bases in Mexico, Clover."

"We could get on a boat—"

"We've got bases all over the world, Clover. It'll never work. They would hunt me to the ends of the earth."

"Just forget about that for a moment and think about this. We… I dunno. Find a little village in Peru and get jobs making tortillas." He chuckles here, so I know I've got him. Not got him as in agreeing with me, but he's playing into my fantasy. "We settle in, learn Spanish—do they speak Spanish in Peru?"

"They do."

"So we'd learn Spanish and save our money so we could… open up a little bed-and-breakfast, maybe." I side-eye him. "I could plan weddings in Peru. Isn't that the place where llamas come from? Maybe llama weddings are a thing down there the way horseback weddings are here? That's kinda fun. But back to your fantasy. We'd settle in, sell llama weddings. I'd get pregnant and we'd have twins, of course. A boy and a girl." He chuckles again. "We'd name them… Sophia and Marco. Good Spanish names so they'd fit in. They'd grow up there, working in the llama wedding business. And we'd grow old." I side-eye him again. "Together. We'd have a nice, long, quiet life on the top of some Peruvian mountain. Now isn't that a nice fantasy?"

He wants to pull me back to reality, I can see it in his eyes. But then he sighs and decides to agree. "Yeah. It's a real nice fantasy."

"You're just saying that."

"No. I'm not. I swear, a Peruvian mountaintop has never sounded so attractive."

"But you're not serious, Riggs." He lets out an exhale that feels like surrender, so I point at him and make my voice stern. "Don't do that."

"Don't do what?"

"Give up! You can't give up! There's no giving up. If we decide we're getting out of here and starting over, then that's what we're gonna do."

"Clover, the very idea that we'd make it out of Trinity County on the outside is ludicrous. This is West Virginia. It's three hundred miles to DC."

"So?"

"Everything underground between here and there is military. There are so many access points, we wouldn't get more than fifty miles in any direction. The only reason we're still in this escape plan of mine is because we're in Ike's territory and he's possessive about it. If I tried to leave with you up top, we'd already be caught."

"Well, I don't think this plan is gonna work either. I think if we get on that train, we're gonna get busted anyway. It all feels hopeless right now and all I'm trying to do is make things a little brighter."

He throws his hands up and turns onto his back, looking up at the ceiling. "Fine. Your plan is great. I love it. Let's move to Peru."

Now I flop onto my back and stare at the ceiling. "Maybe I should go back home and pretend you never happened." Obviously, this is not up to me, so I'm only saying this to irritate him.

"You know what? Maybe you should."

I turn back over on my side. "How dare you!"

"How dare I what? I'm setting you free. You should go now." And then he actually throws the covers off and tries to get out of bed like this declaration of his is law.

I jump on his back, taking him by surprise, and then tackle him so he falls over on his side. He starts laughing right away, like my attack is a joke.

But I'm dead serious. I climb on top of him, place my hands flat on his chest, and lean down into his face, looking right into the wolfish eyes of his. And I say, "That is not happening. You are not sending me back!"

"You literally just said you wanted to leave."

"No! I said maybe! This is how women argue! I get angry and make threats, you come to your senses and agree with me!"

"That's not a thing."

My eyes go wide and I'm about to lose my shit when his hands suddenly come up and begin to fondle my breasts—which I now notice are hanging right in his face.

I had forgotten we were naked. But our ending position after our tussle brings it all front and center. Because he's getting hard underneath me and I'm beginning to wonder myself if maybe we should pause here for a little quickie.

So instead of going off again, I give in and stare down at him, ready to beg. "Please. *Please*, Riggs. Don't give up on this."

He pinches my nipples, rolling them between his fingers. But not in a rough way. He uses just enough pressure to tease me. "Should we keep fighting? Or should we find something better to do?"

I answer him by wiggling my bottom, teasing him back.

His smile is sweet, and genuine, and a little bit sad. But it all looks so good on him I can't feel anything other than desire.

I commit his face to memory. Wanting to hold on to this moment forever because who knows what's gonna happen next.

He slides his hands up my chest and then they slide around my neck so he can pull me down to him.

We kiss. Lingering in it for a little bit. Just enjoying how good it feels.

I lift my hips up, ready to put him inside me so I can forget about the walls closing in around us and just live in blissful ignorance for a bit longer.

My hand is wrapped around his thick, hard shaft and then the door bursts open and suddenly the room is filled with people.

I scream. Someone else screams too, but she says, "Get on your knees with your hands behind your back!"

And when I look up, I know who this woman is even though Riggs didn't mention a single distinguishing physical feature.

Hattie Miller is here.

And she is pissed.

Not only that, she's got four men with her. One of them grabs me by the hair, pulls me off of Riggs, and I crash to the floor. His boot finds my ribs and the next thing I know, I'm doubling over in pain as three other men take Riggs down. This isn't as efficient as my submission because Riggs—every buck-naked inch of him—is resisting pretty hard. He's yelling, telling the men to leave me alone, but his attention is on the wrong person because Hattie Miller comes up behind him with her rifle raised.

I yell, "Behind you!"

But it's too late. Hattie cracks him in the side of the head with the butt of her rifle and he falls over sideways, already unconscious before his head hits the floor.

Then Hattie Miller turns her gaze to me. Her lip is curled up in a savage sneer as she takes in my naked body. When her dark eyes meet mine, she huffs out the word, "*Pathetic.*"

She comes at me, and the next thing I know that rifle butt is hitting me too and everything goes black.

CHAPTER 20 - RIGGS

Reality comes back slowly, accompanied by a sharp pain in my temple every time I attempt to open my eyes. I hear nothing at first, so I take my time, just trying to breathe and remember where I am.

Where was I?

What was I doing?

At first there is nothing but a gray fuzziness, but then—my eyes fly open as I try and stand up. Only to realize I'm sitting down and tied to a chair.

"Welcome back, lover boy."

My head whips to the side and there she is. Hattie. Sitting on the concrete floor of an interrogation room with her knees drawn up to her chest and her back pressing against the wall. Her long, blonde hair is pulled back, as usual. But it's not neat. Little wisps have fallen out, framing her rather long face. She's always been tall and muscular, but she's never been pretty. Handsome is the word most people use to describe women like Hattie Miller. But her outward appearance isn't ugly, either. She's just not feminine.

Inside though, Hattie Miller is a hideous monster.

She is the definition of depraved, her personality encapsulating all the worst vices one might find in a person. She is haughty, and greedy, and envious of peers who have more accomplishments, or possess more power, or take better advantage of opportunities.

Her smile, when she looks my way, personifies evil.

I don't even think she does this on purpose. It's not a cultivated identity, it's just who she is.

"Well." She gets to her feet. "Look who's awake." I watch her as she approaches me with that sinister smile that comes so easy to her. "Are you cold?"

This is when I realize I'm naked. And what I was doing when Hattie burst in. "Where's Clover?" My voice is raspy and I swallow, suddenly understanding that I must've been blacked out for a while because my mouth is so dry, this one simple act feels impossible. Still, I do my best. "Where is she, Hattie? Where is Clover?"

Hattie circles me, stops behind me, and then her fingertips are touching my hair. "I didn't interrupt anything when I pulled you away from your prisoner, did I, Riggs? I mean, I know the two of you were in bed, and naked, and—"

"Where is she!" I've recovered enough now that my words come out strong and commanding.

Hattie laughs. "Don't worry," she says, still standing behind me, stroking my hair. "We gave her some clothes. I wasn't going to, but my men were getting a little frisky with her unconscious body, so—"

"You bitch. If they touched her—"

"If they touched her… *what*, Riggs? What are you going to do about it?"

I take a moment to calm down, all the while reminding myself that Hattie isn't like that. She's not moral, or anything. She's just rigid. By the book. She loves rules. And there are rules of engagement when it comes to prisoners. None of her men are touching Clover.

Me, though? Different story. I'm not a prisoner, I'm a traitor. So she continues to stroke my hair.

I shake my head and roll my shoulders, trying to push her off in the only way I can.

This makes her sigh, but it comes out with a lot of satisfaction. She walks around to my front and stands there, looking down at me with an amused grin that comes off so wicked, I nearly recoil. "Do you understand what is happening, Riggs?"

"You burst in on my plan—"

Her guffaw cuts off the rest of my sentence and I go silent as she tips her head back, laughing. She takes her time recovering, but when she does, that smile drops. And as nasty as it was, the expression that takes its place is something altogether vile. She grits her teeth. "Do not even bother with whatever lie you've come up with to hide the fact that you—once again—betrayed us."

"You don't know what you're talking about. I took her prisoner."

"You were fucking her, Riggs."

"So what? I was horny, she was there. And I didn't force her. She was willing. Who cares if I was fucking her. I was bringing her back—"

"*Stop!*" Hattie says this one word so loud, and with such animosity and conviction, I actually do stop. "Just stop, Riggs. You weren't bringing her back."

But I don't agree. I shake my head. Because there's no way she could know this. She can't read my mind. She doesn't know my plan, she only thinks she does.

Hattie sighs and shakes her head. "I feel sorry for you."

"Don't bother," I sneer. "I don't need your pity. I was bringing her back with me because I wanted to keep her. There. Is that what you were waiting to hear? I was lying to her about getting her out, but I just wanted to keep her for myself. That's why I was fucking her. That's why she was with me. I like her, Hattie. She's my prize for a job well done."

This is absolutely *not* what Hattie Miller wants to hear and I am very aware of this. Clover described

Hattie as either a bitchy jilted ex or a bitter, scorned woman looking for vindication.

She's both. Though I didn't admit to the first one with Clover—it's my past, so it's my business. But Hattie and I were dating when I left that first time. It wasn't real. I was using sex to lower her defenses and mitigate any growing suspicions she had about my loyalty to the Colony. And it worked.

I tricked Hattie into thinking I cared about her.

That's why she hates me.

It wasn't because I broke the rules.

It was because I broke her heart.

And what I just said about Clover breaks it all over again. It's got nothing to do with love, though I can see myself loving Clover if we had the chance. But it's not my emotional attachment to Clover that bothers Hattie, it's my *claim*.

I basically just called her mine.

Something Hattie wanted to be, but never was.

It's dangerous to use Clover in this way. Hattie is capable of hideous things. But I need to take control immediately or this will end badly.

Hattie believes me. I've known her my whole life so I can see it in her face.

This belief fades though. In real time, as I'm looking at her. And in its place comes certainty. Not in what I just said, but in herself.

She turns, walks over to the wall, and turns again,

leaning against it with her arms crossed. She's about six feet away and she is glaring at me. "Your father's not here yet. Won't be until tomorrow."

"So?"

"So that means I'm in command here."

"And? Are you trying to impress me, Hattie? Because if so, you've missed the mark. Subservience doesn't impress me."

She scoffs. "That's funny. Because from what I saw on the surveillance footage at Clover Bradley's house, her submission was your downfall. It was the food, I think. That's the night she gave in. When you went all the way down to Fayetteville to get her those burgers."

"You were *watching* me?"

Hattie's scoff is now a condescending rumble of laughter. "Of course I was, Riggs. Do you really think anyone from the Colony trusts you? Please. That's absurd. You're a *traitor*." She grits that word out between her teeth with disgust. Like she just got a taste of spoiled food. "No one trusts you. Especially your father. That's why he sent me along to keep an eye on you. And this little story you're cooking up about bringing her back with you? Save it. I heard your whole plan. It was like..." She stops here to smile at me. "Like I was in the room with you."

Then she pushes off the wall, laughing, and walks around behind me again. Her fingers once again playing with my hair. "This was nothing but a test. And you failed. So guess what happens next?"

Involuntarily, my mind conjures up an image of the tunnels. Of me, stuck in them for the rest of my life. Dirty, and hot, and starving, and sick and coughing from the dust and debris of the job.

"Those tunnels are your forever home, Riggs. The darkness is your future. You will never get another chance. And I'm sad for you, I really am." Her fingertips begin tickling my neck, sending a chill down my spine.

I grit my teeth, putting a stop to the reaction she is so carefully cultivating. "You've never been sad for anyone in your life, Hattie."

"It's not true. I love you. You're my best friend, Riggs."

"You're delusional."

"Maybe." She walks around in front of me again, her fingertips lingering in my hair until the last second when she has to pull them away. "It's a weakness, I know. My fatal flaw, or something. But my misplaced sense of love and loyalty to you can save you."

"What are you talking about?"

"Your father's not here yet, so I'm in charge."

"So what?"

"I could… make a deal with you. In fact, I have the authority to do just that." She reaches into the long pocket along the right thigh of her tactical pants and pulls out a piece of paper folded into quarters. I watch as she carefully unfolds it, all the while grinning.

I don't wanna ask, but the question comes out anyway. "What's that?"

"This?" She holds up the unfolded paper. "This is the deal I'm gonna offer you."

I swallow and steel myself for what's coming. Because it's not going to be good.

"The offer is... your freedom in exchange for Clover's life."

I scoff. "You want me to kill her?"

"To save yourself, Riggs. Yes. I want you to kill her. Then, when your father gets here, I'll back up your story about why you brought her down here. With one minor substitution. You weren't bringing her home to keep for yourself, you were bringing her as a hostage. He'll believe it."

"No, he won't. Do you think my father is stupid?"

Hattie takes offense to this. "Of course not. And if this story were coming from you, there's no way he would believe it. But from *me*, Riggs?" She smiles at me. "He'll believe anything I say. I'll destroy those recordings, I'll back up your story, I'll mark your assignment complete and give you a commendation. You'll get all the perks and privileges of being the general's son. A new house, a wife." She points to herself. "You'll come home to me every night." Hattie pauses here. Sighs. "Or... you go back down to those tunnels and die there the way a traitor deserves." She straightens her spine, lifts up her chin, and crosses her arms. "I'll save you from that fate and you'll get your life back."

"If I *kill her.*"

"That's right," Hattie says. "If you kill Clover Bradley, I will save you."

CHAPTER 21 - CLOVER

I wake up tied to a chair in front of a metal table in some kind of concrete block room with one door and no windows. My head is pounding and my ribs are screaming, but I manage to look up and around and note the cameras. It's some kind of interrogation room.

When I look down, I'm wearing gray surgical scrubs and my feet are bare.

At first, I'm confused. Unable to recall how I got here and why I am wearing these hideous clothes. But then the face of Hattie Miller fills my mind and I replay what happened in the embassy penthouse.

They found us. I was right. I knew it. The broken trains were a ploy, not so Ike could spend the day with me, but so Hattie could catch up with us.

Of course, I wasn't really expecting it to be her. But I felt it. I knew our plan was failing and someone was coming to get us.

I gasp, then look around for Riggs.

But I'm alone. He's not here.

The moment I think this, the door comes bursting open, scaring me so bad, I squeak.

Hattie Miller comes in with two very big men. I can't tell if they're the same ones who were accosting me back in the room, but it seems likely. Which means they saw me naked. Someone put these clothes on me because Riggs and I were in the middle of—

"Good. You're awake." Hattie's voice is loud and commanding as she slams a folder down on the metal table. All this noise echoes off the walls of the nearly empty room and my body begins to shake the way it did the other night. There's a chair across the table from me and she pulls it out, dragging the legs along the floor with an earsplitting screech.

She takes a seat, opens the folder, and starts flipping through pages.

I don't say anything. Neither does she. She just keeps flipping pages. Then she abruptly grunts and closes the folder as she looks me in the eyes. "You're Lowyn McBride's best friend."

It doesn't feel like a question, so I don't say anything back.

Hattie sucks in a breath between her teeth like she's getting ready to deliver bad news.

As a child growing up in the town of Disciple, West Virginia, I learned a thing or two about non-verbal cues and gestures. Specifically, how to use them to convey emotion while performing in the Revival.

Everyone in fourth through sixth grade attended acting classes over the winter break. This was about the age when some of us were getting too old to sing in the children's choir and were moving on to other roles—newsie boys and girls, or dancers, or sometimes, if you were particularly adept at the acting side of things, we got to be cripples in wheelchairs who were healed in the tent.

I was a cripple once. But just the once because I kept laughing when the people started crying over me. An actor, I am not. But I certainly recognize this teeth-sucking thing Hattie just did as an act.

She's about to lie to me.

"It really sucks to be you," Hattie says.

Which is sorta confusing, because it's not a lie. I'm in a very unfortunate situation at the present. Again, this is not a question, so I decide to say nothing.

"I think I owe it to you to tell the truth here."

I can't help it, I scoff. It's just a tiny one, but more than enough for Hattie to take notice.

"I know," she says, putting up a hand, palm towards me. "I get it. I don't know how much Riggs told you about me, but I will assume it's enough to understand how I operate. So I don't expect you to trust me. But I'm gonna tell you anyway. Riggs has accepted an offer to save himself."

My eyebrows go all crinkly trying to decipher what this might mean.

"Yes," Hattie says. "Unfortunately, saving himself involved throwing you to the wolves. Or the wolf, as it stands. Which is me. I'm the wolf."

I sigh, tired of this whole thing—the kidnapping, the emotional turmoil that came with falling for my captor, and now this. "Can you just get to the point?"

Hattie leans back in her chair and crosses her arms. "I thought I just did."

"Try again," I say. "And use more words this time."

"All right. I'll be blunt. I like to be blunt." I bet she does. "He sold you out, Clover. I made him an offer. In his defense, it was a good offer. Hell"—she laughs— "who am I kidding? It was a great offer. He gets to pass his little test—because that's what this assignment was —and go home with me. He'll never see the inside of those dark tunnels again. He'll never know that feeling of hopelessness. He'll get promoted, I'll retire, we'll get married, make ourselves a little home, throw parties for his comrades, and live out our happily ever after, just as we both imagined it as kids."

I'm not sure when, exactly, I started laughing during her little speech, but by the time she finishes, it's a full-on incredulous chuckle. "Come on, Hattie. You don't really expect me to believe that? I mean, he hates you. He told me."

Her face doesn't change. Not even a twitch.

But her eyes—bright blue as they are—go dark.

It only lasts for a moment, though. And in the next

one, they're shining again. "Yeah. He hates me. Always has. Because I remind him of all his shortcomings. I was the child his father wished he had. Riggs was… well, to call him a disappointment would be an understatement."

"What do you want?"

"Calm down, I'm getting there. I painted a rosy picture of a fictitious future between the two of us. To make you jealous. Oh, let me be very clear here, though. Everything I just said *will* happen. He might not be in love with me, but we're getting married."

"I thought you were getting to the point?" I hiss these words out through clenched teeth.

"Don't be offended, Clover, because it was either kill you or be sent back to those tunnels. So I wouldn't take it personally." When I don't respond or move, she adds, "His killing you, I mean."

I roll my eyes. "Well, where is he then? If he agreed to this, why isn't he in here killing me?"

"Oh, I can't let him do that. You're Lowyn McBride's best friend. And Lowyn is Collin Creed's love interest. Killing Colin Creed's love interest's best friend would cause all sorts of problems between the factions. It was just a ploy on my part to see how committed he was to the idea of *you*."

It takes me a few seconds to parse all these words. But even when I'm done doing that, I still don't understand what she's really trying to say.

Hattie raises her eyebrows at me. "You're not following, I take it?"

I shrug. "OK. So he decided to kill me and you're saying no. What am I supposed to do with this information?"

"You're supposed to use it to make your next decision, Clover. That's what you're supposed to do with it."

"Is there some kind of question in there? Because if so, I'm not hearing it."

"Would you like to walk out of here a free woman?"

I scoff. "Is that a real offer?"

"'If I'm lyin' I'm dyin'!' Isn't that one of those folksy expressions you hill people like to say?"

I'm so over her. "What's the catch?"

"The catch?" Hattie smiles. "The catch is, you leave Riggs behind, of course."

"That's it? I renounce him and walk out of here, free and clear?"

"That's it."

She's not lying about this part. I can tell. It's a real offer and after what Riggs told me about Collin and what he was doing all those years he was missing, it makes sense that they would not want to piss him off, even if it was in some kind of second-cousin way via Lowyn.

"What's gonna happen to Riggs?" I ask.

"I just told you. We're getting married."

"That's a lie."

Hattie scoffs. "Yeah, it is. He hates me. And that's fine." She shrugs, then nods her head to the two men standing on either side of the room. "But I've got my share of what I need."

"OK. You're really not making sense."

"The offer is real. What happens to Riggs has nothing to do with it. And why would you care, anyway? I mean, he really did accept the offer I gave him."

"To kill me in exchange for his own freedom."

"That's right. So it should be an easy decision. And I would take this offer and run if I were you. Because once his father gets here, there will be no deal. If you stay, you die. If you leave, and keep your mouth shut, and forget all about Riggs Russell and the few days you spent together, then you get to live. So." She leans back in her chair, satisfied. "What's it gonna be, Clover? Live? Or die?"

CHAPTER 22 - RIGGS

If you kill Clover Bradley, I will save you.

Her words echo in my head as I play them back. "Get me some clothes."

"First, you give me an answer."

"Why, Hattie? What difference does it make if I answer you first? Are you enjoying this?" I nod my head down to my naked body, then scoff when she smiles. "Well, I'm not surprised. You've been after me since I was a kid. And I *never* wanted you. It drives you crazy, doesn't it?"

Hattie shrugs. "It's neither here nor there. Do you have any idea how many men I'm fucking at the moment? Sure"—her eyes linger on my body for a long second before meeting mine again—"you're hot and you've got a nice dick. But I don't pine for you or your dick, Riggs. I've got my share."

"Liar. You're a liar. You're doing this to hurt me because I hurt you."

"I'm doing this to *save you*, Riggs."

I laugh. Loud. Because Clover's words come spilling out of my mouth. "If it weren't for you, I wouldn't need saving, Hattie. You've done nothing but betray me."

"You've done nothing but betray the Colony!"

"Don't act like you're some Colony Charter patriot, Hattie. You cling to those rules because it gives you power. My fuck-ups *give you power*. And if the only way to control me is to hurt me, then that's good enough for you. You'll never have my love, but you don't need love to thrive, do you Hattie? Because you're not driven by love, you're driven by hate."

"So many words. My God, you're dramatic." Her eyes narrow and she stares at me. "But before you make a hasty decision, let's paint a picture of your future, shall we?"

"Oh, I know. I know better than anyone what my future in the tunnels looks like."

"Do you?" She scoffs. "Because I don't think you do. I think you've already forgotten what it was like in those tunnels."

"That's hilarious coming from a person who's never been down there. You have no idea what I went through. So I don't need your reminders."

"You're wrong, ya know."

"About what?" I'm sneering now. So angry. If I wasn't across the room and tied to a chair, I'd choke her out and never think of her again.

"I *was* down there. I went to see you. After six months of me begging my father, he finally arranged a day pass for me with your father's permission."

"Well, obviously you never followed through because we never saw each other down there."

"You're right. *We* didn't. But I did follow through. I did see you. You just didn't see me. I don't know what your days were like. If that was an average day or a bad one. But I didn't even recognize you, Riggs. It wasn't the beard, either. Or the dirt, and grime, and sweat that was caked all over you. It was the look in your eyes. That empty, dark look in your eyes. It was hopelessness."

"You never got that close. I would've seen you. Hell, everyone down there would've noticed a woman walking into the tunnels."

"I was watching on the surveillance system. And let me tell you, I was… shocked. At how bad you looked. But I was still gonna see it through."

"Except you didn't. So what happened to change your mind?" I hate that I'm interested in her little story. I hate it. But I can't help myself. I need to know why she didn't come. I would've given anything for a visit—even from Hattie Miller—while I was in the tunnels. There was no hope. A familiar face—even if it belonged to the woman who put me there—would've been better than nothing. At the very least, it would've marked the day as different. Would've lent a sense of time to a place where time almost ceased to exist.

"I wasn't allowed. While I was watching security monitors, you killed a man for stealing your food."

Something comes over me here. Some kind of hysteria, I think. Because I am suddenly laughing out loud. "You're so full of shit."

"Am I? Didn't you kill someone over food, Riggs?"

"Yes. But if you saw that footage, you weren't on your way to see me and it wasn't six months in. It was week two. I was still in holding. So I'll give you a few points for reading my file, but the take-home message for me here is once a liar, always a liar."

Hattie comes towards me, grabs my face with both hands, then bends down so we are eye to eye. "Are you going to kill her to save yourself? Or do you want me to do it and let you rot in the tunnels? Either way, she dies and you live with it. The only question left is… would you rather live with it as a free man or a prisoner?"

"You're evil. You're ugly, too."

Hattie smiles. Laughs. "Your insults don't hurt, Riggs. Because you're a liar as well." She leans in, pressing herself against my chest as she stares down at me. "How about this? How about one more chance, hmm? One last shot to save her."

"Just another lie, I bet."

"No. It's a real offer. All you have to do is *kiss me.*"

I'm already laughing. "Kiss me one time, Riggs. Good, and long, and make it as real as you can stand. And if you do that, I'll let her go."

"What about me?"

"Well, if you're not gonna kill her, then you're still fucked. Unless, of course, you'd like to take that kiss to its logical end?" She winks, eyes dancing with malevolence. Then she actually climbs into my lap, pressing herself down on my legs, grinding herself into my dick as she loops her arms around my neck and leans in, like she might kiss me without my permission. "Just one," she whispers. "Just one stupid kiss with me and I'll let her go."

I inhale deeply, steeling myself for what I'm about to do. And then lean towards her.

Hattie smirks at me. Snickering with satisfaction.

I lean closer, our lips a breath apart.

She's waiting for it, I can tell.

"You are nothing but a rotting piece of filth under my fingernails, Hattie Miller. You disgust me. And if I wasn't tied to this chair right now, I'd wrap my hands around your neck and then gleefully watch your eyes pop out as I choke the life right out of you."

Her smirk fades and I'm laughing, fully enjoying the fact that finally, my colorful threats have found an appropriate target.

Clover would approve.

Hattie screams, headbutts me, then does it again.

My forehead splits, blood gushes out of my nose, and a moment later, she punches me in the ear, the chair topples over to the side, and I hit my head on the floor.

But this time, when the world wobbles and starts to fade, I'm wearing a satisfied smile.

CLOVER

CHAPTER 23 - CLOVER

If you leave, and keep your mouth shut, and forget all about Riggs Russell and the few days you spent together, then you get to live.

Hattie's words linger in my head as she studies me from across the table. She looks extremely smug and satisfied. But instead of projecting an air of confidence, all it does is make me question everything.

"What's the problem here, Clover? You're that attached to him that you can't leave him behind?"

This *is* part of the problem. But I'm not going to tell her that. I fell for Riggs. And even though it happened during a kidnapping and I'm properly embarrassed at how well the Stockholm syndrome is setting in, I'm still having trouble envisioning a life after he's gone.

I'm not even sure it's his absence that causing all this angst inside me. It's just… in a weird way, he's a part of me now. And if I leave here—thereby leaving him behind forever—I don't think I'll ever be the same.

Obviously, I can live without this man. I understand that life will go on, I'll spend the next two years in therapy parsing out every minute of what happened to me, and eventually, I will find myself a new normal.

"The problem, Hattie"—I say this out loud, even though I didn't really mean to—"is that... I don't really have anything going for me right now. You see, I lost my job, I lost my cottage, and my life was completely upturned."

"*So?*" She sneers this word out at me.

"So maybe this was just all meant to happen? Maybe this is just my path in life?"

"Oh, please." She scoffs, chuckling. "Are you trying to insinuate that you think Riggs and you were..." She almost snorts. "Destiny? Oh, come on, Clover. Nothing about your encounter with Riggs was destiny. That's crazy. I'm the one who got you fired. I'm the one who made them pack up that cottage of yours. I'm the one who set this whole thing in motion."

"You're lying. You've been lying about everything since you came through that door."

"Oh, but I'm not. If you get out of here you can ask Mr. Sutter yourself. We paid him, Clover. He's on the take. Fifty thousand dollars to fire you and kick you out on your ass, thereby forcing you to go home. Everything about your encounter with Riggs was a setup. His entire mission was a setup. What kind of dumbass do you think General Russell is? I mean, he knows his son better than anyone. He knew Riggs would fuck it up."

"So you sent me in to trap him?"

"Trap him?" She's snarling now. "No one trapped him. It was a test. He was passing with flying colors for nearly three days. We were so proud of him. Everyone watching the security footage was cheering with each and every threat he spit at you. And then…" She sighs. "Well, then he went and fed you. And took you up to some room in the attic where we didn't have cameras. What happened in that room, Clover? Did you use your feminine ways to change his mind? Is that what you did? Did you corrupt him with offers of sex?"

My anger is building the whole time she's talking. *These people were in my house.* They put cameras up. They violated me, and used me, and now she's got the nerve to *insult me*?

But anger is not the way forward here. So I internally calm myself so that when my words come out, they are even and steady. "It was bliss, Hattie. That night with him. It was bliss having his body next to mine. All those muscles pressing up against my bare skin. He hugged me, all night long. He held me tight and made me feel better. And he told me all about you."

She doesn't know what to think about this. She

wants to say something smart here. Something to derail me. But she's too slow and I keep going.

"He told me you were a brawny lumberjack compared to me." Then I bust out laughing. Because the look on her face is priceless. She was expecting 'bitch,' I think. That's what she thought he called her. And while it's still an insult, I think she wears that persona like a badge of honor. It can't cut her, that word.

But 'brawny lumberjack' is a much more personal attack. And she feels it.

Hattie stands up, kicking the chair back so hard, it topples over backwards. "Fuck him."

"No. Fuck *you*, Hattie. And fuck your offer too. He didn't sell me out, did he? He refused. So guess what? I'm gonna refuse too. You can take your offer and shove it up your ass. You can kill me if you want, but know this: You were right about one thing. I am Lowyn's best friend and if I never come home, trust me, Lowyn will never rest until the mystery of me is solved."

Hattie narrows her eyes at me.

But I narrow mine right back. And then I make my last threat. "Kill me and you people will be looking over your shoulders until he finds you. And he *will* find you. Mark my words on that. Collin Creed will hunt you to the ends of the earth and you will die for your sins against me."

Hattie holds my gaze, unflinching and, apparently, unmoved by my warning. "I'll take my chances."

Then she gets up and walks out.

CHAPTER 24 - RIGGS

After toppling over and knocking my head, I must've feel asleep because I slowly wake up to the sound of someone clearing their throat. Immediately, and without opening my eyes, I know who it is.

"You're awake. Don't be a coward, Riggs. Open your eyes and look at me."

My father's voice is low and commanding. Like his words are law, leaving no room for discussion.

An old urge to rebel manifests inside me. Like muscle memory, the need to disagree just for the sake of disagreeing is nearly overpowering.

But I control it. To give in like that is weak. And it reminds me of when I was a prisoner in the tunnels. When I had no power and no other choice but to react.

I refuse to react. I might be a prisoner again, but I'm done bending to these people and their tyrannical ways. It should not be a crime to want something else.

It should not be a crime to crave freedom. It should not be a crime *to leave.*

I open my eyes. Not because he commanded me to, but because I will not play the role of petulant child just because that's how he sees me.

I'm in a bed. Rather, I am strapped to a gurney. Hands and feet tied to the railings that run along my body. I'm also wearing clothes now. Gray scrubs. Prison garb.

Well, I guess I didn't fall asleep. Someone drugged me. It bothers me that I don't remember this. Do I have a concussion? Probably. But it's more probable that my lack of memory is due to some kind of drug cocktail, so I take a breath and let it out, studying my surroundings.

The room is small and square and General Russell is in the far corner to my right, sitting in a chair. He's leaning back and he's got one leg propped up on a knee.

He's in full dress uniform, which isn't out of the ordinary. One only needs to look at history books—fake or not—to discover that all tyrants love the dress uniform. The general's chest is adorned with medals and ribbons that tell a silent story about his past.

If you buy in to what the Colonies are selling, that past is filled with valor and decades of patriotic service.

But if you're me, well. It's just another lie.

His hair is nearly white, which contrasts his short, neatly trimmed beard. He's over sixty now, but the color of his hair is the only thing that gives it away. His face is surprisingly devoid of wrinkles, his shoulders are still broad enough to fill out the perfectly tailored uniform in a way that makes him look much younger, and his blue eyes haven't yet gone blurry. They are cold, calculating eyes that miss nothing. As he stares at me, his lips form a flat line depicting something between indifference and disgust.

"Where am I?"

That flat mouth lifts up, but in a sneer, not a smile. "Not in the tunnels."

"Then where?"

"No 'hello,' Riggs? No 'how are you, Father?'"

"You set me up. You *set me up*."

He shrugs up one shoulder. "We all knew you would fail. I needed the evidence."

"Oh, I get a trial this time? How generous."

My father laughs. It's kind of a loud chuckle, which is completely out of character for him and makes the muscles of my stomach clench with dread. "A trial? That's quaint. Your treason is showing, Riggs. Trials are for up-tops. You know very well there's no such thing down here."

"So why? Why set me up like this? Was Hattie watching me the whole time?"

"Yes. But from afar and from the other side of a

screen. As was I. And I'm not going to lie here, Riggs, I had money on you."

My eyebrows go up. "You bet on me to win?"

"No." His laugh, again, conjures up a sense of dread inside me. "Hattie had money on you to win. She hunted you down and brought you back, but she was a firm believer in your reeducation down in those tunnels. In fact, she's the one who put you there. I was going to have you hanged. She talked me out of it, insisting—bless her heart—that more than half a decade in the dark would rehabilitate you. She had picked out a house and everything. And, though she would never admit it, she was planning the wedding."

I'm so stunned, I don't even bother answering back. Hattie thought I would marry her? That I would, what? View her betrayal as… altruistic? As if she was saving me from myself?

I saved you.

In my head, these words come out in two voices. One is Clover's. One is mine.

And the irony is not lost.

"Hattie has always been delusional."

"Yes." The general laughs. "She has loved you since you were children. Always sticking up for you, and covering for you, and believing in you."

Now it's my turn to laugh. "Well, with friends like that, who needs enemies."

"As I was saying. There was a point there, during

your reeducation test, where everyone was betting on you to win. And for a moment there, I was sure she had me. But you never disappoint, Riggs. You came from my seed. I know you better than anyone. And now Hattie knows the real you as well. You hate me, you hate her, you hate the Colonies. You hate everything we hold dear. You're like a sick animal. Something that needs to be put down."

This is when I glance at my arm and notice the IV.

"Yes," the general says, noticing my noticing. "There are a lot of drugs in your future, Riggs. But don't worry. That's not how you'll die. Drug overdose? That's way too cliché. You need a more fitting exit from this world. So…" He shrugs with his hands as a smile creeps up his face. And for the first time I think I really see my father for what he is. Evil. "Hattie came up with something very creative for you."

"I bet she did." The words are just a whisper, not even meant for him, just me. And that feeling in my gut is back. That feeling that I missed something very obvious here. And that whatever happens next, it was put in motion long before now.

"Hattie discovered a lot of things about you today, Riggs. A lot of things about that woman you brought down here as well."

"Leave Clover out of this. She had nothing to do with it. She didn't even want to come."

"Well, that's funny. Very funny. Because she was offered a way out and she said no."

"What?"

"That's right. Hattie offered her a deal. All she had to do was forget she ever met you. If she did that—and kept her word, of course—she would be returned to her quaint little town and Collin Creed would be none the wiser about any of this."

"*What*? There must be a catch. Why the hell would she say no to that?"

The general laughs out these words. "Well… loyalty, of course. Isn't that hilarious? You kidnap her in her own house, threaten to kill her five, six different ways, bring her down here where her discovery would mean certain death, and still, she refuses to leave you behind."

"Let me talk to her." I try not to sound desperate, but I don't entirely succeed. "Let me talk to her and I'll tell her to take the deal. I can—"

"It's too late." He waves a hand in the air like he's erasing my words.

"No. It's not. She'll take the deal. Let her go and she'll never say a word."

"Oh, I'm sure. She's weak and rather stupid. But she's got a rebellious streak in her. Hattie was being compassionate and nice and Clover insisted on insulting her. So." He shrugs with his evil smile this time. "She withdrew the deal."

"But Hattie's not in charge here. You are. You're the fucking general. All you have to do is make it so."

"True." My father stares at me, his eyes poison personified. Not even bothering to hide his malice. Not even trying to dress it all up in a pretty frosted bottle with a shiny satin ribbon. "But her replacement plan for Clover Bradley was even more fitting."

"Why do you hate me?"

The scoff he responds with is filled with disgust. "Why are you such a disappointment? Hmm? You were born into the highest level of privilege, Riggs. You were given the best education, placed in the company of the best children, raised up as a warrior for all that is just and right in the world and you threw it all away for what? Life up there?" His eyes drift up to the ceiling of the room and stay there for a few moments before returning to me. "It's filth. It's sin. It's corruption—"

"And down here isn't?"

"You tell me. Blackberry Hill is the poorest Colony in the entire world and it's clean, and filled with polite people who are happy to do their part and live their lives to the fullest extent possible. They do not waste their days doing nothing. They all have purpose. Can you say the same for the poorest cities up there? No. They are filth. They are crime-ridden cesspools overflowing with people with the impetus of insects."

"At least they are free."

My father guffaws. "They're not free, Riggs! They're food for the spider who weaves an invisible web all around them. They are chewed up, and spit out, and used for… whatever. They are nothing but a bit of meat. You gave up everything I set in motion for you for that, Riggs. For a bit of filthy, rotten meat."

"That's not true. It's not even close to true. I just don't want to be here. I want to live in the sun. In the fresh air. I want to be free to go anywhere I choose. It should not be illegal to *leave*."

"But it is." His smile is sad now. "Leaving is high treason and you are a traitor. We can't have traitors running around the Colonies, now can we? It's a problem. *You're* a problem, Riggs. And, well… if there's no you, then there's no problem, is there?" He stands up. "We're done here."

"Wait! What about Clover? Don't kill her. Please. None of this is her fault."

"Kill her?" My father scoffs as he side-eyes me from over his shoulder. "We're not going to kill her. Killing her would incite Collin Creed and send him careening down a path of revenge and retribution. No one wants that. It will all end badly. We're just going to kill *you*, Riggs. Actually, *we're* not." He smiles again. A pretty poison frog. "*Collin is*."

It takes several moments for me to parse these words because I just can't make sense of it. Why would

Collin kill me? I never betrayed him, *he's* the one who betrayed *me*.

As if he's reading my mind, my father says, "You're on a lot of drugs right now, Riggs, so allow me to elucidate. You see, everything that happened inside Clover's house was recorded. It was a test, son. We were keeping tabs on you the entire time."

"So?"

"So…" He shrugs with his hands. "We have all those threats you made. All those times you tackled Clover to the ground. All those times you tied her up and gagged her. All those times she begged you to let her go. And right now"—he looks at his watch—"Collin Creed is watching all that footage. And since his one true love is Clover's best friend, Collin is forming some opinions about how you might meet your true end, Riggs. He's also very confused about something. He's about to start putting things together and while he won't have all the answers, he'll have a start. He's a smart guy. So I have no doubts whatsoever that he'll figure it out. And when he does, that'll be the end of you."

"What's the point of that? You're acting like this is some great scheme, but who the hell cares if Collin kills me?"

"Who cares? Why, Clover Bradley cares, that's who. She said she wouldn't leave here without you, remember?"

Suddenly, I get it. My father is going to scar her. That's the point of this. He's going to hurt her in a way that cannot be fixed. And the worst thing about this is that I built it. I laid the groundwork for this pain he and Hattie want to inflict on Clover because I kidnapped her, and fucked with her head, and made her loyal to me, and it worked so well that when given the chance to save herself, she couldn't leave me behind.

This entire thing is my fault.

My father opens the door to the little room and a nurse comes in. "He's ready. Let's do this."

"You're sick!" I say, struggling against my bindings. "You people are fucking sick! She didn't do anything!"

"But she did, Riggs." I look past the general and find Hattie, the owner of that voice. She's smirking at me. Just as evil as the rest. "She's a prissy little bitch. But, somehow, you convinced her to love you. She insulted me. Threatened me. If I *could* kill her, I *would* kill her. But having you killed and making her responsible?" Hattie chuckles. Her smile is big and satisfied. "Well, I guess it'll just have to be enough."

My vision starts to go blurry and when I look to my right, I realize the nurse has pushed more drugs into my IV.

A moment later, there's nothing left to live for.

CHAPTER 25 - CLOVER

I'**ve been chained** to this metal table for hours now and there is nothing in the room with me but the sound of the air conditioning, which doesn't seem to have a cut-off temperature because the room is freezing and my body is shaking as bad, or worse, as it was the other night when Riggs held me.

But he's not here to hold me now and so there's no hope of stopping the shivers that are getting worse by the second. Pretty soon, I'll be convulsing if someone doesn't take me out of here or turn that damn AC off.

Maybe that's how they'll kill me. They'll just leave me here and let me freeze to death.

For fuck's sake, Clover. Get a hold of yourself. You're not going to freeze to death. It's probably not even that cold in here, you're just... frightened.

Which is the truth. I am scared.

What are they going to do next? Will they kill us? Will they torture us?

The door slams open, banging against the wall. I

lean back, shocked, and stare at the huge man filling the doorway.

Ike Monroe.

He's wearing jeans today. Boots, a leather jacket, and a black t-shirt with some kind of faded logo on it. He looks like his twin brother, Lasher—member of the Revenant biker gang—right now. And it's such a contradiction from the last time I saw him in a suit that it takes a few seconds for me to make sense of the paradox.

I knew he was dangerous the other night. I know what he did to Lowyn. But it was hard to see him in that light when he was all dressed up and acting like some kind of high-society host.

He looks nothing like some high-society host right now. Nothing at all.

Ike looks over his shoulder, leans back a little so he can look down both sides of the hallway outside, then directs his gaze right at me. His eyes are squinted and I can't tell if it's rage or hate.

But then, right as I'm staring into them, they soften, he steps inside, and the door closes quietly behind him.

I hold my breath as I wait to see what happens next.

He puts up both hands, pressing his palms at me. "Don't scream."

I notice that his accent is thick now. Filled with the

drawl of a man who grew up in the hills of West Virginia. Not all polished like it was the other night. He must've been putting on pretenses or something, because right now he sounds just like everyone else from the Trinity. "Do I have a reason to scream?"

"No. I'm here to help. We're gettin' out of here."

"*We?*"

He points to himself. "I'm going with you. It's just two checkpoints. We'll be fine." Then he's coming at me, pulling something out from his back pocket.

I recoil, unable to picture what that something might be, but then I let out a breath when I realize it's a very big set of bolt cutters. Ike doesn't hesitate, just puts the cutting end on either side of the chain link attached to my cuffs and presses the handles closed. It slices through the metal like butter and my hands, while still cuffed, are free.

I stand up, rubbing my wrists.

"Come on. Let's go." He makes a grab for me, but I pull away.

"You're crazy if you expect me to trust you, Ike. You're running this place. You're one of them. For all I know, you got Riggs captured on purpose. For all I know," I say again, "you called Hattie here yourself."

He sneers at me. "Hattie's been here, Clover. The entire time. And you're wrong about me. I'm not one of them."

"What the hell are you talking about? This is *your* city. You work for these monsters!"

He glares at me, his eyes so narrow they're nothing but slits. "So you think… what, this was my dream? Do you think I was just sittin' around when I was sixteen thinkin' to myself, 'Gee. I sure wish there was some secret underground cult I could join up with to save my *entire. Fucking. Village?*'"

These last few words of his come out like a snake spitting venom and everything cordial and charming that I once saw inside Ike Monroe disappears.

He's bad. He's a bad, bad man.

He's also my only hope at the moment. Because I wouldn't even know where to look for Riggs down here, let alone the safest way to the exit. So I defuse things by stating something obvious without making it feel accusatory. "Well, you sure looked like you were having a good time last night."

His whole expression relaxes and he scoffs. "Well, you sure did too."

"I was faking it."

"And what makes you think I wasn't?"

He makes a grab for me again, but I pull away just in time. "Why should I trust you?"

"I'm pretty much your only option, Clover. And we're wasting time."

"That's not good enough. Not after what you did to Lowyn."

His eyes go narrow again. "What do you know about it?"

"I know… you're *bad*."

For some reason, this characterization makes him chuckle. "Oh, bad doesn't even come close to what I am, Clover. But if you think this life I'm living was anything other than the best-case scenario in the face of many bad options, then… whatever. Find your own way out."

And then he turns to leave.

"Wait," I say. Because I'm not sure he's bluffing. In fact, I'm pretty sure he's not bluffing. He *is* my only option.

Ike doesn't turn, just side-eyes me from over his shoulder. "We can argue about this later, OK? You can call me every name in the book. You can accuse me of anything you want. Hell, I'll even stand still and quiet and let you do it. But we need to *go*, Clover. Right now."

I wilt here. Because I've got no choice and I hate that. But I do want to live. So I rally and nod. "Deal."

"Stay right behind me and no talkin' now. Don't say anything. Look at your feet and if anyone confronts us, make some pathetic sniffling noises or something. Like you're afraid of me."

I look up at him. "I *am* afraid of you."

He smiles. "Woman, I am a fuckin' saint compared to these Colony people. Look down, sniffle, and shake a little if anyone talks to us. Got it?"

I nod, then look down at my feet.

"I'm gonna be a little rough with you, so don't take it personal."

He starts pulling me over to the door, but I resist. "Wait! What about Riggs?"

"They're gonna kill Riggs, Clover. That's why we gotta get outta here."

He pulls me towards the door, but I lean back, planting my feet. "I can't leave him behind."

"You don't understand—"

But just as he says that, the door comes crashing open again. Hattie appears, apparently alone, and she just stands there for a moment, trying to sort out what is happening. She's just about to open her mouth and start asking questions when Ike grabs the bolt cutters from the table and hits her in the side of the head with them.

She goes down like a fuckin' sack of flour. I'm talking crashes to the floor, banging her head on the side of the door as she falls.

"That's gonna hurt, no doubt about it. And I'll pay for it in the end. But it can't be helped." Ike looks at me and grins. "And anyway, she's a bitch."

"Who *are* you?"

Ike side-eyes me. Like he's angry. But then his eyes soften. "Not what everyone thinks. Let's just stick with that for now. When we're back up top, I'll tell you everything. But for now, if you wanna save Riggs, then you gotta trust *me*. Let's go."

He turns his back on me, ending the conversation, and then he steps into the hallway, looking both ways. It's empty and silent, like this is some secret, unused section of the underground city, and I start to get the feeling that he's maybe not supposed to be here.

We go left. Ike's grip on my upper arm is very firm. He's very tall and walks fast, so I have to practically trot to keep up with him. I look down, like he told me to, and concentrate on his boots. They make a deep thudding sound on the concrete floor, while my bare feet slap along beside him.

Suddenly, there are voices somewhere up ahead. They are faint, but with every step, they get louder. Which tells me these are people to be confronted, not avoided, and my heart skips a couple of beats.

We come around another corner, and I take a peek up and see two large men halfheartedly guarding a steel door. They look up as we approach, both of them snapping to attention when they realize who it is.

"Ike?" one calls when we're still down the hall a ways.

"Don't look up," Ike says, his words a low growl meant only for me. And then he greets them. "Hey, Mouzer. Hey, Bills." He jerks my arm. "I'm taking this one to the pile." His words are light and happy now, but in a scary way. "Either of you wanna come along and watch?"

The pile? Pile of what? Dead bodies?

The two guards chuckle. "Wish we could," one says.

"I'd hit that," the other one adds.

Which leads me to believe it's some other kind of pile and my whole body begins to shake.

"But we can't." The first one sighs. "The general's here. You shouldn't either, Ike. He's an asshole."

"And that bitch of an attack dog he brought with him?" the other one says. "Let's just say I wouldn't take her to the pile if they paid me."

"Hell, I would." The first one laughs. "I'd fuck her hard, and then shoot her in the head as I was blowing my load inside her."

I look up, forgetting my number one directive, and recoil. What the hell? Did I just hear that correctly?

Ike yanks my arm so hard, I yelp. "Look at your feet, bitch. You don't need to see their faces."

I look down and all three of them laugh.

What if he set me up? What if he really is taking me to some place called 'the pile' where, apparently, they go to rape women before they kill them?

"Well, I gotta go," Ike says. Then he looks at his watch. "I've got an appointment with the general after this." He snickers. "He ain't gonna be mad. She's my reward for a job well done."

I feel so sick, I might throw up. And I don't hear

how the two men respond, because Ike is pulling the steel door open and shoving me through it.

"I'll take a little video," Ike says, just before he closes the door. "Stop by my place tonight and we'll watch it together." Then the door bangs closed and he starts dragging me along the new hallway. "Keep your head down," he whispers. "That was the easy part. Those are my men, but this next group aren't."

"The *pile*?" I ask, my voice weak.

"Not now, Clover. Just shut up and look at your feet. I'll do all the talkin'."

Again, I hear distant voices that become clearer as we walk. We turn the corner, and there's a group of them this time. At least three, but I don't look up to check. Because their conversation isn't banter based on boredom, they are having some kind of official meeting.

They sound like soldiers.

The man who is talking—obviously, the one in charge—says, "Hey. Where the hell is Hattie?"

I feel Ike do something here. But I don't know what until he starts shooting.

One, two, three, four.

I look up just in time to watch every one of the men collapse to the floor. Each one with a smoking hole in the center of their foreheads.

I scream, but Ike's hand is over my mouth before I can really let it out. His hand is so big and he presses it against my face so hard, I can't breathe. I look up at him, eyes wide with terror.

He just killed four men. In cold blood. Four. Right in front of me.

"Do not scream," he growls. "Promise?"

I nod. And he removes his hand. "I thought you said you were gonna talk to them! Not shoot them in the fuckin' head!"

"We don't have time for talking. We've like an hour to save Riggs, Clover. Because they are taking him to Collin as we speak. And he knows we've got you down here. He knows what Riggs did to you. Hattie and the general made sure of it. And if you're not there to set him straight on whatever the fuck is going on between you and Riggs, Collin's just gonna waste him. So if you wanna save your man, then shut up and run!"

He opens the door, shoves me through it, and that's what I do.

I run.

CHAPTER 26 - RIGGS

When I wake up, the only thing I hear is a peculiar squeaking sound. I focus on it like it's my last hope as my head spins and my foggy mind begins to clear. It takes several long minutes to realize I'm lying down, but moving at the same time.

The gurney. You're strapped to a gurney, Riggs.

My entire unfortunate situation comes hurtling back to me like a punch in the face.

Clover! Where is she? What's happening?

Suddenly, we stop. "Where's Hattie?" It's my father.

"I don't know, sir," an unfamiliar voice says. "She went to get the prisoner and hasn't come back yet."

"We can't wait for her then. Let's continue. Open the door."

I start coughing as the drugs wear off.

"Good," my father says. "You're awake. I want you to be awake. I want you to look Collin Creed in the eyes as he kills you. It's a fitting punishment for a traitor."

There's no way to ignore his threat. I've been

conditioned my whole life to care what this man thinks of me. But most of my attention is on what the other guy said. *She went to get the prisoner and hasn't come back yet.*

"Clover," I say, my voice raspy and nearly unrecognizable. Did Hattie kill her? Is that why she hasn't returned?

"Sir?" a third voice says.

"Yes, what is it?" My father sounds annoyed.

"There's..." The new guy pauses.

"Spit it out, soldier. We're in the middle of something here. I don't have all day."

"There's been a... an incident."

"What kind of incident?"

"Ike Monroe. There are reports that he... well, he shot four of our men at the Blackberry Hill checkpoint."

"What?"

My eyes aren't even open and I can see my father's angry expression. I've been on the receiving end of that glare so many times, it's burned into my retinas.

"What the hell are you talking about?"

"He took the prisoner—his men claim he was taking her to the pile for a..." This soldier hesitates. "Final rite, or whatever."

"He wasn't told to do that."

"No, sir. No one thinks he's actually doing that. They think he's setting her free."

I don't know what comes over me, but I start laughing. There's a good bit of coughing in there too, because I get an elbow to the jaw and my mouth fills up with blood.

"You think that's funny, Riggs?" Oh, my father is pissed.

"I do," I manage, spitting the blood out with my words. "She's free. She's free and she's gonna go right to Collin. So your little plan is—"

But before I can finish, an alarm starts blaring, cutting me off.

My father leans in to my ear to make sure I hear him over the roaring sound of the klaxon. "You wish. Blackberry Hill won't help her. Ike might be willing to risk everything for a woman, but that village of his has been living in prosperity for over a decade now. They're not going back to that sad, poverty-stricken life they had before we took over. And even if she does make it out of Blackberry Hill, she's miles away from Disciple. She'll never make it home before Collin gets his hands on you. Because this alarm you're hearing? It's Collin's alarm, not ours. He knows we're here. And now he's coming for you, Riggs. This is your end, son. I wish I could say it's been a pleasure."

Someone is next to me, pushing more drugs into my IV.

And then the fuzzy fog turns to darkness.

CHAPTER 27 - CLOVER

"*Keep going!*" Ike passes me as we run down the hallway, grabbing my arm and pulling me along with him.

I'm faltering. So out of breath, I'm gasping. Not because of the running, though. Because I can't get the image of those dead men out of my head. I might be in shock.

"Come on!" Ike insists. He's gripping my arm so tight now, I'm sure there'll be a massive bruise when this is all over.

If it ever ends, that is. Because right as I think these words, an alarm starts blaring. It's not close, because it's not that loud. But an alarm is an alarm.

"Run faster!"

"I am," I yell back. "I'm running as fast as I can!"

"That's Collin's alarm, Clover! Which means they're leaving Riggs somewhere Collin can get him. We don't have much time and I still have to convince everyone up top that getting you out is worth the reprisal!"

"What? What's that mean?"

"It means that they might not help us."

"But they're *your* people!"

We come around a corner and slow as an elevator comes into view. "Doesn't work that way. I'm in charge down here, but ever since Collin came back and that shit with Lowyn—"

"They demoted you! You're not in charge up there!"

He shoots me a warning look, but doesn't deny it.

"So… all this is for nothing?"

We stop in front of the elevator and Ike pushes the call button. "No. It's the middle of the night. If we can get up top without making a commotion, no one will even know we're there. I've got a truck hidden in the woods for emergencies. Don't worry. It's gonna work."

"'Don't worry, it's gonna work?'" My mouth just kinda falls open and doesn't recover, that's how stunned I am. "That's your plan?"

"It got us this far, didn't it? We're home free now. All we gotta do is—"

And this is when we hear *her*.

"I'm coming to kill you, Ike Monroe! I'm coming to kill you!" Hattie Miller is yelling at the top of her lungs. It's close, too. A few hallway turns away. And she's not alone. There is a thunder of boots as a group of people come running towards us.

Ike and I both look at the elevator, but there's no ticker thing at the top of it letting you know what floor it's on, or how soon it'll be here. It's a thousand feet to the up-top. And even though the elevator I came down in was fast, there's no sign that this one will be here before Hattie.

Ike grabs me by my shoulders and spins me around to face him. "Listen to me. I'll hold her off. As soon as the elevator gets here, you get in and leave."

"What about you? Hell, what about *me*? I don't know where your stupid hidden truck is!"

"Ike Monroe!" Hattie bellows. And she is dangerously close now. "I'm coming for you!"

Ike shakes me. "Listen! When the doors open up top, the stairs that go up to my house are right across from it. Go up, leave my house, go right. There's a stable at the end of the village. My horse is in there. He's a big buckskin, can't miss 'im. You take him home."

"What! I can't—"

"You have to! You can find the horse, there's no way in hell you'll find the truck. His tack is next to his stall. You ride him down the trail behind the stable. Eventually, you'll come to a highway. There's a barn there. Don't stop. Cross the road and head back into the woods."

"Ike Monroe!" Hattie is right around the next corner now. But she's hanging back, being careful. As she should. Ike Monroe has already knocked her out once and killed four men tonight.

"There's a trail in those woods." Ike shakes me again. "Are you listening?" I look up at him and nod my head. "That trail comes out by the waterfall at Sleepy Creek."

"I know where that is!" My words are breathless.

"You'll find your way then."

"What about you?"

He shoots me a crooked smile. "I'm right behind you. But don't wait for me. Just get up there and go! Otherwise, Riggs is dead. And Collin will be the one to do it."

And just as he says this, the elevator doors open with a ding and Hattie Miller starts shooting.

Ike presses something into my hand, pushes me inside, pulls his gun, and starts shooting back.

Bullets come flying at me, pinging off the walls and shattering the mirror inside the elevator. I put my hands over my head, crouching down near the call buttons, then remember I need to push one to make the doors close.

I look up, press the top button, and then huddle in the corner as the bullets keep coming. They pelt against the closing door and the last thing I hear is Hattie Miller screaming, "I'll see you up top, Clover Bradley! I'll see you up top!"

CHAPTER 28 – RIGGS

The fog is now my friend. That's how it feels. The spinning head, the shooting pain, the sense of dread. We're all best friends here now. And the darkness. Don't even get me started. The darkness is my brother, that's how close the two of us are. Blood relations.

There is a cracking noise coming from above me. Something familiar, but also out of place. I want to open my eyes and look up, but they are *so* heavy.

"I think he's waking up."

"Mmmm."

Before I can think about it, a grunt escapes past my thick, numb lips. Because I know these voices. They were brothers once too. We go way back.

Someone kicks the chair I'm sitting in. "Can you hear me?"

Amon. Oh, I hear him. He's off to my right, but when I try to turn my head and look at him, it lolls, my muscles too loose to hold it up. I let out a long breath, already tired.

Amon kicks my chair again. "Wake up, dead man."

To my surprise, I actually manage to say, "I'mmmm aaawaaaake," in someone else's voice. Well, no. It's my voice. I just don't recognize myself.

They've pumped the cocktail into me. I'm being interrogated.

Then a sharp realization kicks me in the gut. *Clover.* "Whaaaat happp—" But that's as far as I get. I'm suddenly too exhausted to keep going.

"Shoot 'im the next one," Collin says. "Let's get on with this."

With great effort, I manage to crack one eye open. Everything is blurry and bright. I look up, squinting. The crackling noise is coming from a single light bulb swinging above my head. It's attached to a concrete ceiling and instantly, I know I'm still underground.

I didn't even make it up top. I'm gonna die down here.

When I look down, I realize I'm in a wheelchair. *Strapped* to a wheelchair. "I'm gettin' the full treatment today," I mumble.

Collin is right in front of me now, crouching down and staring into my eyes. "You fucked with me, Raleigh. What'd ya have to go and do that for?"

His eyes are not right. They are wrong in every way. The blue in there isn't the blue of skies or the blue of birds. It's something else. Something not blue. Something not green, either. It's the color of a blue pit viper. And the brown in his eyes isn't brown. It's not orange, it's not yellow. It's gold. Like amber. Something born thousands of years ago and trapped in sticky sap.

All you have to do is look at this man. Look him straight in the eyes and you know what he is.

A pretty poison frog.

Pretty enough that he doesn't even need the frosted glass bottle and shiny satin ribbon. When people look at Collin Creed, it's like looking at the Devil himself.

God knows what Collin is. He told me that once. It was my first mission with the crew. We were in the middle of the fuckin' desert on our way to some middle-of-nowhere oasis on the Arabian Peninsula and we were chewing khat leaves. It was my first time and after a few hours, I was tripping. Collin said, "God knows what I am, Raleigh." That was my name back then. To these guys, anyway. "God knows what I am. He sees right through me. So you know how I deal with that?"

I wasn't too interested in this conversation because, aside from the fact that we don't have a god underground, I was drinking arak. I was thinking about God, and how if we had one it might be the boring machine that drills our tunnels. That's about as close as we come to God. I was high on those leaves and buzzed on the drink, and could care less what

God thought about Collin Creed, or his reaction to such thoughts.

But he told me anyway. Collin said, "I just don't believe in him." And then he laughed and shrugged. "I just don't believe."

I think I laughed too. In fact, I'm laughing right now.

Hysterically.

Because it was a good time in my life. I hadn't seen them kill yet. I didn't know what was gonna happen next, but I was in a desert oasis, getting buzzed, having fun. I had friends, and the place was beautiful. There were half-naked women dressed up in bells or something, shaking their hips at me. And the whole thing felt like a dream.

But then Collin leaned in, just like he's leaning in now. And his eyes are tiny little slits. Like he really is a blue pit viper. And he says, in a weird, echo-y voice, "I don't like liars." And then something about burning bridges. "Bring him all the way up, Amon."

Amon is suddenly right up next to me. This is when I realize there's a IV stand next to my shoulder. Amon bends down and I see a flash of a syringe. A moment later, my arm is burning.

And a moment after that, the fog is gone. It's like a light switch. One moment I'm all hazy, the next everything is crystal clear. But with the new cognitive function comes the pain.

Everything hurts. I feel like someone ran me over with a truck.

I stare at the face of Collin Creed. He's like three feet away, kicking back against the concrete wall and frowning at me with his arms crossed.

Amon stands behind me and I feel something cold against the back of my head and I can see him in my mind's eye. All dressed in black. The mask over his face. The only thing visible are his ice-blue eyes.

How many men has Amon had in wheelchairs just like this?

Twenty?

Fifty?

More?

I'd say more. It has been over six years since I've seen them and just that one year alone, where I was on the crew, I'd have to guess I'd seen Amon do this very thing to at least a dozen men.

"Good," Collin says. "You're back. We're gonna take a moment here to have a little chat, *Raleigh*. And then" —Collin grins at me, and this is when all those good times fade and I go from being crew member to enemy number one—"then, *Riggs*, we're gonna take you to the boneyard so you can rest in peace."

CHAPTER 29 - CLOVER

My *mind is racing* as I ascend in the elevator, Hattie's words ringing in my ears. *I'll see you up top, Clover Bradley!*

I stay crouched in the corner of the elevator, staring at the floor. Listening to the pinging of bullets below me. Gradually, they become distant, then they stop altogether.

The elevator jolts to a stop and the doors open.

My heart is racing, my head is pounding, and for a moment, I can't move. Because I don't understand how the hell I got here or what the hell is actually happening. Did I really just spend the last week as a prisoner in my own house and then a guest of a secret underground military installation?

Laughing is the only response I have. It's all I've got. It's just a few chirps at first, but a few seconds later, I'm nearly hysterical.

The doors begin to close and I panic, snapping myself out of whatever psychological reaction I'm in the middle of having. I thrust my arm between the doors, stopping them just in time.

Then I get to my feet and step out into the brightly lit room, blinking for a few seconds as I try to come to grips with my reality.

This is really happening, Clover. And if you don't snap out of this paralysis, you're dead, girl. You're dead!

OK, think. Think. It's an office, that much is clear. But it's not very big. The size of an average bedroom. A desk lines three of the walls and above the desk are dozens of monitors depicting various scenes. Black and white streams of different rooms—even the one I'm standing in—and the dirt roads of a what appears to be a village. The front gates of the Revival grounds and a couple of driveways that look to be in Disciple. The parking lot of the diner down in Revenant. There's even a few shots of Bishop. But most of them show nothing but woods. All lit up green with night vision.

The doors begin to close behind me and I panic, hearing Hattie Miller's voice in my head. *I'll see you up top, Clover Bradley!*

Oh, no, you won't, bitch. I swing around, grab a chair, and roll into the closing doors of the elevator, taking it out of the equation.

Oh, shit! But what about Ike? He said he was right behind me.

I stare at the elevator, wondering if I should send it

back down. It's a crazy idea. But what if he's waiting for it?

What if he's already dead?

What if the only person coming up behind me is Hattie?

I can't risk it. It makes me sick to turn my back on him, that's not the kind of person I am. But I'm practically free. If Hattie came up instead of Ike, I don't know that she'd kill me, but my life would be over even if she didn't.

No. I can't worry about Ike when Hattie Miller is on the hunt and she's got my scent. I leave the chair in the door and force myself to think clearly. I think that elevator is the only way up here. At least the only convenient way up here. Which might not buy me a lot of time, but it should be enough.

I look down at my hand, because this is when I realize that Ike pushed something into it at the last second. It's a phone, but there's a piece of white notebook paper wrapped around it and secured with a rubber band.

I take the rubber band off and open up the note.

It's a letter to Lowyn.

Dear Lowyn,

These are my dying words and I want them to be for your eyes only.

I suck in a breath and stop reading.

His dying words!

I fold the paper back up.

Ike's not coming. He knew he wasn't gonna make it. He knew we'd get caught and still, he helped me. Everything he just did was to get me out of here so I could give this note to Lowyn.

No, Clover! You're supposed to save Riggs!

Holy shit! Riggs! I forgot about him!

I am not at the top of my game here. I am faltering because I can't hold on to all the important information Ike gave me! I grab my hair, trying to pull myself together. I need to save Riggs! That's the whole reason Ike got me out.

Collin is gonna kill him.

My head snaps to the side when I notice movement on one of the monitors. It's a… an armored truck? Pulling in to a driveway. Is that… I walk up to the monitor, pushing my face up to the grainy green images as I squint my eyes, trying to decipher what's happening. Is that Lowyn's house?

Collin Creed gets out of the driver's side of the truck as Amon hops out of the passenger. They both go around the back and open up the doors.

A moment later, they are pulling something out of the truck.

It's a body.

I actually gasp and then start crying. Because it's Riggs. I'm too late. Collin has already killed him.

But then Collin kicks the body and it moves.

Riggs isn't dead yet! I still have a chance.

But then Riggs gets to his feet and they start pushing him towards the back of the house where the woods are.

They're taking him up there. That's where they'll do it. High up in the hills so no one can find his body.

No. No, no, no. I did not come all this way to just give up now.

I look down at the phone, shove the paper into my pocket, and bring the home screen up. I expect it to be locked, but it's not.

Of course it's not. Ike gave me this phone to use! I tap it away and pull up the contacts. Does he have Collins' number in here?

Oh, you bet he does, Clover. Because Ike thought this whole thing through very carefully. I watch Collin on the screen as I press his number, then wait. Smiling.

Just in time. I'm gonna save Riggs just in the nick of time.

But all I get is a beeping noise. I look down at the phone and realize there's no service.

Well, of course there's no service, Clover! You're still underground!

I glance back up at the monitors, but none of the men are in the one I was looking at. I scan the other and then there he is. Riggs. He looks up at the camera like he knows it's there. And my heart sinks. Because that look on his face has no hope in it.

"No. No, no, no." I say it out loud this time. "You hang on, Riggs. I'm coming."

I look around for the door out of here, find it, throw it open, and then pause at the bottom of a steep stairwell.

There's a door at the top.

Is there anyone on the other side of that door?

Ike must've been certain there wouldn't be, or he would not have sent me here. At the very least, if there is someone up there, he would've made sure they would be people who would help me.

It's foolish to trust this man. He kidnapped Lowyn. He threatened her, probably hit her, since she did have a mark on her face when Collin brought her to the Dixie Yonder after all that shit happened. But I didn't ask, so I don't know for sure.

Still, Ike meant for me to get away, if only so I could deliver his final words in the form of a letter to Lowyn. I didn't read it, but I don't have to. It's an apology. And the reason he helped me escape was to make sure that Lowyn accepted that apology, even if he was too dead to appreciate it.

I go up the stairs, acutely aware that Collin and Amon are minutes away from killing Riggs, and don't even hesitate at the top. I come out into a house. A very nice house, actually. But it's dark, and silent, and empty. I close the door behind me and press Collin's contact again.

Beeps. Nothing but beeps because there's no service.

Of course, Ike knew this. If he thought I could just call it all off with a phone call, he would've said that. But he didn't. He told me to find his horse and ride down the mountain.

I go outside, pause, but only briefly, to make sure no one is out and about, and then take off running down the road in the direction of the stable.

When I enter the barn, I trigger the lights and the horses start making noises. I figure it's close enough to dawn that they think I'm here to give them breakfast, and their excitement makes me nervous. Because clearly, this is Blackberry Hill and that means this village is filled with people just like Ike Monroe. People who do not know that he told me to take his horse and rescue my man.

So I hesitate, peering outside to see if anyone's coming. Because if they are, fuck the horse. I'm running.

I count to sixty, then turn back and walk the aisle, looking for the buckskin. He's massive. And snorty. And by the pawing he does, I'm like a hundred-percent sure he's a stallion. Because that's the kind of horse Ike would own.

I talk to him for a moment, acutely aware that I'm wasting time here and Riggs is gonna be dead before I even get tacked up. So I grab the bridle, skip the saddle, and go into the stall.

He's a massive horse, but Ike would not have told me to take him if he didn't think I could do it. So I say, "Head down," in a soothing voice and he does just that. He lowers his head, accepts the bit, and follows me out of the barn. There's a mounting platform just outside and when I swing my leg up and get on him bareback, he takes off running, heading straight down the hill.

I haven't ridden in years and I bounce along, grabbing hold of his mane for dear life. But he's got a nice smooth gallop and he's *fast*. So for the first time tonight, I have hope.

I hold the phone out in front of me, praying for a signal to appear as we race down the hill.

CHAPTER 30 - RIGGS

The fog fades like it was never there and I realize that Amon gave me something to counteract whatever drugs were in my system. Suddenly, I am acutely aware of everything.

Collin lets out a breath and squats down a little so we're eye level. Those eyes. So much poison inside them. They narrow down into slits, like the serpent he is, as I stare back at him. "They told me you were dead, *Raleigh.*"

"They lied."

"They told me you died from a vaccine."

"They *lied.*"

"They told me that if we didn't do what they said and drink their stupid fruit cocktails every week, the rest of us were all gonna die too."

I lean forward, closing some of the space between us. "They fuckin' lied, OK? How many times do I gotta say it? They *lied.*"

"So you say, *Riggs.*" Collin sneers my name. "But

what I'm not gettin' is *why*. Why the fuck would they tell me you were dead? That's what I wanna know."

"Why?" I laugh. It's normal now that the drugs have been flushed from my system. "Fuck you and your why. You're the liar here, Collin, not me. Because I was on the run and you sold me out for a bonus. That's what really happened. Tell him." I nod my head to Amon. "Tell Amon what you did."

Amon walks around to my left. "What the fuck is he talking about?"

"Just more lies," Collin says. He never breaks eye contact with me.

"Lies?" I ask. "No. I spent six years in darkness over what you did to me."

Collin stands up. "I didn't do shit to you. You, on the other hand, were part of some big ol' conspiracy, right? Some underground military city thing? You infiltrated my team, pretended to be our friend, and then sold us out. What were you lookin' for, huh? Why did you join up with us? And who sent you?"

I scoff. "Why did I join?" Then I laugh. "Let's start with the who. My defection coordinator's name was Clayton Boseman. At least, that's what he was calling himself when we met. He's the one who turned me into Raleigh Winston. It wasn't my idea. He recruited me, I escaped from Hattie, and then he sent me in for an interview with you."

Amon looks confused. "Who the hell is Clayton? Who the hell is Hattie?"

Collin shrugs. "Lies."

"You wish." I sneer back at Collin Creed. "You *wish* I was lying." Then I turn my attention to Amon. I wasn't close with him the way Collin is, but we had our moments that year I was on the crew. "He sold me out to Hattie Miller, who took me prisoner, dragged me back to the general, and I was became a traitor and spent the last six years digging tunnels in the pitch fucking dark. All because of *him*."

Amon looks at Collin. "I'mma ask one more time, Col. What. The fuck. Is happening here?"

Collin leans back against the wall again, staring me straight in the eyes. "Whatever's happening, it's just a ploy. He's buying time." Now he looks at Amon. "What you need to focus on now *is Clover*. Now put him back down."

"Clover!" I say her name, because somehow, she had slipped my mind. I look at Amon, ready to tell him about Clover because at least he's halfway listening to me. But as I do this, Amon's fist connects with my face.

My head jerks to the side, blood flies out of my mouth, and then everything starts to go blurry again.

"Yeah." Amon's behind me now. "Clover. Consider that a deposit on the payback for what you did to sweet little Clover."

The last thing I hear is Collin saying, "Let's go. We got a boneyard to see."

There's a yank on my IV and a burn running up my arm.

Then my brother is there.

The darkness takes my hand and leads me back into my own personal hell.

THE NEXT TIME **I wake up**, I'm rolling around in the back of something. A truck, probably. But I can't be sure because my eyes are still too heavy to open. All I know is that we're on the road.

We got a boneyard to see.

That's the last thing Collin said. He's really gonna do it. He's really gonna kill me for kidnapping Clover.

Where is she?

Is she still down there? Did Hattie take her somewhere?

The truck makes a hard left and I roll, bumping into something. Then we come to an abrupt stop. I can hear Collin and Amon talking, but it's outside the truck and muffled, so I can't make out any actual words. But then the doors open.

"He's awake," Collin says.

"Good," Amon answers. "Because I'm not carrying his ass up that fucking mountain."

They pull me out by my feet. I brace myself for the fall the best I can, but my hands are tied behind my back so when I hit the ground, a sharp pain shoots through my shoulder.

"Get up," Collin says. "We're goin' for a little walk now."

I force my eyes open and glare up at him. "I should be killing you, Collin Creed. You're the traitor, not me."

He kicks me in the ribs. Not a warning kick, either. It's hard. Not hard enough to break one, but close. "Shut your mouth and stand up."

There's no easy way to follow his command with my hands tied, but I don't even bother asking them to release the zip ties. Collin and Amon watch me struggle, but after several attempts and a lot of wriggling, I manage to get to my feet.

Amon grabs my shoulder and spins me around. "Walk."

I'm in a driveway, facing the woods. This is Collin's childhood home. Lowyn owns it now. I've got cameras hidden in the trees here. That was part of the job I was doing. Or, more accurately, the job I thought I was doing.

So I look up, searching for them. I find one and

stare into it, wondering who's watching me. My father? Someone in Blackberry Hill security?

No one, is the more likely answer.

This is it for me. When Collin Creed decides you're gonna die, well. That's just all there is to it. You might as well consider yourself dead.

Collin pushes me, making me stumble. "Walk faster and quit lookin' around."

Amon leads the way and we enter the woods out behind Collin's house. It's a steep climb at first, so I struggle because my hands are tied, but Collin keeps pushing me so I do my best.

We walk in silence until we reach the top of the hill and I can catch my breath. Amon and Collin don't say anything. Amon just heads into the moonlit meadow and Collin pushes me again to keep up with him.

There's another set of woods on the other side, and when I look up, there's nothing but hills.

We enter the woods again and I'm not sure how much further we'll be going. This could be the woods with the boneyard for all I know. So I have to speak up. "You know I didn't betray you, Collin."

He snickers. "Doesn't matter now, *Riggs*. All I need to know is that infiltrated my team, spent an entire year with us gathering information, and you're a liar."

"I'm not the one who told you I was dead! I was captured."

"So you say."

"Yeah." I whirl around. "So I say. You're the traitor."

"You said that too."

I narrow my eyes at him. "You didn't even come *look* for me."

Amon spits on the ground, an indirect insult to me. "Why the hell would we look for you?"

"Why? Because I was on the team, Amon! I went *missing!*"

"You didn't go missing," Collin growls. "You went dead."

I sneer at him. "Everyone thinks you're so fucking smart. But you're nothing but a dog on a leash. I told you my defection coordinator's name was Clayton Boseman. But that was a lie. His name wasn't Clayton, it was Charlie. Charlie Beaufort. He was kissing your ass all those years. Building you up so you'd kill for him." I look at Amon now. "And you too. Though Charlie liked you about as much as he liked me." I don't wait for Amon's response. Just direct my attention back to Collin. "Lift up my shirt sleeve." I nod to my right shoulder.

Collin makes a face. "What?"

"Lift it up, motherfucker! *Lift it up!*"

He won't though. Because he knows what he's gonna find.

I lean my head down, grab my shirt sleeve with my teeth, and pull it up. "Look," I growl. "Look at it!"

Amon lets out a sigh.

Collin just glares at me. He doesn't look at my shoulder. He doesn't need to. We've all got the same tattoo.

"Silence," I spit. "Silence, remember that? The oath? I took it. I got the tattoo. I was on the team, you piece-of-shit, megalomaniac fucking killer! *Look at it!*"

Finally, his eyes fall down to my shoulder to the tattoo.

It's a bald eagle with wings stretched out and a shield covering its chest. Inside the shield is the word 'silence.'

"That was us," I say. "We were the silence. I was one of you. I didn't do shit but follow your goddamned orders! I saved your ass twice. *Twice!* And I lived to tell about it. Which is more than I can say for Rick and Naveed!"

I'm looking at Amon when these two names come out. I know for a fact they're just the beginning of those who died for Collin. Because the only ones left from our team are Nash and Ryan. So Amon lets out a breath here that is part heartbreak and part regret.

"We existed," I say, growling my words out in Collin's face, "to get you out alive. And we did. I did. Twice. I got inked up just like everyone else. I paid my dues. And some motherfucker—some fat, fucking D.C. bureaucrat motherfucker—comes along and just... tells you I'm dead and you... what? You *believe him?*"

"All right," Amon says. "All right. Just… shut up for a minute while I think."

"Amon," Collin cautions him. "Where did we find him? Huh? Where? Down there." He points to the ground. "You saw the footage. You know what he did to Clover!" Collin pulls out a gun, then looks me straight in the eyes. "Fuck that boneyard. I'll end you right here."

Amon puts a hand between us. "Collin—"

And that one word is my one way out. I bend over and ram Collin right in the chest with my head. The gun goes off. The boom from the discharge echoes into the night. And even though it's not even dawn yet, birds take flight and fill the inky sky in a thunder of wingbeats.

CHAPTER 31 - CLOVER

*I*ke's horse rears up when the gun goes off.

Partly because it's a gun goin' off, but also because I scream, "*Riggs!*"

In the same moment there's a swarm of birds up in the trees and they're not far. Maybe a mile away. I kick the horse and he takes off again, heading in that direction.

"He's not dead," I say. "He's not dead, he's not dead."

I'm gonna make it.

But then there's another shot and some yelling.

"Riggs!" I scream again. But the wind from the galloping horse makes me swallow those words and there isn't a chance in hell anyone heard them.

Another gunshot, and I lose all hope.

He's dead. It's over. I'm too late.

But it's like Ike's horse feels my desperation and he kicks it up a notch, tearing down the trail in the direction of the ruckus so fast, I have to drop the phone and hold on to his mane for dear life. If I fell off now, I'd probably die. And then everything would be lost.

So I hold on and then there's a clearing up ahead and people fighting.

"Collin Creed!" I scream. And this time, my voice makes it past the wind trying to steal it away. "Collin Creed, you stop right now!"

And then I see them fighting in the tall grass. But Amon turns in my direction and he tackles Collin to the ground.

For a moment, they both disappear in the tall meadow grass and there's no one else there.

The horse stops short, practically flipping me forward over his neck. The only reason I don't crash is because I grab hold of his neck at the last moment. It's just enough to slow my momentum, so even though I do end up on the ground, it's not as bad as it could've been.

I roll, and then everyone is yelling. I'm calling out, "Riggs!"

And Riggs is screaming, "Clover!"

And so are Amon and Collin. They stand up, looking at me like I'm some kind of ghost. I run past them and throw my arms around Riggs, burying my head into his chest as everything that happened to me over the last week suddenly becomes too much.

Riggs is yelling, "Untie me! Un-fucking tie me!"

And then Amon does just that and finally, Riggs'

arms hug me tight and I let out a breath that I swear I've been holding in for days.

There's no discussion. No talking at all. No mention of Collin and Amon trying to kill Riggs.

That's a conversation that needs to be had, but not now.

Now, all I wanna do is feel grateful.

WE WALK BACK **down** the hill, Ike's horse following us. Even though this path is not really a trail and he seems too big to make such a steep descent, he still follows and manages just fine. Like he's been climbing up and down mountains his whole life. Which, of course, he probably has.

When we get to the back of Collin's house, Lowyn and Rosie are pacing in the driveway. I did manage to get a signal while I was tearing down the mountain, so I called her and told her to meet me here.

Lowyn and Rosie both rush at us when we approach. They hug each other. There's other people too, Disciple people, all standing around at the end of the driveway. They must've heard the shots.

Collin looks at Riggs like he's got something to say here, but he doesn't say it.

"You can sleep here tonight, Clover. The key is under the back doormat. Just…" Lowyn points to her house, which is Collin's house too. "Just get some rest and we can sort it all out later." She looks at Collin. "Right?"

Collin is still staring at Riggs. But then he looks away. "Right."

He pulls Lowyn towards him, and they head towards Lowyn's car in the driveway. She looks over her shoulder at me one more time. "I'll be back this afternoon. We'll talk then."

I just nod as Rosie and Amon follow them, and get in the car. The Disciple people disperse, deciding that whatever this Collin Creed drama is, it can wait.

A moment later, Lowyn's backing out the driveway and then, like people weren't shooting at each other just twenty minutes ago, and I wasn't escaping from a crazy woman down in a secret underground military city—the night goes quiet and things are back to normal.

Riggs lets out a long breath. "What the fuck just happened?"

Which, for some unknown reason, make me laugh. That's all I can do, just laugh. He looks at me like I'm crazy, but it takes me several seconds before I get myself back under control and point at him. "I saved you."

He scoffs. "Woman, if it weren't for you, I wouldn't have needed saving."

Which makes me laugh again. He scoops me up in his arms, carrying me like he's about to walk me over a threshold, and then he says, "You like me."

"*You* like *me*."

He admits it. "I do like you. Come on. There's got to be a bed in this house somewhere."

And then he does walk me over a threshold and that's that, I guess.

As happy an ending as one could've hoped for.

Considering.

I DON'T KNOW what time it is when I wake up, but by the low light outside, at the very least, it's late afternoon.

As much as I would've liked to talk things through with Riggs after we came upstairs to the bedroom, he passed out mumbling something about Amon and IV's, which I took to mean drugs.

Despite me releasing that breath outside, my body

was tight with tension and my mind was racing so it took me a good long while to finally fall asleep.

Once I did, though, I guess it all caught up with me because I can't remember a single time where I slept the day away.

Riggs has his arms around me tight when I finally come to enough to open my eyes. He's awake, I can tell. Might've been awake for a while now, in fact. But he stayed in bed with me instead of getting up and going downstairs, where there are people, because I can hear them.

Collin and Lowyn are down there, making enough noise to let me know that they've been here a while and are probably trying to wake us up at this point.

"You awake, Your Highness?" Riggs's voice is all low and grumbly.

I smile. "Do I have to be?"

"Well, I think Collin Creed is about to come up here and drag me out of bed by my feet if we don't make an appearance soon, so…"

My sigh is long. But he's right. I can hear Collin saying something about Jim Bob Baptist down in the living room and there are dishes clattering, like maybe Lowyn is cooking up something in the kitchen.

I push the covers off, get up, use the bathroom—practically scaring myself when I look in the mirror—and come back out to the bedroom to find Riggs standing up, holding up his gray scrub shirt to look at his ribs. There's a big ol' bruise there.

"Who gave you that?" I ask him.

He glares at me with squinty eyes, which I interpret to mean Collin.

"Are you gonna be mad about that?" I ask.

Riggs looks at me like he'd like to be. "Maybe."

I grimace. Collin Creed is what you'd call an alpha male. If this were a wolf pack, he'd definitely be in charge. There wouldn't even be a discussion about it. That's just who he is.

Riggs is more of a lone wolf than a pack leader. And regardless of what his relationship with Collin was in the past, there's no way in hell he's gonna give in and follow him again.

It worries me for a moment. But then I think of Amon. And while he's no lone wolf, he's no beta either. Every team has a leader. And a good leader doesn't have any use for followers. A good leader wants equals.

That's what Collin and Amon are.

So I have hope that whatever happens next, Riggs can find a way to get past last night.

But it's not up to me. Nothing about Collin and Riggs has anything to do with me.

So when we go downstairs and Collin points to the door as he looks Riggs in the eyes, I don't say a thing when Riggs follows him out.

I don't say anything when they get in Collin's Jeep and drive away, either. I just watch from the window.

Then I turn to Lowyn and find her staring at me with a soft face. "He'll be back soon."

I nod, and then we sit at the bar between her kitchen and living room and eat pancakes.

LOWYN **and I spend** the evening cleaning up the kitchen and talking about anything and everything except last night.

With one exception.

She says, "There's a horse in your backyard."

To which I say, "Is this my backyard?"

And she replies, smiling at me, "It is now. For as long as you need it."

Ike's horse has stuck around. I'll probably have to take him back to Blackberry Hill. But I'm pretty sure he knows the way home—all horses do—and he's still here, so… he can stay for now, I guess.

It's nearly ten at night when Collin's Jeep returns, pulling back into the driveway. Lowyn and I have been playing cards for about an hour now, both of us getting worried about how things are going over at Collin's compound, though neither of us mentions it.

Then there they are. Collin. Lookin' just like Collin.

And Riggs. Dressed up in an all-black Edge Security uniform. He looks at me and says, "I guess I got a job."

And then that final breath comes out of me and I know, somehow, some way, it's really gonna be OK.

EPILOGUE — RIGGS

Twenty-two of us enter Blackberry Hill and you'd think, with so many guys, it would be a shit show. Some would know what's up, some would be confused, some might be scared, some looking for blood.

But that's not how this goes.

That's not how this goes at all.

When you've got a team of nearly two dozen men, there's almost no way to get everyone in synch. But Collin, Amon, Nash, and Ryan somehow pulled this all together. Watching their new crew work is like watching a ballet. Everyone has a job to do and no one deviates.

It is seamless, and serious, and I would not want to go up against any of these men. They're all damaged. The military was the only thing they had. The only thing they knew. So when they got discharged, they were lost. Homeless. Drug addicts. Criminals. That's all they were before Edge Security.

Now they've got a nice compound to live on,

friends they can count on, a regular paycheck, and a dog.

A *dog*.

I mean, is that brilliant, or what?

They've all got their own attack dogs. Some are puppies in training, and about half the guys share a dog, but they don't mind because there's always puppies coming up. I take my hat off to Amon Parrish for thinking this scheme up. Talk about inspiring loyalty and a sense of belonging. It's fuckin' genius.

Last time I worked with Collin, we were just a crew of ten and Ryan and Nash were special, of course. All of us were hand-picked by Charlie Beaufort, but not in a standout way like our fearless leader. They just happened to make it out the other end alive. It was a whole lot of 'right place, right time' so they're partners now.

It was Collin running things. It's always been Collin running things. And, of course, since they grew up together, Amon has been his number one from the start.

Twenty-two guys is a lot, so we've been broken up into four teams—Ryan has six men, Nash has six men, and then Collin and Amon are their own team. Which leaves one team without a leader. I am not a leader. I'm lucky I'm even here.

Well, not here specifically because this is my mission, actually. But on the Edge team at all.

Clover really did save me when she came riding in on her big old horse. Collin really was gonna kill me. He wasn't buying the tattoo thing, which was meant as a pledge of loyalty when each of us guys under him got them done. He has said as much in the weeks since.

"You infiltrated my team," he said. That was the first day, when I left Clover with Lowyn at her house and Collin took me back to the Edge compound. We have a very long debrief. I told him everything, several times over, and by the end this was what he was stuck on.

I infiltrated his team.

He can't get over it. He might never get over it.

But it wasn't me. It really was Charlie. And even though the last time I saw Collin he and Charlie were close, something happened to that relationship because they're not close now.

If they had been, I'm sure Charlie would've denied it and I would not be wearing this uniform.

Even now, Collin still doesn't trust me. I'm working for Edge because I'm here, for better or for worse, and unless Clover kicks me to the curb, I'm staying.

"I'm gonna give you once change, *Riggs,*" Collin said. He sneers my name every time. Like he can't get over that Raleigh thing either. "And if you even think about betraying me or my men, I'll slip into your bedroom at night and end you and Clover won't have any say over it."

He will too.

I believe him.

So. Here I am. A bona fide Edge Security employee. Collin's gotta do something with me. He can't just let me live in his childhood home, hang out in Disciple, and make friends with everyone until I become a default member of the community, now can he? I guess he figures keep your friends close and your enemies closer.

When I'm not on a secret mission sweeping Blackberry Hill, I'm Revival tent security, Jim Bob Baptist's personal bodyguard when he needs to 'do city work,' as he puts it, and kennel cleaner when there aren't enough hours to keep me busy.

It's gonna take time, I guess. But I've got that, so I don't mind.

This mission here, though, this one's all me. Because we've been doing recon on Blackberry Hill for about three weeks now and we think they bailed out.

Clover and Lowyn drew us a map of the place, including Ike's house and the secret bunker underneath it, so we're going in to see what's up.

It only takes a few careful minutes of sweeping to determine that this little mountain village is indeed empty. Not a single person here. It looks like they left in a hurry and didn't take much because the closets are all full of clothes, the kids' backpacks are overflowing with homework, and some of the houses even had breakfast rotting on the kitchen tables and full cups of coffee sitting next to them.

They probably left that same morning Clover escaped.

After the sweep is over, we all meet up in front of Ike's house. Collin nods to me. "You're coming with us. Let's go. Nash, you're in charge." Collin's voice comes off all tinny because we're wearing full-on state-of-the-art body armor. It's all black and super-soldier as all fuck.

Amon leads the way, opening Ike's door and heading in with his rifle at high ready. I follow and Collin comes in behind me.

We go straight to the door that leads down to the bunker. There's a security pad on it, but the door hasn't been shut properly, so we don't need to break in.

"It's probably been like this since Clover came up," Amon says.

Collin looks at me and I nod, but neither of us says anything.

"What's that noise?" Amon asks.

Collin goes to the door, pushes it all the way open with the end of his rifle, and then we all lean in. Because there is definitely a noise coming from down below. Something that sounds familiar, but I can't quite place.

"You're up, *Riggs*." Collin still sneers my name every time he says it. I told him he could call me Raleigh if it made him feel better, but he found that funny. He nods his head to the door and I let out a breath, which forms a bit of steam on the inside of my visor before the helmet air conditioning can fade it away.

I go through the door and down the steps with my rifle ready, and when I get to the bottom, there's another door, also partly open.

I'm a hundred-percent sure there's no one down here, but I slice the pie anyway, peeking around the corner in appropriate military fashion, just to be extra careful.

And that's when I understand the noise we're hearing.

It's a set of elevator doors trying to close, but it can't, because Ike Monroe's dead body is in the way.

I sweep the whole room, then go back to the stairs. "It's clear."

Amon and Collin come in and they both sigh.

The body has been here for weeks. It's badly decomposed and if we didn't have these helmets on with filtered air, it'd probably smell pretty bad.

"What's that?" Collin points to the body. "Is that a note?"

It is indeed a note. Pinned to Ike's shirt like he's a second-grader going home to his mama.

Amon rips it off and hands it over to Collin. Collin reads it, then hands it to me.

It says: *You're up next. Love ya, Hattie.*

"What's it mean, *Riggs*?"

God, the way he sneers my name is really getting old. "Obviously, I'm the next target."

Collin just grunts. Then he opens up Nash's line. "We've got a body we need to bring up. Get a bag and take care of this for me, will ya?"

"I'm on it," Nash replies in the open channel.

The three of us kick it, leaning against the wall, until the guys appear with a bag and take Ike's body up. Then Collin points to the elevator. "Let's go, *Riggs*." Because of course, this isn't all there is to Blackberry Hill.

I argued with him for an hour, at least, back at the compound about this part. I mean, what if there's an army down there?

But Collin wasn't hearing it. Partly because he can't leave this thread dangling, but mostly I think he's just curious. He wants to see it with his own eyes.

So fuck it. I enter the elevator and Collin and Amon come with me.

I press the bottom button and the doors close.

Elevator music plays as we descend, which I think Hattie probably did on purpose to make this whole thing just that much more creepy, and the three of us stare at the doors until we stop and they open.

Immediately, the three of us are in high alert mode, practiced actions taking over. The tunnel ceiling is weeping water, the ground has puddles, and it's pitch fucking dark, so the hybrid night vision kicks in, making everything seem very first-person-shooter video game.

We don't say anything now. It's all business as we carefully walk down the long corridor.

We come to a crossroad of hallways and Collin stops. "Where to?"

"I have no idea," I say. "I've never used this tunnel. I don't even know where this is in relation to the actual city. It might be military."

"It's pretty quiet for military," Amon says.

"That's because they're gone."

"Gone?" Collin lowers his rifle to face me. Then he even opens his visor so he can see me properly.

Amon and I open ours as well and I shrug. "They're gone."

"I thought you said there was a city down here?"

"There is."

"So what'd they do? Evacuate the whole damn place?" Collin doesn't believe a word I say in the best of situations, and this isn't the best of situations.

I shrug again. "Let's go check it out, but I'm telling

you, they've shut it all down and sealed it off. To keep you out, probably."

Amon and Collin look at each other, have some kind of private conversation, and then Collin looks back at me. "Lead on, *Riggs*. Because I'm gonna need to see every fucking inch of this facility."

We spend five fucking days down in the newly abandoned Blackberry Hill, people coming and going, relieving each other in teams of ten. There isn't a single crevice that we don't photograph and map. Just like the village up top, it's empty and people left in a hurry.

I go to the consulate and find my pack, Clover's too. Hell, our clothes are still there, strewn all over the floor, because Hattie took us out of there naked.

I pack them up, grab both packs, and then make my way back to the exit.

There's only one way in and out now. Every exit has been either sealed with concrete or blown up. The train tunnel below has been collapsed. Even the door that Clover and I came in from has been sealed with concrete.

And it kinda blows my mind that the Colony gave this place up.

It's a win for Collin Creed. A very big win.

Edge Security—sixty-five men, give or take—just

defeated the Colony and captured an entire underground military installation.

And that's it, I guess.

This is war.

Collin, Amon, and I enter the Gavel and Quill Tavern in Capitol Hill and push past the maître d'. He immediately opens his mouth as if to object, but you don't get to be the gatekeeper at the Gavel and Quill by being stupid, so that mouth closes just as fast because the three of us are dressed like we're on our way to ambush some underground city people, up to and including brandishing properly permitted weapons.

The brazen display of these weapons is almost enough to get past the maître d's better senses and make him chase after us, but the whole thing happens too fast and by the time he makes up his mind on how to handle the situation, we're deep into the restaurant, twelve more Edge men are coming up behind us, and each of them has a dog at their knee.

Charlie Beaufort hasn't seen us yet. He's sitting in a big booth in the middle of the room and looks to be having a serious conversation with a senator's staffer, so Collin is already slipping into the booth next to

Charlie before he even takes notice that the whole restaurant has gone silent.

When a team of 'private security' dressed up in black tactical and carrying GhostMachine rifles enters a restaurant and starts surrounding people like a brick wall, it tends to garner one's attention.

Unless you're pompous Charlie Beaufort, that is.

Amon points to the staffer. "Get out." Then he hooks his thumb over his shoulder.

The staffer sitting opposite of Charlie—young guy, early twenties, I'd guess—is properly intimidated and scoots out of the booth without saying a single word.

Amon takes his place, sets his rifle on the table in front of him, and I slide in next to him, but face the open side of the booth so I can keep an eye on things while Collin has his chat.

He still doesn't trust me, but Charlie Beaufort seeing the three of us together is something Collin was pretty set on, since Charlie was the one who recruited me and told him I was dead.

"Hey, Charlie," Collin says. He even says it nicely. "How's your day goin'?"

I peek over my shoulder to catch Charlie's reaction and find him looking around, like he's got bodyguards to prevent unpleasant situations such as this, and he's expecting them to appear and take over.

He does have bodyguards, but we took them out

first. They're tied up in Charlie's limo in a parking garage down the block.

Charlie, realizing that no one is coming to save him, forces a smile. "This is an unexpected visit, Collin." He's sincere when he says this because he still hasn't seen me. Because this man is so rich, and so insulated, and so powerful—I am no one right now. Just one of Collin's men.

It blows my mind that he lives and works in a city as dangerous as Washington D.C. and doesn't even bother to understand his surroundings. He reeks of privilege.

"Is it though?" Collin asks. "Unexpected?" Then Collin nods his head towards me. "Remember Raleigh, Charlie?"

Charlie mumbles, "Fuck," under his breath as he meets my side-eye gaze. Then he looks at Collin. "I can explain." He chuckles these words out. And they are so calm, and so easy, and filled with so much certainty, it kinda makes me sick. He's still not afraid.

"Wow," I say. "You are a lot stupider than you look."

Charlie's face goes red and he's about to have one of those blowhard, blustering reactions he's known for, but suddenly the tip of Amon's rifle is pressing up against Charlie's lips. Amon says, "Shut up, Charlie," before Charlie even has a chance to spit out excuses.

"Listen," Collin says, "we're all busy men, so I'm gonna get to the point. Well, points. I'm gonna make a few right now while I have your full attention. One, I do not owe you ten hours of work for helping me save Lowyn from Ike Monroe last spring. Two, you burned a bridge with me, so we're through. I'm keeping all the money you paid us for this current job, but all the active Edge men were pulled out this morning."

Charlie's eyes go wide—perhaps thinking of the consequences of this pulling out. I don't know what this job is, so I can't be sure what he's thinking, but I'm gonna go out on a ledge here and say that Charlie might be in the beginning stages of a panic attack over this. He even starts his infamous blustering.

But Amon's rifle pokes right into Charlie's pie hole and makes him choke those words back.

"Three," Collin continues, almost seamlessly, "Trinity County wants it to be known that we own all airspace above our county, as well as the ground below it. Blackberry Hill now belongs to us. If I see one drone, Charlie?" Collin stares at him with those viper eyes of his. "One. Drone? It's on. If I find one stranger in my new underground city, they are dead and so are you." Charlie is about to object to this, since it's hardly something he can control, now is it? But Amon shakes his head at him, and no actual words come out. Only a squeak or two. "Are we clear here, Charlie? No debts. No drones. No strangers." Charlie just stares at him, trying to process what is happening. "I'm gonna need a verbal answer at this point."

Charlie huffs out a breath. I'm expecting him to just agree, and that would be that. But instead he looks right at me, his eyes narrowing down. "You're making a big mistake, boy."

Collin scoffs. "That wasn't the answer I was looking for, Charlie."

But Charlie holds my gaze and his eyes are filled with threats. He might be afraid of Collin Creed. Maybe. He should be, but sometimes people don't know what's good for them. But one thing is for sure, Charlie Beaufort is not afraid of *me*.

"Your father," Charlie continues, "will never forgive you for what you've done."

"I don't think he's clear, Collin," I say, growling my words right back. "I really don't think he gets it."

Amon puts his fingers in his mouth and a sharp whistle fills the tavern. There's the clattering of toenails on hardwood, and then, a few seconds later, twelve K-9's trained to military standards are surrounding the booth on all sides. People are gasping, and starting to panic, but not a single person tries to get up and leave.

"Oh, he gets it," Collin says. "Don't ya, Charlie?"

"Collin, you don't understand what you're doin' here, son."

"I'm not your son. And trust me, I know exactly what I'm doin'. I'm cutting ties with you, Charlie. You and all the other liars in this town. You stay the fuck away from us and we'll stay the fuck away from you. But if any of my men, or Amon's dogs, get hurt? I'll come for you, Charlie. And you'll be dead before you even understand what's happening."

Collin slides out of the booth, I stand up and take a step back, and then Amon gets out. He snaps his fingers and those dogs line up on either side of him like foot soldiers.

I smile, give Charlie Beaufort a sloppy salute, and that's how we leave it.

EPILOGUE – CLOVER

No one protested more about having Ike Monroe's funeral in the Revival tent than Collin. But after I passed Lowyn the note that Ike gave me addressed to her, and explained how many ways both Riggs and I owed him our lives, he gave in.

Of course, the entire town of Revenant was insisting on it, especially Ike's twin brother, Lasher, and this seemed to be a sticking point with them. They would not back down when Collin initially said no. It's not like Collin's even in charge of Disciple, so it wasn't even his decision.

But then again, he kinda is and it kinda was.

Anyone from Disciple can request a Revival funeral, just as they can request a Revival wedding. But only the leaders of Bishop and Revenant are afforded the same courtesy. Otherwise we might be having funerals and weddings every weekend. All things need limits.

So here we sit on the first day of fall and the entire county has been shut down so we can honor Ike

Monroe with a proper Trinity County sendoff and there's not a damn bit of space, both inside and outside the tent, that isn't being filled with a person.

And, of course, they did come to see Ike off. But that's not the only reason this place is packed.

They came because Collin Creed is gonna speak after the sermon. He's gonna stand here on the Revival stage and say something to us.

There isn't a single person alive in Trinity County over the age of twenty who hasn't been waiting for this. Not whatever it is he's gonna say, but just him. Up there on that stage. Where he belongs.

So we quietly sit through the children's choir singing 'Amazing Grace,' and we try not to fidget as Simon, our replacement preacher, gives Ike a nice sermon—having us all reflect on the idea of redemption—and we say our 'amens' and a few people even faint because we're so conditioned to do these things during Revival, some of the older ladies forget this isn't a show.

But when all that is over, and Collin Creed stands up, there is a collective holding of breath as he makes his way up the sawdust aisle, climbs the steps to the stage, and takes his place behind the pulpit.

Simon, who I suspect has always known he was nothing but a fill-in-the-blank until the real preacher of the Revival decided to take his place, has the good grace to stand aside and bow his head.

Of course, Collin's not gonna be the preacher, so Simon isn't at all worried about his job.

That's why everyone from all of Trinity County is here. This is probably the only time we'll ever see Collin up on that stage and whatever he says next will be the only gospel he ever speaks.

"Ya know," Collin starts, "when I left here after high school to join the Marines, I couldn't get out fast enough. Of course, I think I had a really good reason to feel that way, even though some of you never understood it." He flicks a passing glance at the guilty party—Jim Bob, of course—then puts his attention back on us. "I was away for twelve years and I can honestly say I didn't think about Disciple, or miss it, for a single moment of those twelve years. But after six months of being back, I can't imagine ever leaving again."

This is what we want to hear. Me more than most, I suspect. We want to hear that we're doing it right. That we're not missing out on anything out there in the wild, wide world. That home is Trinity County, and Trinity County is where we belong.

I didn't come back on my own accord. And if I hadn't been forced by Hattie and her sneaky plan to trap Riggs, I might never have come back. Sure, I was renovating my childhood home to turn into a wedding venue, but it wasn't a priority. If it had been, the place would've been finished years ago.

"I think about my father," Collin continues, "every time I hear the call to Revival. Because these words meant something to him. And they mean something to you all, too. Because why would they be the call to Revival in the first place if they didn't?"

We all nod. Because those words are special.

"Each part of the call has meaning. 'Behind the rumble comes the glory' is about stickin' it out. 'The echo on the water' is all the things behind you. All the things that make you you. But the part I think about most these days is 'the comfort in the brave.' Because that's who we are."

He pauses here to point to us, then himself.

"*We* are the brave. But not because we do heroic things. We're the brave because we have each other. And that's all we need. It is the 'we' that gives us comfort."

There is a lot of murmuring here. A lot of agreeing.

"And this is what I want to tell you today." Collin looks over at the casket holding Ike Monroe's remains. He points to it and my heart flutters because there's a second here where I think he might say something mean about Ike. Who would deserve it, one hundred percent, but not in this moment.

But Collin doesn't say something mean. He says, "Ike Monroe was one of us. Even though we didn't know it until after he was dead. And that needs to change. We need to know each other. We need to trust each other. Because the world doesn't like people like us. And I'm not talking about weird hill people who play pretend for profit. I'm talking about people who stick together. And the reason the world doesn't like us is because out there"—he points down the sawdust aisle at the open flap of the tent—"out there is the damage. Out there is the danger. Out there they are nothing but angry liars. In here is where we find grace."

We all let that breath out. Everyone looks around, whispering the same question. "Did he just rewrite the call to Revival?"

He did.

Because of course he did.

We are the brave and it is our commitment to each other that brings us comfort.

"From now on, it's all about *us*." Collin points to the left side of the Revival tent and his finger sweeps across the crowd. "*Us*. Everyone in Trinity County— above and below—is one of us. And everyone else..." He stops here and stares at the crowd for dramatic effect. "Everyone else," he says again, "is *them*. It's always been a coalition. Revenant depends on Disciple, Disciple depends on Bishop, Bishop depends on Revenant and all the dependence comes right back around the other way in a giant circle. We are the righteous. We are the brave. We are each other's comfort. May the circle be unbroken and may Ike Monroe rest in peace."

And then, like he really is the preacher, we all say, "Amen."

"Well," Riggs says as we make our way out of the tent after Ike's people, who are carrying his coffin, "that was some sermon."

"Oh, that wasn't a sermon. Collin Creed doesn't give sermons. That was a promise."

Riggs laughs a little. "Yeah, it sure was. And I feel like I slipped through that tent flap just in the nick of time. Because what I took home from that speech was that he is kinda pissed. Did I read it right?"

I just smile at Riggs, but don't answer him. We are entering the boneyard now. It's behind the tent and butts up against the private park along the river. Ike's big buckskin horse is waiting in here, like he knew Ike was coming. Lowyn's backyard is far too small to keep a horse in grass, so I brought him over here a few days ago. There's no gate that connects the boneyard to the park, so he must've jumped the fence. Which was never intended to keep giant stallions out, so it probably wasn't that hard.

But that's not really the reason why I don't answer, either.

It's that... seeing that horse makes me realize something. My dream is what got me here. And my dream was a horse. Without that dream, I wouldn't have bought that SUV. And if I hadn't bought the SUV, my house would not have been empty of workers. And if it hadn't been empty, I would've never been kidnapped. And if I hadn't been kidnapped, I wouldn't've have had to escape Blackberry Hill on a horse.

And that's that. Full circle. Just like Collin said. We are the unbroken circle.

Funny how dreams come true.

Funnier still that they never quite turn out the way you plan them.

I look up at Riggs and smile.

Because this dream is perfect all the same.

END OF BOOK SHIT

__Welcome to the End of Book Shit__. This is the part of the book where I get to say anything I want about the story you just read or listened to. It's not professionally edited and really has nothing to do with the reader, it's just my thoughts and feelings about the story and writing process.

__Well... this escalated quickly__. Kind of. If you're a new reader then maybe it was quick. But if you've been around a while, ya'll knew that book three was never gonna look anything like book one. Rumble was a bit sweet compared to what I usually write. But that's fine —these Disciple girls are kinda sweet, after all. They deserve all the gushy stuff.

But I don't write sweet romance. I don't write gushy romance, either. I write dark romance so if you're not here for that, well I hope you enjoyed books 1 and 2 and maybe it's time to move on. Because the story from here goes places. Some of them dark, some of them erotic, some of them sad. But I don't have another sweet and gushy story in my head at the moment so there isn't one on the horizon.

But again, sweet and gushy was picture perfect for both Lowyn and Rosie. And although Clover's story was not anything close to what I consider dark, Comfort was a small step in the right direction. If I had really meant to make this dark, our boy Riggs would've been exploring his more sinister side instead of driving twenty miles away to get Clover burgers.

So this is what I would call "Captive Romance Lite". If you want to read a real captive romance, try my book Meet Me in the Dark. I don't really do warnings but that book has a very serious and strong warning attached to it.

I came up with this idea pretty early. I knew that Clover was our third heroine and that she was never going to hook up with Ryan or Nash. I wanted to bring in someone new and so we get Riggs.

The big thing between these two characters was trust. Clover had no reason to trust Riggs and Riggs had no reason to even care about Clover, but over the course of the week they grew on each other. And in the end, that's what it all came down to. Trust.

Would Riggs sell out Clover to save himself?

Would Clover sell out Riggs to save herself?

It would be pretty easy to imagine both of those scenarios because Clover knew that Riggs was lying to her at times. She saw through his charming, handsome façade. And he told her, several times, that he would kill her to complete the job.

So I thought the big scenes with Hattie telling them lies in separate interrogation rooms was a pretty good way to test their new relationship.

And, if you think about it, the Revival Wedding Vow is all about trust too. The man promises all these things to the woman he loves and all she is asked to do is trust him to deliver.

I like that vow. It's very old-fashioned, I think. But I like it.

Blackberry Hill and the rest of the underground cities and people have been in the story from the very beginning. The room that Lowyn saw when she was "married" to Ike Monroe back when she was nineteen was the same room Clover used to escape. So all the seeds of this story were planted back in The Rumble and the Glory.

I love me some secret underground tunnels. I have been writing tunnels since Junco. Which was my very first book, so that's almost 15 years. I didn't think much about the tunnels back in Junco but I do recall getting a lot of messages form people that they really thought they were fascinating. It was a little bit surprising because everyone knows there's tunnels all under the Denver airport. Whether they have secret shit in them or not, I don't know.

I think I told this story before. I know I've said it

out loud, so maybe I've never actually written it down. But anyway, I knew this guy way back in the day and we were just hanging out drinking a little and he started telling me this story. He was a plumber (Denver area, of course) and he started telling me how he was working on one of the decommissioned bases out by the "new" airport (which is like 25 years old now).

And he said they took him to a tunnel. It was not under the Denver airport (The airport tunnels are real, you can see them online. Just like the tunnels in Cheyenne Mountain down in Colorado Springs). But these tunnels were a little bit south, according to him. And he starts telling me about these underground highways. Like seven lane freeways under the ground. I'm pretty sure that's what he actually said – seven lanes. Big and wide enough to drive very large things down them.

Like I said, we were a bit drunk. But he had details and he said he had to sign some NDA or whatever. And yeah, that's really all I remember. The only other detail that stands out to me is that my grad school for my PhD program was over that way and at the time I was there the campus was brand new and it was all built on top of an old US Army medical center.

And when I was there you could still see a whole bunch of things left over from the base. There was clearly something under the ground because you could see the vents. Not small vents, either. Like manhole structures except they were not all sealed up. It's hard to explain but it was very apparent that there was shit under the ground. And we'd walk right past these vents (across a big open concrete lot) to go to go get lunch at a sandwich shop.

So is it true? I don't know. This is the extent of my personal knowledge of underground military tunnels. It was just a little factoid I held on to until I started writing the Junco books. So that's where the whole tunnel thing came from—this drunk guy I knew twenty years ago and grad school.

But whether or not they're real doesn't matter because this whole story is fiction. But there are most definitely underground bases, all over the world, in many countries, where secret shit happens away from prying eyes of foreign governments and it's all very interesting to me.

I didn't want to spend a whole lot of time down there in this book, so the trip was short and we never left Blackberry Hill. We might never go back underground, to be honest. I just figured that since Collin and Friends found the entrance to the tunnels in The Echo on the Water we should explore that place at least once and now it's done.

I will tell you though—I'm a little sad I had to kill Ike. I feel like he kind of redeemed himself a little and there was potential there. But, he's dead. He really is dead. He won't be back. But wow—lots of leftover strings with that bitch Hattie Miller. lol I feel like she's gonna be the girl we love to hate.

But not in the next book. The next book is a little bit darker, a LOT spicier. Like 10x the spice in book 4. And there will be more than two narrators for the audiobook, if that give you any hints.

Which leads me to the fact that this is a FOREVER SERIES. Which means, I'm never going to end it. It's always going to remain open for future books. And I will continue releasing them 3 at a time like I did with this first trilogy.

Book four will be my next project after I finish the one I'm currently working on. And then I'll write 5 and 6 and when all the audiobooks are finished, I will do a rapid release. That might be early 2025 or mid 2025, I can't say for sure due to narrator schedules.

So that leads me to the next book on my release schedule which is my **ADULT ROMANTACY SPARKTOPIA!**

YOU CAN FIND SPARKTOPIA ON AMAZON

This is an adult romantasy with four main characters—two men and two women. Plus a couple of important side characters. There are seven narrators and it's a full cast production.

What is it about, you ask? Love, of course. And trust, of course, of course. Because those two things go hand in hand.

Sparktopia is a MASSIVE tome of a book. At 177,000 words and eighteen hours of narration, it is BY FAR the longest book I've ever written. But there's a good reason for that. Because it's actually two books in one. And there's a third story running in the background that some people might not even pick up on until they get to the end.

So it's not fluff. There isn't a single bit of fluff in all those sentences and paragraphs. And if you like epic romance mixed in with big mysteries and grand adventures—then you're going to love it. It's a heat-pounding page turner that feels much shorter than it is once you start reading or listening.

That is my September 2024 release and I'll talk about what comes next in the End of Book Shit in Sparktopia.

So that's it for now. Kind of a short EOBS—some readers really hate the short EOBS. But that's really all I have to say about this one and I don't want to bore you.

Thank you for reading, thank you for reviewing, and I'll see you in the next book.

Julie
JA Huss
July 16, 2024

ABOUT THE AUTHOR

JA Huss is a scientist, New York Times Bestseller, USA Today Bestseller, and a cowgirl who rides English. Five of her books were optioned for TV/film, several of her audiobooks have been nominated for the Audie and SOVA Awards, and she was a RITA Finalist in 2019. She has been an indie author in both fiction and non-fiction for seventeen years and lives on a ranch in Colorado with her family, horses, dogs, goats, donkeys, and chickens.